THE LATE
Harvey Grosbeck

THE LATE
HARVEY GROSBECK

GILBERT MILLSTEIN

DOUBLEDAY & COMPANY, INC.
GARDEN CITY, NEW YORK
1974

Portion of lyrics from "My Melancholy Baby," words by George A. Norton, music by Ernie Burnett, on page 123. Copyright MCMXI by Ernest M. Burnett. Copyright renewed MCMXXXVIII by Ernest M. Burnett and assigned to Shapiro, Bernstein & Co., Inc., New York, N.Y. Copyright renewed MCMXXXIX and MCMXLII by Ernest M. Burnett and assigned to Shapiro, Bernstein & Co., Inc. Copyright renewed MCMXXXIX by Chas. E. Norton and assigned to Jerry Vogel Music Co., Inc. Copyright MCMXL by Shapiro, Bernstein & Co., Inc. All rights reserved. Reprinted by permission of Shapiro, Bernstein & Co., Inc., and Jerry Vogel Music Co., Inc.

ISBN: 0-385-01133-4
Library of Congress Catalog Card Number 73–83658
Copyright © 1974 by Gilbert Millstein
All Rights Reserved
Printed in the United States of America
First Edition

For my wife, Barbara

THE LATE
Harvey Grosbeck

At middle age, the horizons of Harvey Grosbeck's life were severely circumscribed . . . pressed down and bound in iron under a heap of detritus he had allowed to accumulate in a peculiar combination of agony, fear and an erratically enforced indifference. At the moment, these horizons were circumscribed by his wife's thighs, between which he was applying his head and hands and mouth so assiduously as to bring forth a series of gratifying responses in answer to his importunities. These importunities consisted mainly of pinchings, strokings, lickings, suckings and noises he considered stimulating (but, ah, just as often, they were unbidden) and, when he could manage it, which he did, though it tore at his eyeballs and sent tiny tremors of pain through his skull, eye rollings, the purpose of which was twofold: to see what was happening, and so to intoxicate *him* further, and to let *her* know the intensity of the enjoyment she was bringing him.

But, in fact, her eyes were closed. She had ideas of her own. She had her own horizons, no less circumscribed than his, but her own. This irritated him, but he acquiesced in it, well aware that in the end he had contracted for at least as extraordinary a bargain as a man was likely to make in a lifetime. He had always sought out women through whom he might read the barometer of his emotions. Through the woman he felt . . . felt his lacks and his advantages . . . but *felt*. Then, all of the tics and tropisms by which he was

9

really governed assumed the appearance of a rational whole. In this way, he had felt his way through three wives and an indeterminate number of complaisant women and produced three sons, none of whom, he told himself confidently, promised to become either a murderer or a drug addict. Indeed, one of them had completed college.

When he was with a woman, any woman, Grosbeck had no need to run a finger down his arm to assure himself that, surely enough, he *was* he. With a woman, he knew quite well he was he, although *what* he was would forever be a mystery, certainly to himself if not the woman. Both of them often had quite interesting theories on the subject. Certainly, neither of them ever wearied of talking about him. Or, when she did, he left or was thrown out. He was adept in searching out such women and they did not fail him (for a while, at any rate); nor for that matter, did he fail them. He eagerly confirmed their hysterias and their raptures, their broodings, their glowings, their misgivings, their certitudes. He referred to his third wife as "the present Mrs. Grosbeck," but only warily out of her sight and broadly in it. One day, he told her that a new feminist magazine was about to be published and when she expressed some interest in it, he told her, "They're putting it out once every menstrual period." The present Mrs. Grosbeck was terribly indignant (as she put it) for fully a minute; then she laughed. She was no feminist.

This wife was a Victorian . . . full of shames and lusts and appetites bearing no relation at all to the facts of the last years of the twentieth century. She had a devoutly purposeful *nostalgie de la boue.* She was a camisole thrown in pretty confusion over an antimacassar laid on the back of a Biedermeier chair. Broughams, painted black and yellow and quilted inside, creaked through her days, though she rode the subway and submitted, head bowed, to having her splendid behind grasped by hot, intent strangers. Her underclothing was extreme, what there was of it.

Now, she lay on an extravagantly curved, uncomfortable, red-velvet couch, upholstered in covered buttons with ornamented, golden-black nailheads on the dark wood . . . amid throws and pillows . . . surrounded by dark, small oil paintings of romantic landscapes of the nineteenth century and watermarked lithographs of New York, with which Grosbeck had supplemented the oils. There were seven Battersea boxes on a round oak table, some bits of chinoiserie, five *netsukes*, all grotesque; two *étuis*, a fragment of a German Christ of the sixteenth century, an ivory Chinese doctor lady and several dozen souvenir silver spoons in sterling, arranged on a piece of silk embroidery; all enameled, one with a representation in the bowl, of Fort Sumter. She had never been in Charleston, South Carolina.

The lights were low. For all of her anachronisms, she knew the possibilities of a three-way electric-light bulb; the air reeked of jasmine, cigarette smoke, and . . . yes . . . sherry fumes. She had blackened her eyelids with kohl and she wore a wig. The harsh chemical hair, black also, reached her shoulders. It was three o'clock of a Saturday afternoon in midsummer; the sun was shining; the temperature was well over ninety degrees; and the air conditioning hissed in the room, occasionally stirring the ball fringe on the portieres behind which she had hidden the machine. He had told her about that. "All you're doing," he had said, "is wasting it." "I don't care," she had answered, "I like it hot. Hot! Hot! Hot!" For her, he knew, the weather outside was always lowering and cold, even in midsummer.

Madeline Grosbeck was a stately woman of great intelligence who claimed . . . and he never knew whether she was joking . . . that she was half Arab. Somewhere in her background, he remembered her telling him, was a Palestinian Jew from a hundred years back . . . a roisterer, a drinker, a slapper of women, a roarer . . . a Jew whose mother might very well have loved a Bedouin in Hebron. Madeline read Tarot cards, collected porcelain, told fortunes, dressed well, was an excellent cook, and, when in a state of sexual excitement, talked baby talk; it was a signal. She was full of signals and to transgress any of them was to arouse in her a fury which she expressed by biting on her thumb with her capped teeth. At such times, she spoke in tongues and headed for the door. These excesses often lasted as long as fifteen minutes. He was utterly enchanted with her and inexpressibly saddened whenever she gave way. He called such times "Ramadan."

This afternoon, having arranged herself, lighted a cigarette and sipped . . . she sipped, not drank . . . some sherry, she said, "Heavens to Betsy." It was not just bathetic; it was revolting. But, by an act of will, he managed to transmute such expressions into the equivalent of a code for the coarsest and most dissolute of propositions. And, so they began.

For the occasion (all couplings between these two were occasions, however frequent; as ceremonious as the passage of a glass hearse with jet plumes and black horses to a corner of Père Lachaise), she had spent some time and given the matter much thought. Beneath the wig and the kohl was a choker of half a dozen strands of small, irregular, but real pearls set in gold. She knew where to find such things. Beneath that, nothing to the waist. Beneath that, a round skirt, black and taken up so short by her that it was not a skirt at all, but an abstraction meant to fulfill a convention both had settled on. Beneath that, pearl-gray stockings, gartered with blue-silk ribbon. On her hands, half a dozen large rings. On her feet, shoes with extremely high heels, of a kind women no longer wore. Who knows where she had found them.

Grosbeck stopped for a moment, sat up, ran the back of his arm across his mouth, and reached for his drink. The ice had melted, but he nevertheless took a long swallow, lighted a cigarette for himself, took hers out of her hand, since it had gone out, and asked her whether she wanted another one. She rolled her head from side to side . . . slowly . . . and licked her lips . . . and then lay perfectly still. Grosbeck heard the city outside and made it recede. His wife arched her back slightly, opened one eye and then closed it, and moved her legs still farther apart. Her hands strayed languidly over her breasts and then gave up, the long fingers flopping at the ends of the thin arms and the arms thrown out at either side . . . the *haetera* expectant. Grosbeck was well suited to this sort of thing . . . the owner of a mind full of bits and pieces which had only to be shoved around in the right patterns for him to react. He was near tears, quite drunk and pleasantly inflamed.

He would return to his *devoirs,* but meantime he drank, holding the glass with one hand and examining one of her legs with the other. He realized, with humility, that they were spectacular legs . . . far out of proportion to the eight heads required for the figure. The legs alone must have been all of, say, six heads. "So, how," he said aloud, not realizing that he had opened his mouth, "do we cram the rest of it in two heads?"

His wife opened one eye again and said, "What?"

"Nothing," he answered. He looked at the leg he was holding. For a long time.

Plinth, he said to himself.

Base.

Shaft.

Shaft! he thought and squeezed. The words ran on and on in his head, and he bent down again.

Echinus, volute, abacus, guttae, he screamed at himself. Architrave, capital, entablature, metope, triglyph, dentils, fascia, frieze.

He rummaged around in his head as he applied himself. Tuscan! Grosbeck told himself, the triumph somewhere off in the distance as the drums rolled. Tuscan! A Tuscan column. The hell with the details.

And, at last, cornice. The pediment rolled slightly and suspired.

It was time for the ascent, for the slow climb from the penultimate (hee-hee!) to the ultimate. Once more, he rose . . . reverently, but unsteadily. The crowd surged forward to watch, but he swept it away with a wide swing of his left arm. His glass was caught in the arc of his arm, fell to the floor and broke, and a wide stain spread on the carpet. The noise was deafening; dogs barked; functionaries implored and yelled; the people muttered angrily; a great cloud of dust arose; the motes sparkled in the flickering light.

"Madeline," he said, "Madeline," and entered the temple to pray; laid aside the altar cloths; took up the censer, and began swinging it gently. The altar moved against the censer, the censer against the altar. The scent was overpowering. The deity said, "Oh," and turned up her face.

"Oh," she said.

"How goodly are thy tents, O Jacob, thy dwellings, O Israel!"

"Do me, Harvey," she said. "Do me."

"O Lord, I love the place of Thy House and the abode in which Thy glory dwelleth."

"Harder."

14

"And so I bow down, and adore Thee, O God, my Maker."

He felt a fumbling at him. The censer was arrested in motion. A floor above, a young engineer . . . a thick young man with doe eyes and a long, drooping mustache, practiced a karate chop, all alone on the way from green belt to brown to black, and fell on the floor. The thump sent down a flake of plaster on one of the Battersea boxes, the one reading "Glorious 1st Aug. English VALOUR TRIUMPHANT and French Perfidy DEFEATED." The young man's wife was black. She was black and Jewish and liberated and contentious and bored and she spoke in a voice that squeaked and broke. When she directed it at their two children, *they* fell on the floor.

But the service was not interrupted. Once more, the hoarse voice rose, the raven clamoring among the cypresses.

"Ream me, ream me," she enjoined Grosbeck.

"The Lord is upright, my Rock, in whom there is no unrighteousness."

"Jesus Christ! Oh, Jeesezzzuz!"

"Open to me the gates of righteousness; I will enter into them; I will give thanks unto the Lord."

"Move! Move!"

"I will give thanks unto Thee, for Thou hast answered me, and art become my salvation."

"God damn you!"

"The stone which the builders rejected is become the chief cornerstone."

The storm broke; lightning filled the corners of the room; rain fell in heavy drops; the words ran together.

"ThisistheLord'sdoing;itismarvelousinoureyes.Thisistheday whichtheLordhathmade;wewillrejoiceandbegladinit.WebeseechThee,OLord,saveusnow!WebeseechThee,OLord,make usnewtoprosper.Liftupyourheads,Oyegates,andbeyeliftedup, yeeverlastingdoors,thattheKingofglorymaycomein.Whoisthe Kingofglory?TheLordofhosts;HeistheKingofglory."

Bingo.

Mr. and Mrs. Grosbeck writhed and turned for, it seemed, forever. Without mind and jointed. One. Disjointed, but one; he, the small, gray acolyte with meager buttocks and stringy hams and a face that had seen better days (but he was not concerned with that for the time being); she, enlarged, the belly Grosbeck called her "bowl of plenty" stilled, sated. Madeline Grosbeck sat up, blowing, disheveled, warm, a bead of perspiration on her long upper lip. The wig she was wearing was off center and it caused her long nose to look as though it were out of joint. She resembled a Gaudi cathedral or the Watts towers, an eccentric masterpiece hung with flags and encrustations of bottle glass. He kissed her passionately. She pulled the wig off as he kissed her and kicked off her shoes, slowly and carefully. There were other removals; her body was closed for the day.

Grosbeck left the room . . . left the masterpiece to pull itself together . . . and went into the bathroom. There was an abomination in the toilet bowl. Who did it? Who did it? He tried to think, but the doorbell rang. Grosbeck left off his reconstruction of the crime. "I'll get it, Madeline," he said, and flushed the toilet. "The bathroom's all yours." He knew her habits and respected them. "I'll get the door." The recent debauchee realized that he had not had time to void and this distressed him. Everything in its place and a place for everything. He and Madeline passed each other in the hallway without a word.

He went to the door just as he was, naked except for the

sport shirt he was wearing, and opened the door. A man and a woman, of no readily ascertainable age, were standing there. Each had a briefcase under one arm. The man had a face like brown pudding, the woman one like vanilla sauce.

"Can I help you?" Grosbeck asked. He scratched himself in the groin. He was about to pull up the shirt and search for lint in his navel, but he stopped himself; best not overdo it.

But the calm of the man and the serenity of the woman prevailed. Brown pudding and vanilla sauce go very well together. Grosbeck was impressed. The women turned herself on. "Good afternoon," she said. "I hope you are not too busy to spare a few moments for some important news."

"Of course not," Grosbeck said. "I don't say I've got all day, but I'm always ready to listen. I hope it's not bad news. I suppose I should have asked who was at the door. The thieves and the muggers come right in these days." He rubbed his chin, and added, "Anyway, I'm in the news business, you know, so it's all grist for the mill." Hah! he thought, mill-wise that is. Suddenly, he was enormously happy.

The phonograph record continued. "My friend and I would like to come inside and visit with you for a while."

"I'm afraid that's impossible," said Grosbeck. He looked from the woman to the man. "You understand," he said confidentially, and smiled. They were impervious. Grosbeck hurried on. "But I'll be glad to hear anything you've got to tell me in the way of news."

It was the man's turn and he turned *himself* on. "We represent a new organization bringing you a piece of information that will change your entire life and renew your power to live on this earth. Perhaps forever."

"Oh, is that so," said Grosbeck. The woman took up the

parched litany. "We bring a message from the Son of God who taught that the traditions of creed bind man . . . make the commandments and teachings of God of no power and effect. We want to give you the message of the new world, to show you how God's word can shine forth, to show you the snare of tradition, which is a pagan creed. 'Whosoever shall call on the name of the Lord shall be saved.' Acts 2:21."

"Why, I do that all the time," said Grosbeck. "Excuse me a moment; would you please hold the door?" He darted back into the living room and took a book from the shelves that ran the length of the room and reached the ceiling. The couple had a good look at his backside and he wished, knowing the wish to be fatuous, that something remained of his youthful musculature, instead of the ruined wall with its wrinkled drinking fountain.

"Here," he said, back at the door. "Look." It was a Gideon Bible he had taken from a hotel room.

The woman resumed. Grosbeck could not be sure whether she had seen him or heard him. "We only ask that you listen," she said. "We have no formal church, believing that the Holy Bible is Almighty God's written revelation given to mankind."

"Well, then, I've got it, haven't I?" Grosbeck asked reasonably.

"I see you have the Bible," said the woman—patient St. Simon Stylites ignoring the peck of the crows—"but we would like to leave you this gift of several of our written messages." The two of them opened their briefcases simultaneously and pulled out pamphlets printed on what looked like newsprint, and extended them to Grosbeck. He took them and made an effusive thanks. They ignored that, too.

"We will call again next week," said the man, "in case you have any further questions you might like to ask. This is Miss Chatham and I am Mr. Price. If it happens that we can't come back, we will send our friends who can explain Jehovah's message and give you the comfort of God's word. Thank you and good afternoon." The two smiled and mingled, the vanilla sauce covering the brown pudding, and left, to go on to the next apartment.

Grosbeck closed the door. He threw the pamphlets into a garbage can. He was disappointed. They had had no news and he had made no dent in them. "Madeline," he called. "Madeline, for Christ's sake, we've been saved. I mean, *again.*"

There was no answer. He heard the shower running. He put the Gideon Bible back in the bookshelves and stretched. What the hell, he told himself, I tried. Madeline was still in the shower, so he peed in the kitchen sink. He was a small man and he had to stand on his toes to get over the edge. He inspected the inside of the refrigerator and decided that there was nothing there that he wanted. He was sleepy and went to the bedroom, and, just before falling asleep, said to himself, You're hardly the second coming of Christ, Grosbeck. The happiness he had felt naked and unashamed before that obsessed couple had dissipated. *Le cafard* had descended upon him; he was vaguely displeased with what he had done; and the last thing he had to say to himself before falling asleep was (one) That's mostly a physical reaction and (two) God takes the insane to his bosom, too.

❖

Harvey Grosbeck had no metaphor by which to live; no syllogism; no system that was not rotted at the edges or rusted into holes in the middle. Neither the cant of the middle-aged; the mysterious grunting of the young; nor the confident vocabulary of the fashionable intellectual or the ruling class was enough to distract him from his vision of Hell. He strained to see signs and obey signals. There were none. True, he had mastered the intricate iconography of his wife, the mad, delicate cryptography of her ways, but that wasn't big enough for him, not the kind of cosmic, simple-minded thing he had in mind.

He waited to turn dizzy in the presence of manifestations. But there were none. There was nothing, nothing save his thin squeal of rage and fright, fortuitously disguised as a hiccup. He had reached middle age bereft and gasping. He drank just enough to let irony stain him. Daily, he went to the office of the newspaper for which he worked to have his worst fears confirmed and the clutch of vomit rise in his throat. Not for an instant did he imagine he was alone; if anything, the fact that he was one in the commonalty, an attendant lord, one to swell a progress, enraged and depressed him further.

Daily, tens of thousands of words, thrown together in plain disregard of their meaning or significance . . . the work of blithe Yahoos . . . passed across his desk, to be read, accepted or rejected, edited and passed on to a composing room which set them uncritically and a pressroom which printed them as impartially as an arsenal turning out defective shells. The copyboys brought these things to him and he judged them in silence and hatred. Some, he saved, such as this one:

"Advisory 7/8 NX. EDITORS: We interrupt the transmission of the day's top news stories—most of which seem to deal with crisis, confrontation, gloom or doom or despair—to bring you a brief interlude of good news. We have been carrying these periodic wrapups of good news for several months and the word from news desks across the country has been unanimous: 'Give us more!' We're glad to oblige."

What were today's glad tidings? The first was an essay entitled "Of God and Man." It began, "The most common of all human sins is putting other people down. It's so common that many of us who are guilty of this kind of psychological aggression never stop to think how wrong, how truly evil, it is." The writer . . . Grosbeck imagined a man of about his age, born in the Midwest and educated there in something calling itself a university . . . had thought it necessary to define "putting down." "You know what 'putting DOWN' means, of course." If it were of course, Grosbeck wondered, then why bother to define it? "It's an exceedingly useful phrase that young people [young people, of course] have added to the English language. It means substantially the same thing as 'belittling' or 'denigrating,' but it's so much more vivid." Vivid, eh? "It manages to suggest both the motivation and the effect of remarks and gestures that are calculated to make another person feel stupid or inferior or gauche."

Grosbeck thought he would frame the story. But, meanwhile, he read on, fascinated. Eddie Guest at this late date. "Some people use put-downs out of deliberate cruelty. But most of us put others down because we're trying to build ourselves up—to gain some edge of moral or intellectual superiority that will give us an advantage in our relations with the target of the put-down." There was much more, all of it delicious. "Put-downs may be directed at strangers or casual acquaintances. But they are most vicious when they take place in the context of an intimate relationship. Husbands use put-downs against their wives, and vice versa. Some parents consider it almost a holy duty to put down their teen-age children whenever the slightest opportunity arises. Children subjected to this treatment quickly become adept at making their parents feel foolish." Kiss my ass, Grosbeck thought mordantly, and went on reading.

"It is characteristic of the put-down that the person administering it thinks he's being terribly subtle, whereas the victim immediately recognizes the slap for what it was intended to be. To pretend you really didn't mean to hurt or embarrass someone, when in fact that was precisely what you hoped to do, is to compound malice with hypocrisy. People who think of sin in terms of earthier vices of the flesh ["Earthier vices of the flesh," Grosbeck marveled, "earthier vices of the flesh" . . . Oh, Augustine, Oh, Aquinas, Oh, Bruce Barton] may be surprised by the assertion that it's sinful to put another person down. They should reread their Bibles—especially the teachings of Jesus. He said the supreme moral law, the one commandment in which all other rules of human conduct are subsumed, is that people should love one another." I'd like to subsume you, you son of a bitch, Grosbeck murmured.

"When Jesus spoke of loving others," Grosbeck read, "He did not mean being fond of them or feeling affection for them. He meant that we have an overriding duty to deal kindly and charitably with everyone with whom we come into contact—to treat others as we'd like to be treated ourselves. Putting down is sinful because it is an offense against charity. It is essentially an unloving act, no matter how hard we try to justify it in our minds as a comeuppance which the other person needs." What's he after, Grosbeck wondered, and skipped a few paragraphs. Aha, he thought, here we are. "Does this apply even to parent-child relationships? I think it does. A parent has a duty to teach, correct and admonish his children, provided it is done in a spirit of genuine love. But he has neither the duty nor the right to condemn them, to judge them unworthy, to put them down. Perhaps if we could all grasp this truth, there would be less alienation and antagonism between generations." Ummm, thought Grosbeck, and if my aunt had balls, she'd be my uncle. So that's it; he's got a kid who's a junkie. Poor, stupid bastard. Take off that paper turnaround collar, you brokendown, benighted hack. Give him a Bible, maybe? Preferably one stolen from a hotel room? Grosbeck folded the copy carefully and put it in his pocket, intending to give a reading . . . with expression . . . at home.

The next item on his desk was a cable to the office from a correspondent in Calcutta, who had covered the war between India and Pakistan. Copies of these cables were circulated to him and from them he was sometimes able, sometimes not, to gauge the distance between what was published and what was not . . . to discover again the enormous difference between what it was a correspondent wanted to say and knew to be true and what it was that he sent to be printed, printed only after it had been "Osterized," sprayed with deodorants, pounded, kneaded, smoothed, molded, placed in the implacable ovens of the busy, self-assured chefs who decided which raisins should be placed where . . . and baked only after a cooks' conference . . . the temperatures evenly distributed, the last solecism and tautology removed and the faintest blemish of intransigence against received wisdom with them.

At Grosbeck's newspaper, the indignation aroused by a split infinitive seemed to be no less than that generated by rebellion in the field. But, of course, it was. Every now and then, a split infinitive appeared in the newspaper, but the pencil reserved to excise received wisdom lay in a drawer unsharpened, a curl of dust grown on the broken point.

There was nothing of that in today's cable from Calcutta, nothing of the teeming bazaars this day, of the bodies ripe or rotting in the streets and the dogs avoiding them in frantic pursuit of rats; nothing of the brazen sun in which those bodies cooked; nothing of the click and chatter of the voices; nothing of the dark alleys and the smells; nothing of the highly polished, Briticized Indian gentry and military (nothing, either, of the highly polished, Briticized Pakistani gentry) for a change. They had all, Grosbeck told himself, fought their war and gone up to Simla . . . to the cool uplands . . . against the rains and the heat. All. Except, of course, the correspondent. And he had cabled, "I feel you should pull everybody. Everyone is too tired to go on more. Today is my fortieth consecutive day of work. I am exhausted. I am ill." The sentences revealed anew to Grosbeck the poignance of which humans were capable when they least expected to be. "I am exhausted. I am ill." The Lord is your lousy goddamned shepherd, Grosbeck assured the correspondent. You shall not want . . . except when you're alone or with someone else. He maketh you to lie down in a charnel house, for His name's sake, while everybody else goes up to Simla. Grosbeck pulled out Mister Goodnews' homily, "Of God and Man," and laid it alongside the cable.

Lastly, his eye fell upon another piece of news. The President of the United States that very morning had made another of his pitches to the God of the Israelites. He was off to China, in a couple of days, was the President, and he asked his assembled Janizaries and bogus opponents alike a single rhetorical question: "Will you," he demanded to know, "pray primarily that this nation, under God, in the person of the President, to the best of our ability be on God's side?" The simple *chutzpah* of the man, so bald, so stark,

24

was breathtaking. The assemblage at the prayer breakfast . . . for that is what it was called; staged in the ballroom of one of those cavernous commercial hotels in Washington . . . nodded between the frozen orange juice and the linoleum fried eggs. What was it he would promise them in return for their devotion? A full generation of bullshit. Grosbeck's patience was very nearly at an end. . . . But that was nothing new. . . . It was always very nearly at an end.

Perhaps there was something outside the windows of the city room . . . the windows carefully sealed off from outside contamination like . . . like what? Like the White Room at Cape Kennedy? Grosbeck wasn't entirely sure about the White Room at Cape Kennedy, but it would do. The newspaper building, old and revered, was set down in what had become a scabrous landscape of freaks, panders and murderers near Broadway and a block away from Forty-second Street. Grosbeck wandered over to his particular window.

Across the street was a hotel catering to all of the gangrenous effluvia in the area. The highly transient occupants of its rooms were a notoriously open lot. They never pulled down the shades. They were athletic to a degree Grosbeck secretly envied. They were catholic in their tastes, too: They assembled in groups of two, three, now and then, four or five . . . men, women and children. . . . Grosbeck was never positive, although there was nothing wrong with his eyes and he wore glasses only for reading. He was never positive even when they had removed all of their clothing which, to be sure, was not all the time. He found their couplings of such dimensions and ingenuity that they made the Laocoön look like a square knot.

Once in a while, Grosbeck was treated to the touching, rustic spectacle of a young man and a young woman . . .

both naked and only fornicating. At those times, he told himself that his faith in the eternal verities would have been restored, had he had any such faith.

It was always a mixed bag . . . some fellatio, some cunnilingus, some masturbation (sometimes mutual), bits of exhibitionism, some play acting, a few slaps and punches; disappearances into bathrooms and returns to the arena; coffee being drunk from paper containers by men in their shoes and socks and nothing else; women washing themselves between their legs with palms full of cheap whiskey daintily poured from pint bottles.

There was sound, but Grosbeck could only imagine that; his windows were sealed and so were theirs. The daily spectacle (it went on, uninterrupted, day-night-day) resembled one of those question-and-answer games on television, in which the participants sit in boxes on several tiers, watched by a man who had turned the sound down. Nothing much there, today, for Grosbeck . . . two homosexuals monotonously taking turns flogging each other . . . when they weren't handling each other's bodies as though they were sacks of meal on a weighing scale . . . their faces green, their bodies pale, new red weals and old purple ones rising above the rancid skin; three indeterminates racing around a bed and falling as one in a tangle; two women, played out and sitting naked in chairs at either end of a small room, their bellies slack, their hands still mechanically exploring themselves.

"I give up," Grosbeck said aloud to a woman at a desk near him. Perhaps he had become jaded. "Mr. Grosbeck," she said, "if they won't pull down their shades, at least why can't we?" Her shade was down; Grosbeck's the only one undrawn in the immediate vicinity. "Never," he told the woman. "Dishonor before death," and returned to his desk.

The German-Jewish founder of the newspaper did not foresee what would happen to the neighborhood. He had erected . . . with the mixture of both Gothic *and* Romanesque decoration so beloved of Gentile architects of the late nineteenth century . . . an enormous, thick, squat bastion of respectability, prudently intending at some future date to sell it to a department store and move on uptown to some cheaper promised land. But all that had changed and fortunately the founder was not there to see it. The newspaper lately had, of necessity, become highly solicitous of its employees, one of whom had been shot to death on the street near a loading platform and others of whom had been stabbed, beaten or robbed the instant they stepped outside the bastion.

The newspaper now saw to it that the women were accompanied to subways, buses or taxis at night by guards and it sent reporters around regularly to the steaming warrens in the neighborhood to "expose conditions" and so chasten the laggard and corrupt police. The reporters purchased endless examples of the bad, monotonous pornography purveyed in the stores along Forty-second Street and on Eighth Avenue; attended any number of 16-millimeter movies (sound *and* color); allowed themselves to be cosseted in the massage parlors. The newspaper gave them generous expense accounts and the reporters were conscientious. Ultimately, they did their stories and took several days off to rest up. There were some police raids . . . as stylized as the Grand Guignol . . . including camera crews from the television stations. A day later, the hum of hustling going on, the pullulations of the resident flora, the flicker of random violence (mayhem or worse) had returned. It was almost reassuring: decline as usual.

The newspaper was a highly moral one and its relations

with the police were exasperating to it. It did not scruple to bribe the police to permit its trucks to run the wrong way up the one-way street at edition time. At the same time, it ran long, involved stories and editorials about the evils of double parking on Park Avenue. When this happened, the police invariably retaliated by ticketing the newspaper's trucks for several days; the circulation manager then had to see to it that the publisher listened to reason. The practicality of the newspaper was beyond reproach.

It was exemplary, even exquisite, and compared well with the practices of other large corporations which were not so moral. Some years before, on the first anniversary of the Berlin Wall, the newspaper had run a picture on the front page of an old woman, a West Berliner, in a sagging sweater, with a bun on top of her head, weeping at the Wall. Most of her face was hidden by a handkerchief. Grosbeck surmised that she was not so much wiping her eyes as smearing sausage grease from her face. But this was a minority view.

The next morning, the newspaper received half a dozen letters from readers, the burden of which was that it was rather late in the day for such people to be crying, that they had been composed, dry-eyed and cheerful and had said nothing when six million Jews and an unspecified number of other kinds . . . Gypsies, Communists, *goyim* and so on . . . were being killed before and during the second of the great wars to end all wars.

The newspaper *was*, indeed, Jewish; it was circumcised and attended Temple Emanu-El (Reform, on Fifth Avenue), but it was diffident in the presence of Jews and only in recent years had it promoted them to positions of authority. Possibly, the attitude was only lingering and reflexive, but the founder and his Jewish contemporaries had done their best in the previous century to prevent the immigration of Jews and similar riffraff from Eastern Europe; they had failed: the *goyim* needed the labor badly and Congress brushed off the founder and his friends.

Latterly, the newspaper had become fond of Negroes and Puerto Ricans; they couldn't be wished away, could they? However, it did not hire them in overwhelming numbers, because the blacks and Puerto Ricans had difficulty performing the intricate rites expected of them, but it did sympathize with them and deplore their condition in print. It was very good at deploring behind the sealed windows. And, naturally, within the law. (The trucks running the wrong way were only a peccadillo and there was an accommodation to be reached among accommodating men.) For the newspaper, the law was the Tablets brought down from Sinai by the manager of VanCleef & Arpels.

The phenomenon of the letters about the West-Berlin-woman-weeping-at-the-Wall upset Grosbeck's superiors. A meeting was called to deal with it. It was decided that of the half dozen letters received, one should be published. Another would be written in the office and signed with a fake name and address, expressing sympathy for the woman and all the courageous people of West Berlin, and published, too.

Grosbeck, knowing better, had protested. "Why," he wanted to know, "do we have to fake this sort of thing?" Normally, he maintained what came to be known some years afterward as a "low profile" with "minimal visibility," but this time the imp of the perverse had pinched him. "*La guerre est finie, n'est-ce-pas?*" he added. There was a dainty pause and then Shalit, the assistant managing editor, raised his chin and spoke.

"Harvey," he said patiently, "you know as well as I do.

We need a balanced editorial view." The words fell from his mouth like little men all dressed in black business suits, one indistinguishable from another, but all pregnant with purpose.

"What do you mean balanced?" Grosbeck asked. There was a perceptible shifting of chairs away from him, a scraping of throats. Grosbeck was no hero; the movement and the disapprobation made him lonely and afraid. But he was too far gone; he had missed lunch and that day's news he had found to be more wearing than he could stand. "You *did* get six letters against the woman," he said.

"That's true," Shalit went on, "but are you or anyone else going to tell me that that really represents how people feel about the Wall? I think we owe it to our readers to put the whole thing into perspective."

"I know, I know," Grosbeck continued, "but why couldn't you have waited a couple of days before you rushed into print with a fake letter? If things are as you say they are, you would have got plenty on the other side."

"I don't think you understand, Harvey," said Shalit, "but you should. You've been in this business long enough. Right now, the thing's on people's minds. In a couple of days, it'll be gone and there'll be something else. What we're doing here, I would say, is simply *anticipating . . . anticipating* what we're *going* to get. There's always an—uh—time lag in these things. Maybe I shouldn't even say that, come to think of it.

"You know as well as I do that a good many times people who are in favor of something won't bother to tell you about it. It's the *aginners* who write. We're speaking for those people who don't write. I grant you we're going to have the letter written here in the office, but what we're really doing is speaking for all those people who are either too lazy or so confirmed in their beliefs that they don't think there's any need to let us know how they feel.

"What we're doing, as I said, is just giving people a balanced editorial view." His voice took on a hypnotic quality. "A balanced editorial view," he repeated. He looked around him and several of the jackals wriggled and waved their tails. Shalit was a man with an adenoidal voice and acne on his face. At his age . . . my age, Grosbeck thought . . . and he's still got pimples. Like some snotty little kid. Shalit was tall and ungainly and he looked like a Talmudic modeling of Abraham Lincoln. He ran the news department . . . subject to the imperial dicta of Mister Baleen, the managing editor, without raising his voice, which was, *mirabile dictu*, the voice of Mister Baleen, the voice of the founder, of the German Jew of Temple Emanu-El. "I think," Shalit said, getting up, "that Mister Baleen would go along with that."

Grosbeck bet that he would . . six, two and even. Mister Baleen's *spécialité de la maison* as managing editor was freedom of information and the need, the crying need, for a public that would *know*, so that it could hold public servants everywhere to strict accountability. Baleen always neglected to mention that the newspaper had had advance word of the unsuccessful invasion of Cuba by a group of exiles encouraged, financed and trained by the United States Government, and had suppressed it. When this became known later, Baleen's explanation had been . . . and Grosbeck admired him for his gall . . . that considerations of national security had been uppermost in his mind and that of the management of the newspaper . . . that, weighing one thing against another . . . the security and reputation of the United States overrode any possible gain the newspaper might have made in the esteem of its readers

31

from what Baleen called a "premature disclosure." He denied that there had been any pressure from the White House . . . "only some informal exchanges of opinion" . . . and the reporter who had stumbled on the silly, dangerous project was transferred from Washington to San Francisco with a raise in pay.

In pursuit of the public's right to know, Baleen spoke frequently . . . all over the FREE WORLD . . . in simultaneous translation . . . before assemblages of journalists with troubles of their own . . . advertising, bullying governments, revolutions and a more realistic notion of the facts of life. They suffered Baleen's inanities and devised honors for him which had no significance anywhere outside of his mind. If these honors were inscribed in copper and mounted on wood, he hung them in his office, in which he sat at a desk raised eight inches from the floor. He was not a tall man, but neither had Mussolini been. The foreign journalists and publishers did not have to live with the constant hortatory whine of his voice and his painful presence. His staff was not so lucky. Twice a year, he wrote a signed article on the subject of the public's right to know, the contents of which never varied, the words being very nearly the same each time. It was possible . . . and members of the staff had once done it . . . to substitute an article written, say, in 1954, for one written in 1967, and hand it in to Shalit, freshly typed up, every bromide intact, every banality in place. Shalit was not a stupid man, but he was a busy one, and he had failed to recognize the deception. He was rescued by the men who had played the joke on him. Otherwise, they would all have been fired. Shalit bore them no rancor.

He could hardly. The marks of Baleen's beatings were all over his face. On Baleen's face, there were no marks at all . . . none . . . nothing but the impression that Shalit and others had laved him with their hands, smoothing away the wrinkles. Many were summoned to Baleen's office in the course of a day to be beaten or pelted with pieties. Baleen grew larger then and the recipients of his ministrations smaller.

His employees were not the only ones who visited Baleen. Baleen took a very expansive view of himself. He was . . . and he said so . . . a Renaissance man; at the very least, a man who moved with grace and ease in all areas of life, among all kinds of people. He frequently told this to his chauffeur, when the man drove him to work in the morning and took him home in the evening. Because he had a car and chauffeur paid for by the newspaper, Baleen had never been assaulted or solicited on the awful streets around the newspaper and so the Renaissance continued, undisturbed. But he read a good many publications and so he kept in touch. Also, he had a large, enforced acquaintance among people in show business, and, every now and then, to demonstrate the breadth of his tastes, he would prevail on some well-known actress, whom he had never met, to visit the office . . . see the composing room and the printing presses . . . sit in on an editorial conference . . . and see what he was doing about the public's right to know.

These visits were always arranged through the press agents who handled the affairs of the actress. These men were conscious of the newspaper's power in cultural matters. The actress, uncomfortable, but knowing that the visit constituted a personal appearance of some kind, would come to the newspaper. Baleen, swollen and overweening, waving his arms about, explaining, a veritable spastic in his eagerness, would take her through the place.

33

"What the hell," the press agent might say to her. "It's better than making stag movies."

Sometimes Baleen would take the actress to dinner, a ritual at which he summoned up his minimal French and was overbearing toward waiters. One day, one actress . . . a young blonde, widely acclaimed for the size and firmness of her breasts . . . was marooned in the middle of the enormous city room while Baleen excused himself to confer with one of his editors. Grosbeck was passing by and she put out an arm and stopped him. "Would you mind telling me," she asked, "what all this is about? What's this guy got on his mind?" Grosbeck had had the carelessness to reply, "I'll tell you. Here is a man who has striven all his life to achieve mediocrity and hasn't made it yet." Grosbeck hesitated, lowered his voice a little, and went on. "He's . . . I hate to tell you this . . . he's got a fatal illness." "What?" said the actress. "He looks pretty good to me for a guy his age." "All the same," said Grosbeck, "he's dying of obscurity." The actress looked at Grosbeck. "Hmmm," she said. She laughed and passed the remark on to Baleen when he returned. She said . . . the stupid, goodhearted creature . . . that she thought it was cute.

Cute. The next day Grosbeck received a memorandum written not on the letterhead of the newspaper, but on Baleen's own stationery. Grosbeck opened the envelope apprehensively. "Mr. Grosbeck," the memorandum read, "In view of what I am told you said yesterday to Miss Torrance, I am inclined to discharge you forthwith. However, I believe I am an understanding man, not to say a forgiving one, and I am prepared to give you another and last chance . . . with this warning:

"I shall discharge you without severance pay

34

"(1) if you repeat the kind of slander of which you were guilty yesterday;

"(2) or if you use abusive or unbecoming language about me

"(3) or if you use abusive or unbecoming language about the newspaper or about department heads or members of their families, inside or outside the office.

"Will you please acknowledge receipt of this memorandum on one of the enclosed copies."

Grosbeck looked at the memorandum, held it up to the light to examine the watermark on the paper and then put it down on his desk and rubbed his mouth. A memory rushed upon him. As a boy of fourteen, an unbalanced schoolmate who lived next door to him in the Bronx, had thrown him through a gap in the wrought-iron bars surrounding an empty reservoir, and broken his arm. Grosbeck had risen, dazed, and staggered around the reservoir, holding the broken arm, the blood trickling down his face from the scratches inflicted by the dried leaves and sticks at the bottom of the reservoir. He had found his way to a pipe and crawled through it until he saw light above him from a manhole. There was a ladder in the manhole and he climbed it into the meadow surrounding the reservoir. Milton Michaels was waiting for him. Harvey regarded him unsteadily. He swayed and was nauseated. The sharp white stalks of the autumn grass in the meadow penetrated the holes in his sneakers.

Milton Michaels stood before him, hands on hips, whistling. The afternoon was cool and the sky gray and Harvey shivered in pain. "Milton," he said, "your mother fucks the iceman." It was all the defiance of which he was capable and he waited for something further to happen.

"I know it," said Milton Michaels.

"I know all about your sister, too, Milton, big tits and all. I know about Raymond Wilson and your sister."

Harvey could barely see him now for the pain. But Milton Michaels stood still and did nothing, so Harvey said some more. "Your father stopped me in the hall the other day," he said, "and felt me up." That wasn't true.

Milton Michaels looked at Harvey speculatively. He opened his pants and removed his apparatus with care and appreciation. It was a formidable arrangement of parts for a boy his size, but Harvey had heard somewhere that morons were always built that way. He was smaller than Harvey and Harvey, for all the pain and disorder he felt, was drawn by what he saw. Milton Michaels lifted it up, manipulated it skillfully for a minute or two and then discharged . . . blinking as he did so . . . on Harvey's pants. Then he put it away.

"I don't give a shit," Milton Michaels said . . . but his voice did. "Go get cleaned up. You got to do my homework."

"I can't today," said Harvey, "you can see I can't," and the two went home separate ways. Grosbeck's mother received him with horror when she saw his face and arm. Horror struggled with distaste when she looked at his pants. She knew that, from time to time, her son groped beneath the lingerie in her bureau and took out the poorly printed copy of *Fanny Hill* that she kept there. Distaste changed, finally, to concern, and she took him to the hospital. The arm was put in a cast; Harvey continued to do Milton Michaels' homework; autumn passed into winter and winter into spring; life went on much as it had before and Harvey Grosbeck contained his anger out of fear.

And so it was with the memorandum. Grosbeck acknowledged it as he had the breaking of his arm by Milton Michaels . . . with, as they said in the movies, the defiance of the damned . . . and with this salient exception, an exception so subtle that only he, Baleen and Miss Gannon, Baleen's secretary, could have realized what it was he had done.

He went to his typewriter and *typed*, "I'm sorry, Mr. Baleen. I was only making a feeble joke." On the memorandum. And he signed the acknowledgment of the memorandum by *typing* his name on the bottom.

Only he, Baleen and Miss Adeline Gannon knew that if there were one thing Baleen demanded of his employees, it was the thing they called these days "interpersonal relationships." One of its requirements was that memorandums should be answered in handwriting.

Miss Adeline Gannon was a discreet creature with a worn face and hair arranged in a pre-Raphaelite bun who supported a homosexual husband and would like to have been Baleen's mistress (the best of all possible worlds), and she understood.

"Harvey," she said gently to Grosbeck. "Don't. Go back and *write* it out. You know what I mean."

Grosbeck tugged at his forelock, or what would have been his forelock, if his hair had been longer.

"You're absolutely right, Missy Gannon," he said. "I'll write it. I'll do it. By the way, has your husband buggered any goats lately?" That was Grosbeck's double-jointed way of defiling someone even more defenseless than himself while simultaneously asking for absolution.

"Oh, Harvey," replied Miss Gannon sadly. "Please."

She got up from her desk and walked over to a cabinet in the wall. "Here," she said, removing a bottle of scotch from the cabinet. "I think this will do you some good." She poured several ounces into a paper cup.

"Do it and go home, Harvey. He's out for the rest of the afternoon."

Grosbeck drank, went back to his desk, did as he was told, returned his handwritten reply, left the office, went to a dirty movie on Eighth Avenue, and then took a cab home where he quarreled with his wife. She, despite everything, fed him a superb Coquilles Saint-Jacques . . . which was as much absolution as anything Miss Gannon or the dirty movie could have given him.

❖

The assignation postdated the *mea culpa* by a week; Grosbeck spent the intervening days crawling about the office, waiting for his spirits to rise; for Baleen to fall, for Miss Gannon to find her husband *in flagrante delicto* in Flatbush with some ham-handed truck driver. None of these things happened. Grosbeck remained quiet and let the lenses of his glasses grow dirty; that way, what he read took on an unreality greater than anything the *idiots savants* who wrote it could have conceived. At the same time, he wore the glasses constantly. Since they were meant to be used only for reading and since the lenses were dirty, they mercifully distorted everything around him.

For days, wisps of steam rose from the top of his head. During those days, he dressed punctiliously. He rejected frayed shirts; he wore regimental-striped ties; he saw to it that his suits . . . three-button jackets, chalk stripes, sober and somewhat difficult to find in stores nowadays . . . were pressed (he had Madeline take them to the cleaners); he had his shoes shined in the subway arcade daily, risking death or worse. He took a haircut the day after the memorandum. He always wore it short and he was not due for another haircut for two weeks, but, as he told an uncomprehending advertising salesman who wore his long in the mode of the day, "I have a reverse Samson complex. I *gain* strength when I have my hair cut short."

The advertising man, who had a master's degree in business administration from the Wharton School of Finance and Commerce, said the concept of the reverse Samson complex was interesting; he hadn't thought about it that way; he'd like to go into it at some length with Grosbeck when they had a chance. In the meantime, had Grosbeck been reading any of that stuff about the "primal scream?"

"The primal *what?*" Grosbeck asked. "What's your problem, Murray?" Grosbeck asked. "Plain old pipe-rack Freud not doing you any good any more?" He shut up; this was humble week and he had almost forgotten. If thine employee offend thee, cut him off. If I open my mouth again this week, may my vocal cords lose their cunning. He had fobbed off the advertising salesman with several rapid bromides:

"I was just kidding, Murray."

"Why don't we have lunch and talk about it."

"The fact is, Murray, I *have* read some stuff about it, here and there, and I think they may just have something."

Murray said, "We're all right down the rabbit hole, fella, aren't we?" and left the editorial department, appeased, with a wave of the hand, to search through the fifty top markets for a cost per thousand which, delivered, would be inscribed in plexiglass on the brown, chopped-liver walls of the advertising department.

Grosbeck looked at Murray's departing back. One can

live with murder, he thought, and knew he was being sententious, but a pain in the ass is the last straw. It wasn't the last straw. What was? Murder? Rapine? Pillage? Another failed marriage? Baleen? Unemployment? The funny farm? Skid Row? He lived on the edge forever and he didn't want to go over. Haul down the flag. Buy a bottle of scotch. Go home. Eat a TV dinner. Get laid.

"Madeline."

"Madeline!"

The figure on the other side of the bed turned from its side and lay on its back, the nose just above the sheet . . . Madeline Grosbeck in her sarcophagus.

Grosbeck turned on the light. She put an arm over her eyes.

"Madeline, get up."

It was four o'clock in the morning. Grosbeck was unable to sleep any longer and there was a taste in his mouth as though a Chinese family had just moved out. Or was it *in?* Either way, it was what people were sanctimoniously pleased these days to call a racist attitude. Why not a Jewish family? Because Jewish families took a bath every day and had a tradition, thousands of years old, of learning and aspiration. That's why. Should he have thought, a *nigger* family just moved out? No, you shouldn't, you *mockie* bastard, you *kike*.

"I was thinking racist remarks, Maddy," said Grosbeck, for lack of anything better to say.

"For God's sake, Harvey," she said, *"please* let me sleep. I had to clean up after you all over the house. What *were* you doing?"

"How do I know?" he asked. "You were there, too."

Madeline dressed for bed with as much care as she dressed for the street. Grosbeck had no idea what she had on under the sheet, but her face, her eyes, were made up as expertly as though she were going out. He forbore from inquiring into her nuttiness; he had his own and it had imposed tolerance on him, at least where she was concerned; it did not extend to taxicab drivers and salespeople.

Mother, mother what is that, hanging down the lady's back;/ Oops, you naughty thing;/ That's the lady's corset string . . . Lucy is a friend of mine;/ She will do it any time;/ For a nickel or a dime;/ Fifteen cents for overtime. Ta-ra-ra-bom-der-e . . .

"Madeline," he said, "there's something I want to tell you. Maybe it'll help. We need all the help we can get. You just as much as me. They're going to kill us all. Why in the name of God don't we just pick up and leave this goddamned city?"

The day before, while shopping for groceries, Madeline had been accosted by a black man who, after having wheezed his stereotyped combination of political curses and sexual urging at her, had stepped forward, thrown his arms about her and seized her buttocks. On Bleecker Street, in midafternoon. This had hiked up her dress, caused her to be cold and angry and hot with fright, and led her to say, "I would like you to know that I will not tolerate this." His fingers felt like splints and her behind like a freshly dressed wound. She had no idea what she proposed to do if the black man decided that it made no difference to him what she would tolerate. Would she simply sink to the sidewalk, carefully depositing her handbag beside her and spend the next five minutes in submission, in the interest of racial amity, and then go to the *mikvah* to be cleansed? Were there any more *mikvahs*, anywhere in the city of New York? She was past revulsion. The police were past finding.

"I have groceries to buy," Madeline said. "My husband is waiting for me at home. I think you had better stop."

The black mumbled something which ended in "mother fucker," which, she supposed, was a reference to Harvey, and she managed to draw back so that the hands slid down and away from her. The black had a scraggly beard and his long fingers walked in it. At that moment, a hulking Italian, a young man, moved out of the doorway of a fish store, turned the black around and knocked him down. He said not a word to Grosbeck's wife, but kicked the black in the side. Having done this, he spat fastidiously on the black (a professional spitter, the descendant of a generation of spitters who had come from Sicily to build the subways and had spat from one end of Manhattan to the other), and returned to the store, still with no word to Mrs. Grosbeck.

She hated him. She hated the black. She hated herself for all of the hates she felt, for being unable to catalogue them to her satisfaction, eliminating one here, pigeonholing another there, deciding on a round whole of proper political and emotional hates. Her buttocks smarted from the pinching she had received, and, because the young Italian worked in the fish store, she ended up by buying no fish that night. Instead, she bought chicken. She reasoned, finally, that at least the butcher had beaten up no one. Not that afternoon. That was her *ad hoc* decision. The black got up and staggered away. However militant or erectile he may have been, he was not much of a black, not by comparison with the hordes of his kind who, for all they subsisted on welfare, nonetheless grew up powerfully muscled and determined. (Grosbeck knew this was not so, but it was *his ad hoc* decision.) There was a tear in the black's coat, he left one shoe behind him and he limped up the block, around a corner and out of sight. . . .

"All right, Harvey," said Madeline Grosbeck, "we'll go." The nose on the sarcophagus stirred and wobbled. "Where? When? We've talked about this before. We'll talk about it again. And nothing will happen. You'll never go anywhere. You're just upset over what happened to me yesterday." She turned on her side and Grosbeck knew what was coming. He stared at her back with tenderness and loathing. "I'm so busy watching what you do, Harvey," she said, "that I can't hear a word you say." Grosbeck mimed the words as she spoke. "Harvey," she went on, "I'll *go* to Vermont, I'll *go* to Montana. But *you* won't. You won't go as long as there's a rusty piece of cast-iron column left standing on Canal Street or a *bocce* court on Mulberry Street, or . . ." she cast about in her mind . . . "or the Customs House is still standing."

"Custom House, Madeline," Grosbeck said. "There's no 's'."

"Harvey," said Madeline, "you're not talking to one of your copyboys. I'm going back to sleep."

"No, no, Madeline," he said. "Listen to me." Once again, the nose pointed straight up in the air, a monument to annoyance. Madeline Grosbeck held words before her like a Japanese fan of painted paper and invested them with a *fin de siècle* patina. She could ask the grocer for a bag of potatoes and make it sound as though she were ordering a *calèche* from the workshop of Brewster. It was a conjurer's trick, one of the things that had led him to ask her to marry him even as he was clearing away the rubbish of his second marriage. She pretended to have gone with Harvey to a private chamber in the Argyle Rooms in London or a curtained booth of Koster & Bial's Music Hall on Twenty-third

Street. (Had she, unaccompanied, been to see the waxworks in the Eden Musée up the block?) For her, as for him, the year was always 1873 (the silver panic?) or 1895 or 1904 . . . nothing later than 1914, and preferably before Sarajevo.

"Madeline," he said, "I'll go. I swear I'll go. Just give me a little more time."

The nose inclined toward him. "Time, Harvey? Time for what?"

He knew he had to distract her. "Why, Maddy," he said, "time for visions and revisions and so on . . ." He couldn't let it lie there. Things had to be said, if not done.

"Maddy," he went on in haste and panic, "for you, I will obey the injunction of Horatio Greenough: 'Strap your pantaloons over your shoulders to keep them up and under your feet to keep them down; complete the work by a pair of boots that were fitted when your feet were cool.'"

"Talk, Harvey," said Madeline. "All talk." He must make madder music and serve her stronger wine. He reached into the night table next to the bed and pulled out the Wanamaker Diary for 1906. The Wanamaker Diary had been published yearly by the great department store. It was more than just blank pages on which to set down the events of the day: It contained many, many things. This day, at four o'clock in the morning, Grosbeck chose to read for Madeline an advertisement . . . an advertisement for CREX Grass Rugs, of the American Twine Co., St. Paul-New York.

"Why should bedrooms be sanitary?" Grosbeck declaimed. "More hours are expended in them than in any other room." He was still drunk and his head hurt, but he had to press on if he were not to be evicted. "Living more in bedrooms means that we breathe the atmosphere therein to a greater extent than elsewhere." He got to his feet, his face stern and intent. He walked around the bed and pushed the face into hers. "What do you say to that, sweetie?" No answer. He continued to read. "Breathing an atmosphere filled with germs for so much greater length of time exposes us to greater danger of contracting illness."

(You can forget the clap, Maddy. None of that two minutes with Venus, two years with Mercury for us.)

"To avoid exposing our children—as well as ourselves—to the dangers of illness—we endeavor to make and keep our bedrooms as nearly sanitary as possible."

(Jason, my beloved son, have *you* avoided exposure?)

"We know that in contagious diseases carpets are instantly removed—because it has been demonstrated that carpets are the home of germs."

(So you don't get it off a toilet seat, after all!)

"CREX is the most *sanitary* of carpets, being manufactured from the wire grass grown in the Northwest; it is proof against germs and insects, as the large percentage of silica, which it contains, gives it a hard, glass-like surface, impenetrable by dust or germs."

"Harvey," said Madeline, "you're making fun of me."

"You're wrong, darling," he said and turned a page. "Listen to this. Here *is* what we've been looking for all these years: 'Superfluous hair *is curable!* Madam: Are you afflicted with this disease? Are you still using a razor? Are you still using a tweezer? Then you certainly have not used MAJI. . . . Dr. Alexander Grossman, the eminent Hair Specialist, has, after fifteen years of research and experimenting, discovered an *absolute* remedy for this unsightly disease. AND WE CAN PROVE IT. MAJI sets QUICKLY and PERMANENTLY. The action of this wonderful compound immediately commences on its application to the parts afflicted.'"

45

Grosbeck stroked his wife's behind. "You got any afflicted parts, Madeline?" he asked.

"No, Harvey," she said, "I don't. I wish you'd stop."

"Darling," he said, "I can't, I am possessed. I know who afflicts your parts. I do." He grabbed for her breasts and she slapped at him.

"Harvey," said Madeline quietly. "I put up with a lot from you. I don't do this sort of thing to you. I shop and I cook and I clean and I keep house for you. *And,* I work. *And,* we go to bed three times a week. Four sometimes."

"Madeline," said Grosbeck. "Madeline *Smith.* Murderess. Glasgow. 1856." He went away, possessed, to find another book from which to quote. "Here's Madeline *Smith* for you, my dear," he said. "'I shall try and study your wishes more and more each day. It is my duty and I have a right to do so—you have a right to demand it of me. It is a wife's duty —to do whatever her husband likes best.'

"What next, Madeline? How about a cup of cocoa with arsenic in it?" He read again: "'I feel, Emile, yours is a true love. The love a husband should have for his wife. You do not flatter me as others do—you tell me when I am wrong. I love you for all this. It is a kindness to me. Thank you, darling, for being so kind to me.'"

Madeline Grosbeck wept. *Her* husband stood over her. "I don't say you'd murder me, Maddy," he said, "but you do get in the way of what I'm trying to say. Look. The parts of the whole world are afflicted. They won't have to operate. The parts'll *fall* off. There is a specter haunting Europe. It is the specter of Communism. Let me get on with it." He read from the Diary again, tossing the other book on the floor. "'MAJI does not burn the hair, thus making it more coarse and bristly than ever. MAJI GOES TO THE ROOT OF THE EVIL.'" Grosbeck plucked away the sheet and pinched his

46

wife's cheek. Eye makeup had rolled down her cheeks with the tears and Grosbeck retrieved his thumb and forefinger blackened. "'It destroys the rest of the growth,'" he said, his voice now in a dying fall. "'It destroys the factor favorable to its growth. MAJI cures by destroying the productive conditions that cause this disease.'"

Madeline pulled the sheet over her head and Grosbeck pulled it back. "Listen to me, God damn it," he said, "or I won't go to your mother's next week. 'If you want to be cured,'" he read on, reaching peroration. "'If you want to discard the heavy veil you are compelled to wear to conceal this humiliating, unsightly blemish—get a bottle of MAJI now, AT ONCE! If your druggist does not keep it, send $1.00 to us direct, and it will be mailed to you (postage prepaid) in plain wrapper. THE TURKISH REMEDY COMPANY. 161 Columbus Ave. (Dept. 310) New York City, N.Y.'"

Harvey threw the Diary after the other book. "Madeline," he said, "my parts are afflicted, too. But I shall strap on my pantaloons . . . above and below . . . and take a cab forthwith to 161 Columbus Avenue and return posthaste with several minims of MAJI."

Madeline was asleep. She slept efficiently, a slight frown on her face, snoring lightly. He would not wake her. He went into his son's room. Jason did not stir, either. The boy's face was round and rosy and his brown hair lay on his head like a cap. His features were regular and unblemished, of an innocence unbelievable in an urban child. He looked like the child on the wrapper of a cake of Fairy Soap . . . handsome as that girl. Hadn't she grown up to be an actress? Grosbeck didn't even know whether anyone made Fairy Soap any longer. If they did, they were a conglomerate of some kind which also manufactured potato *latkes* in a factory on Taiwan.

The boy was not innocent, although he feigned it skill-fully, and Grosbeck accepted the deception. He knew that the child did it out of the kindness of his heart . . . to shield his father from reality. Or did the young man do it because that was the best way to deal with a peculiar old man. Gros-beck crushed his suspicions. A week ago, Jason had been persuaded into a doorway somewhere near the tangle of warehouses and railroad piers on the Hudson River a few blocks from where they lived and there made to submit to a man. A white man. Regardless of race, creed or color or sex, it went on and on. Jason never went into the details beyond saying that a man had made him do things and Grosbeck had searched the neighborhood looking for . . . what? He hardly knew himself. It was one of the conditions of living in the stricken city. The boy, well versed in living in the city, had had a dollar in his shoe . . . not in his pocket . . . and whoever had done what to him had not taken the dol-lar but put a five-dollar bill in with it. The dirty bastard.

Grosbeck kissed Jason, returned to his own bedroom and slid in beside Madeline. He would make it up to Jason. Sure, he would, he thought bitterly. There's no way out of this goddamned city. He'll just have to take his chances. He tried Madeline again and she repulsed him in sleep. All he had wanted was comfort; it was Jason who needed com-fort and it was his father who was seeking it for himself. His mind was alert, and, alone, there was nothing he could do but reflect.

He had been born in New York and once he had loved it . . . the city of Philip Hone and John Templeton Strong. (It lived in primary colors in his head.) The city of Phelps Stokes and Moses King . . . the streets etched by Bachman and Hill . . . the buildings Greek Revival, Gothic Revival, Italianate, vernacular, cast-iron rococo . . . and red brick from the clay pits on the Jersey side of the Hudson . . . brownstone from the Triassic deposits in Connecticut . . . brick in Common and Flemish Bond . . . brown sandstone in slabs . . . gray, worn, marble fronts quarried out of Vermont . . . Alexander Jackson Davis, James Bogardus, Daniel Badger, James Renwick, Post, Flagg, McKim, Mead & White . . . pilasters of thick masonry . . . sills and lintels of limestone . . . pediments and cornices of tin. "I've had enough chuck steak," said Captain Alexander Williams. "Now, I'm going to have a bit of the Tenderloin."

Much of it was gone before he was born; much of it was lost in the years he had lived. What else had Horatio Greenough told him? "Not from Pliny's page or Buffon's elaborations did man ever learn the mystery of tiger's teeth or fang of deadly rattlesnake. The deadly nightshade 'never told her love' to the eye; 'twas in the writhing stomach of experience that she talked the true, catholic tongue."

Well, Grosbeck had been in the writhing of experience . . . he was no exception . . . and the tongue he had heard undoubtedly was catholic, if not necessarily true . . . at least it was the tongue of the twentieth century. But it was not his tongue. He had no tongues of the kind his wife had in her frenzies. He had only images of disaster and silences erased by the fall of walls, the arguments of pneumatic drills and the screams of victims. He was crazy, he guessed.

He had attended on the destruction of New York City year by year since the end of the Second World War. (The destruction of cities, it seemed to him, was undertaken only between wars, when the money had to be made some way other than killing.) He longed for the old as other men long for money, but there was very little of it to be had these days. He would have settled for pigs rooting in the unpaved streets of the last century as a means of clearing away the garbage. It didn't get cleared away, anyway, even though the streets now were paved.

And, as the destruction marched toward him . . . the contemptuous machines, the terrible drills, the awful cranes . . . Grosbeck retreated. He now lived in that patch of Manhattan to which the banks, the insurance companies and the speculators had only lately begun to be attracted. Here there were still to be found a few of the things on which he had built the metaphor he no longer had. He lived in the southern end of Greenwich Village with the Italians. He liked to say, "Every time I go north of Fourteenth Street, I get a nosebleed."

But even there, they had been too clever for him. His plan had been to move south steadily, believing that before they got rid of him, before they could drive him into the Upper Bay, into the waters where the Hudson and East rivers join, he would be dead.

But they had come at him from the south, too . . . moving from the Battery . . . tearing down the long rows of eighteenth-century buildings, the sail lofts, the plants that roasted coffee and stored hemp, the ship chandlers, the factories. They had ground everything into rubble with the insensate fury with which they did everything . . . and no one to mourn the passing of these buildings but that mincing little fag of an architecture critic on the newspaper. They had obliterated streets and changed the names of others. How *had* they come to leave the Custom House? As they had done to the north, so did they in the south . . . created a desert . . . tawny in color . . . the buildings tall, unidentifiable, menacing . . . glass and copper and sheets of ambiguous metal. . . . They left acres untouched for the time being, waiting on the money to come and obliterate the very ground with more buildings.

To the north of the Brooklyn Bridge, they had constructed a new Police Headquarters . . . a building with hooded eyes, *gigantesque*, which shouted day and night, "I will kill you." The French Renaissance palace, a little farther uptown, had not been a good enough headquarters for the army of thieves, liars and bribe takers who were the police . . . who had been indifferent to his son, who had barely listened to Grosbeck and his commonplace story of the rape of a juvenile, told in pain at the stationhouse.

Beneath the lip of the fine, baroque Roebling bridge, just to the south of it, now stood a concrete college with a black mouth and prissy steel columns for teeth. Once, oh once, on these honorable streets . . . Frankfort, Jacob, Gold, Cliff, William, Ferry, Pearl, Nassau, Hague, York, Jersey, Cuyler's Alley, Gouverneur Alley, Catherine Slip, Peck Slip, Coenties Slip (the names mesmerized him) . . . stood the miserable shacks of tanners; stood the good, heavy, red warehouses with their iron shutters, owned by sensible, cruel nineteenth-century men. Would they have put up with what stood there now? Grosbeck knew, regretfully, that they would.

He was tired again, but still alert . . . no, wild. He lay beside Madeline and told himself, no, they would not have put up with the latest mayor . . . a man bred at Yale on the best that has been thought and said and summarized on index cards. The many scoundrels who had preceded him were, if nothing else, calculable. But this one, with his sonorous voice, his frank, open face and startlingly shifty eyes, was too much to be borne with. He was neither better nor worse than any of his predecessors, but he was a hypocrite, and he neither liked nor understood the city. He was one of those who had presided over its destruction (while Grosbeck could only *attend* on it), at the same time seeking grace, in his manly manner, by walking among the blacks and Puerto Ricans. Why he did it, Grosbeck could not understand.

The mayor's pleasures were much more comprehensible. Chief among them was to appear at receptions in Lincoln Center . . . that Mussolinian series of mausoleums . . . in a dinner jacket, there to put into his handsome face pieces of soggy Swedish bread garnished with tiny specks of rotting French cheeses, not one of which, miraculously, ever fell from his richly curved mouth. Sharks, too, have richly curved mouths.

Madeline, wake up, Grosbeck said to himself. I beg you. She slept. He kept on, alone.

It never made any difference to the mayor what the reception was for. There he was, in his dinner jacket, his physical coordination poor for a man so well set up . . . uttering one earnest triticism after another and showing his good teeth to uncomprehending Hindustani ladies in saris . . . programed stutterings. He had wanted, it was said, to be an actor, but though his voice, baritone, was good, his delivery was not; it was abominable.

The mayor had a deep, insatiable conviction that he would ascend to the presidency of the United States at the side of an Episcopal bishop in white robes; the oath administered by the chairman of the board of the biggest bank in New York City; the Bible held by his wife, a leathery androgyne. The band of the United States Marine Corps would play two selections: "The Whiffenpoof Song" and something from the latest musical comedy. The presidential party would be guarded by the mayor's usual phalanx of jiggling men in their mid-thirties . . . hirsute as was the fashion . . . huge mustaches . . . bouffant heads of hair . . . bell-bottomed trousers and tightly pinched, eight-button jackets

. . . in their breast pockets sheaves of writs of certiorari, position papers and the addresses of the apartments where a client could, if he were so disposed, be whipped within an inch of his life.

There was no sleep for Grosbeck. He got out of bed at six o'clock and decided to go for a walk. He would dress with care for such an early walk, make himself look as neutral as possible because of the random violence in the streets. No one knew what it would take to provoke an attack. He pulled on a pair of dark-green corduroy pants and a navy-blue sport shirt and put on a pair of sand-colored suede boots. He put his card case . . . with identification, but no money or credit cards . . . into a back pocket, his keys in the left-hand pocket. How much money should he carry with him? Too little might get him murdered: too much would be a waste of money if he were held up. Madeline and he had discussed this and decided that between eight and twelve dollars was about right.

Should he wear dark glasses? There were arguments for them and against them. He would take the chance and wear them; they shut out things.

He stroked Madeline's hair and left the room. He entered Jason's room and stroked his hair.

On the wall, in the hallway to the door, he had framed two poems. One had been written by Jason, when he was in the sixth grade. It was a haiku: "A leaf falling down/ Green, yellow, russet and brown;/ Crushed on the ground." The other was also a haiku, written in the sixth grade too, by another son, who had grown up and left him: "Gray rain,/ With sullen flesh mouth,/ In Van Cortlandt,/ About five in November."

He put a hand on the glass of the frame in which each poem was held and stroked. And so set out.

At that hour, the streets were exhausted but not empty. The sun hung in the east . . . white and flat in a filthy sky. The street lights had not yet gone out. Garbage lay on the sidewalks and in the gutters, spilled as in laughing spite . . . coffee grounds, bread ends and orange peels; sanitary napkins used beyond any further utility; the dressings of private wounds torn away by pallid animals looking for refuge, their eyes glaring in the unwelcome light; the droppings of dogs; bedsprings to be uncoiled and made into weapons and burst mattresses to be picked up and transported to broken buildings and slept on again; bones and bottles and half-emptied cans of ambiguous meats and vegetables; beer cans and the sticky pourings of cheap wine; the rinds of pizza and pieces of florid sausage; tire rims and the chassis of a television set swiftly and expertly gutted.

Nothing out of the ordinary.

Overspreading everything was the fine, grainy, secret, penetrating dust of the city. It lay on the ground and swirled in the air and filtered the sun's rays through it so that the sky looked like a sallow cheek badly in need of a shave. The experts, with their language out of which all meaning had long since been wrung or debased . . . in which one thing was described as another . . . called this dust "particulate matter," but it speckled the lungs all the same and made dark, poisoned bags of them and when the air coursed in and out of these lungs a symphony of *râles* chuckled in the open mouth and ended, presto! in a gasp.

When, irregularly, some of the garbage was collected and squeezed together, it was said to have been "compacted" and then it became "landfill." "Biodegradable." "Nonbiodegradable." The terms were an obscenity, for they bore no relation to anything that had ever happened on earth. The military had fined the language down even further: An inconvenient Vietnamese was a "subject" (slope, dink, gook) who sometimes had to be "terminated with extreme prejudice." Then, there was gassing ("beneficent incapacitation"); "slamming," "shouldering out," "denying access to" and "initiatives," followed by "surgical precision bombing" of "targets of opportunity" in which "enemy sanctuaries" were "neutralized" and Communist forces "attrited," their "infrastructure" torn apart. Bombs were "smart" and aimed by the same television which entreated the watcher to empty his bowels so that he could bear the presence of his grandchildren on a weekend and not be distressed by the rumblings in his gut. Shit, blood and pus. A leg on the highway, fingers in a ditch, pieces of a face on a red sand hill . . . collated on cards, run through computers . . . the countryside in a state of ultimate "pacification," no stir among the dead. The economy of the language, its ghastly euphemisms were adumbrated endlessly, and the greater the number of billions of them, the greater and the more hopeless the distance between them and the mind. Darkness had settled on the mind and meaning was not to be found any more than in the cryptic machine numbers on a check . . . Cyrillic or Urdu for all anyone knew.

Upon his deathbed, the first rabbi of Vilna, attended by a *minyan* of Hasidim, ready to rend their caftans, is overheard to gasp, "My sons, Life is like a bottle." The Hasids, tentative yet stubborn, their eyes alight in the search for meaning, their faces beneath their beards and earlocks entreating enlightenment, approach the bed. One steps forward and asks, "Reb, why is Life like a bottle?" The knotted hands are lifted from the covers, the palms outspread. Another wheeze, a last devastating judgment: "So Life *isn't* like a bottle." The first rabbi of Vilna expires with a smile on his face; the *rebitzin* beats her breast; the Hasidim retreat to a corner of the room to examine the paradigm; the body on the bed shrinks; the sphincter relaxes; the paradigm grows larger and explodes with a pop; the Hasidim lose confidence; the *rebitzin* leaves the room; the paradigm lies on the floor in pieces.

❖

Grosbeck's eyes stung as he turned slowly on the corner, making sure that everything had remained in place overnight. To the south, the awful towers of the World Trade Center; to the west, a huddling of loft buildings hiding the Hudson River; to the east, the cement excrescences erected by a greedy, inferior university. And, in between, remnants he could not see: the golden belly of Puck high up on the somber red structure it decorated, east of Broadway, the belly green in the bad light; Firemen's Hall on Mercer Street; the last of the sporting houses on Greene, pinched between two of the massive Roman warehouses which had replaced them all the way from Canal to Houston, and the rest of Greene Street nowhere to be found since the university had had it zoned out of existence; here a hip roof, a mansard, a gambrel; there, hip and valley, gable, jerkinhead, dwarfed but *there.*

Tiny flakes of black settled on Grosbeck's sweating forehead and arms. He was not ready for the day. But who was? The sexton fussing with a dustcloth past the Stations of the Cross and the flickering votive lights in their red glasses? Yes. Baleen? Yes. Shalit? Yes. Blacks? Puerto Ricans? Junkies? Muggers? Yes. The statistical mean? Yes. The mayor?

Yes, thought Grosbeck. Yes. Grosbeck was infantile in his prejudices, but what else did he have to sustain him other than these, other than Madeline, who lived somewhere where they no longer ran trains; and Jason, who had been despoiled and for whom he dared feel no pity, but only love?

The academics had all sorts of explanations for his malaise, for that of the city, for that of the country, for that of the world. They told him nothing. It satisfied him to hate the mayor; the newspaper for which he worked; the people whose effluvia assailed him in the subways; wreckers of buildings and language; *canaille*. He was unable to grasp the particularity of people; a lifetime in the city had made, for him, an undifferentiated mass of the human race. He observed the climate of his mind as through the thickness of a plate-glass window: much activity, storms, lightning, papers blowing down alleys, gobbets of dirt rolling in the gutters, gouts of rain; confusion. Pity Grosbeck and punish his detractors. Purge him of gas and restore the simple declarative sentence. Absolve him of piles for Thy name's sake. Raise him up and lower everybody else. And forgive him his transgressions, for he does not know that he is of the commonalty. (He does. He does. He has admitted it.)

Grosbeck took a deep breath as he stood on the corner. He picked his nose deftly and pulled hairs out of his nostrils one by one. A faint flicker of anticipation went through him. What would happen at this hour? Everything? Nothing? One morning, early, he had stepped into the elevator and found blots of fresh blood on the floor. Unmistakably. It had barely begun to clot. The trail led from the elevator to the street and ended abruptly at the curb. What was that all about?

He had talked to the superintendent, a black-haired Irishman who carried a gun; to the fat, handsome, Italian hairdresser Madeline went to; to Arthur, the flirtatious homosexual Negro who lived with a much older white man in the building; Arthur kissed his fingers at Grosbeck every time they met and Grosbeck was drawn to him in a way that had nothing to do with sex; to Jimmy Perazzo, who ran the candy store.

They looked at him as though he had been out of touch for years. They mumbled and evaded him; he embarrassed them in his ignorance. But he found out eventually; found out that a man had been shot in the building and removed . . . possibly dead. The man had been summoned to an apartment on the top floor, occupied by a tenant who nodded authoritatively, if absently, to other tenants, and whose hours of coming and going were irregular. The tenant owned a dog, a large black poodle, which his wife, a woman with a face that was all black, red and white pigments, walked in the mornings and evenings. Grosbeck had never heard the husband talk to the wife, but when both came down in the elevator, the man extravagantly permitted his wife to precede him out the door.

The tenant's name was M. Catafesta. Apartment 6-R. M. Catafesta. No more. He was said to be a wholesale fruit dealer. That, too, but he was, in fact, a dealer in drugs, one of those dirty, cryptic monarchs, and a great many people came to visit him, putting on their faces in the elevator, long before it rose to the apartment on the sixth floor, a thick dab of deference; a look compounded, yes, of deference, and need and devotion to the business at hand, yes, and anxiety; all men, all moving at great speed, for all that they stood stock-still in the elevator.

M. Catafesta. Dealer and murderer. I often wonder, thought Grosbeck, looking at the men in the elevator, what it is the vintner sells, half so precious as the stuff he buys. Or is it the other way around? Still, Grosbeck couldn't believe it. "My God," he said to Madeline, "I thought they all lived in Jersey now, or Long Island." The superintendent scrubbed away the blood with pumice, the sexton cleansing the steps of the cathedral. The event was no more than a half-hour television program. Grosbeck didn't believe it.

He crossed the street to Jimmy Perazzo's candy store. Perazzo was putting together the last sections of the Sunday newspapers which he would deliver soon. He was thin and bent and he wore an air of implacable melancholy, a cape of misery. Out of this stuck his nose, dotted with pits, large and Roman; on either side of it sat eyes which hid him. He was a minor numbers banker. The store, a bleak crevice in a tenement, was a stage set, Perazzo a poor actor. Once a week, a radio car from the stationhouse pulled up to the candy store and Perazzo disappeared into the back room with a police sergeant; the sergeant transacted his business, ordered a bottle of soda and paid for it elaborately before driving off.

Perazzo's chest and stomach were caved in. He wore, in all weathers, heavy woolen pants too big for him and smoked crooked DeNobili cigars. The collars of his shirts were too large and his black shoes were cracked across the instep. A caricature. His wife was dying of cancer. "What can I do about it?" he once asked Grosbeck. He had made the acquaintance, at Mass, of another woman who lived on Mulberry Street, the tightly laced relict of a truck driver who had sold goods stolen from cargoes at the airports and docks. God obviously had foreordained the meeting. Shortly after Perazzo knew that his wife was going to die, the truck driver died of a heart attack in Jersey City in the cab of his truck. The angels sang. The new widow made funeral arrangements and received Jimmy shortly before midnight in her apartment, first turning a lithograph of the Bleeding Heart to the wall and then switching on a beaded bed lamp with a red bulb.

It was Perazzo who reached across the bed and turned off the lamp. The widow chirped in annoyance and cursed. Perazzo slapped her face. In the dark, she smiled. The bed creaked and groaned as she moved. Thereafter, not a word was spoken. Shoes fell on the floor; elastic snapped; cloth and linen strained and thread parted. Voices floated up from the street. God smacked his lips. Afterward, they slept for an hour. Perazzo snored and recited responses to the Mass for the Dead in his sleep. The widow lay on her back, her arms folded across her chest. She said nothing. Perazzo arose, found his pants, pulled a handkerchief out of a back pocket and blew his nose with great feeling, waking the widow. She offered him coffee. He refused, but accepted instead a glass of wine. She thumped him on the chest. He pulled her ear. They grinned at each other and spoke in Italian. She put a plate of cheese and half a loaf of bread on the kitchen table. He started to eat, changed his mind, put on his clothes, then finished the cheese and the bread and drank the wine, wiping his lips with the handkerchief. The widow ate cold ravioli, holding together with one hand the folds of a purple chenille robe. He belched slightly and excused himself. The widow assured him it was nothing. The two were assuaged and Perazzo went home.

There, he sat at the fetid bedside of his wife as he had night after night, she either comatose with morphine or so mad with pain that all she required of him was another dose. Perazzo crossed himself every time he gave her the pills and promised himself a new pair of shoes for the funeral. The doctor had reminded him that he must take care of himself, too. Shoes; a widow; pasta; a cigar; perhaps an air conditioner, the room smelled so bad. He blessed the bad air with Airwick.

"Anything new with Anna?" Grosbeck asked.

"Nothing," Perazzo said. "She ain't got long to go." He paused. "You didn't have to come out, Mr. Grosbeck," he continued. "I would have been up in another five minutes. You want the papers now?"

"No," said Grosbeck. "It's just that I couldn't sleep and I thought I'd take a look around . . . make my parochial visits."

Perazzo stared at him. "What?" he said.

"I'm kidding, Jimmy," said Grosbeck. "I'm just going to walk around the block or up to Eighth Street and come back."

"Why?" asked Perazzo. "You expect to find anything?"

"No," said Grosbeck. "I guess not."

"Mr. Grosbeck," Perazzo began. Grosbeck interrupted him.

"Jimmy," he asked, "why do you call me Mister Grosbeck? Haven't I lived around here long enough? Why don't you call me Harvey?"

"It wouldn't be right," said Perazzo.

"Are you serious?" Grosbeck asked. "Now? Today?"

"Sure, I'm serious," Perazzo said. "Some things don't change. Some things shouldn't change. You ain't the *padrone,* you ain't the *commendatore,* but you *are* Mister

Grosbeck. What can I tell you? It ain't like it used to be around here. What you're going to find this morning . . . you'll find shit."

"Shit?" asked Grosbeck.

Perazzo nodded. *"Malscalzoni. Desgraziati.* Trash. I don't know where the trash comes from. Good homes. Money. And they're trash. Even our own kids. I can understand bums. But this trash . . . our kids . . . set fire to that bum over on Wooster Street, that wino did nobody no harm. Why? I don't want them around any more than anyone else, they sleep in the lobby sometimes, but to burn them up? What gets into them? Who made our kids trash, Italian kids from good families? The other trash from uptown."

Grosbeck had clucked his tongue when the bum was immolated. But when the Federal town house on Eleventh Street was inadvertently blown up by the radical children of rich people, making bombs to blow up other things for the greater good of mankind, he had been infuriated. Several of them had been left in unidentifiable pieces and now they were one with the bum. Idiots. They couldn't even make a competent bomb. They couldn't even get that right. It was not their politics to which he objected. It was their ineptness and their disrespect or disregard for beautiful things and their inability to spell and parse. Those road-company Bakunins. They wouldn't have known what in hell he was talking about if he had mentioned Bakunin. They gave themselves airs. *They* had invented the telephone. *They* had discovered that something was wrong with the world. Rosa Luxemburg. Max Weber. The sealed train through Germany. Not for them. They fell upon the little Red Book of Chairman Mao, *de nuovo*. They had no past, none at all, and, as far as Grosbeck could see, no future, either.

"Jimmy," he said, "don't bother to deliver. I'll pick up the papers when I come back."

"All right, Mr. Grosbeck."

Grosbeck again asked about Mrs. Perazzo.

"What can I tell you." It was not a question. "They sewed her up at the hospital and sent her home. Days she knows me, days she don't. I sit next to the bed and I light candles at the church, but you and me both know that ain't any good." Perazzo mistrusted the wild-eyed young curates he occasionally caught a glimpse of when he was twisting the dials on the television set. The men who ministered to him at Sacred Heart were graver, more stern, but he was aware that beneath their brown wool cassocks and rope belts they wore T-shirts and elastic-waisted shorts, and that, in the back of the cassocks, there were zippers. He equated that with modernity and came to doubt the efficacy of prayer. When they began to celebrate the Mass in English, he was badly shaken. He was an ignorant man; he did not know a word of Latin; he was a Neapolitan cynic and a Jansenist; his missal was the *Racing Form* and his altar the widow's bed. The church was still his rock.

"She'll be gone before September," he said. "It's just as well. We got a plot up in Westchester. That's where I'll go, too. The undertaker's all took care of. I got a stone ordered from that Jewish monument place over on East Houston Street, that's how far I thought about it. Anna never gave me no trouble."

Perazzo clanged shut the gates of his mouth and turned back to stuffing the pile of newspapers at his feet. Grosbeck felt as though he had been made privy to the diaries of a statesman.

"Let me know," he said.

"You'll know soon enough, Mr. Grosbeck," Perazzo said.

"I'll keep on delivering the papers." He tapped his nose with a forefinger. "Except maybe the week she goes. The store'll be closed."

Grosbeck surprised himself by squeezing Perazzo's arm and making a noise in his throat. He adjusted his dark glasses and walked up Sixth Avenue, keeping to the middle of the sidewalk, careful where he directed his eyes. Things had reached the point where, if the eyes were wrongly directed, someone might leap at one's throat. So, Grosbeck had developed the trick (from his commerce with his wife) of moving his eyes about while keeping his head straight forward. His peripheral vision was not bad. It was advisable to seem to be looking at nothing; to be on an errand which ruled out curiosity, and which, once completed, would return him whence he came and offend no one. He wished, similarly, that he could keep his mouth shut, but the ape of unreason was badly pent and had a tendency to leap over the moat when Grosbeck least expected it to.

At Eighth Street, the sidewalks thickened with the specimens of what the city now threw up. Grosbeck had no explanation for them. They bore no resemblance to anything he was accustomed to. He had tried relating them to the creatures depicted in the wood engravings of Paradise Court, the Five Points, the Fourth Ward, the barrel houses and crimp joints of the East River . . . those creatures with their rotted teeth fixed grotesquely in their misshapen heads . . . soaked in laudanum and rum . . . clubs in their hands . . . the women asprawl in broken chairs, their torn petticoats pulled up over broken laced boots to the fat calves. The connection was not there; the people in the engravings could be grasped and understood; their blood was black ink; the shanghaied sailor, snoring under a quarter of a dram of chloral hydrate, being rowed out to a schooner riding at anchor in the river, was no more than Gothic romance, literature. Mayhem was quaint in old pictures, murder was performed by the light of a dark lantern.

Today was another matter. Who were *these* people and what were they doing out at this hour? The Gothic had been replaced by some kind of modern phantasmagoria for which, as yet, there was no word. Chloral had been replaced by amyl nitrate, amphetamines, cocaine, heroin, barbiturates. One would have thought that *these* people, finished with the concerns of the night, would, by now, have subsided. But, no, there they were, in motion, in ones and twos, coming and going. They sat on the sidewalks, their backs to the walls of buildings, cross-legged, picking at themselves, scratching, sleeping. They walked like lizards, scuttling. They begged of people passing or threatened and they bickered desultorily among themselves. They showed hip and thigh, breast and toe. They smelled of urine and long days without soap, an outrage to a man like Grosbeck who was ready to take an unflushed turd to the Supreme Court.

A young Negro, playing a saxophone and followed by an insouciant mongrel dog, passed Grosbeck as he arrived at the corner. The young man was playing a series of rills and arpeggios . . . discordant notes which, for Grosbeck, added up to nothing, but which must have meant something to the dog, for it howled at the young man's heels, sometimes gravely, sometimes joyously. The dog was the color of putty; the young man, the color of coffee, wore only a pair of dungarees and rope-soled sandals. His eyes were closed, but his step . . . completely at odds with what he was playing on the saxophone . . . was unerringly rhythmic. The muscles of his narrow belly undulated, advanced and retreated as he played.

Who are you? What are you? Grosbeck wondered. Where from? Where going? Why here? Why a saxophone? What in the name of God are you doing here at this hour with a saxophone and no shirt? What playing?

How was a man to know where he was?

The uncertain, persistent voice of the saxophone continued on down the street; the occasional, assenting howl of the dog mingled with the tenor complaints of the instrument. The saxophone player passed out of sight. There were no answers for Grosbeck in him and he pursued it no further. There were other divertissements on the street. Tired though he was, the juices rose in his body. He looked about him. Nathan's. Who in Christ's name would eat french-fried potatoes at this hour, at six o'clock in the morning. The drugstore. The newsstand across the street. Blacks. Puerto Ricans. Washed-out whites. He was upset by the costumes they wore, by their movements . . . not to be anticipated . . . by their beards and chains and sandals . . . by their long hair. He was out of date, even by the standards of the newspaper, where some men had beards and long hair and wore costumes that were expensive copies of the tatters he saw about him in the streets. For the men in his office who dressed that way, he had contempt. They had created for themselves a cheap-jack Versailles in which they played shepherd. But these people were beyond his reach, shut away from him by miles of wire-service copy, books,

66

photographs, rumor and gossip. They had germinated, multiplied and engulfed the city. They ate and they shat and they coupled and killed and robbed, stole and cut and maimed; they inhabited holes of which he knew nothing but the pictures he had been shown of them. He could not fathom them. They had not yet done anything to him, but who was to say they would not, suddenly.

"No New-Yorker who goes his accustomed rounds, who frequents Broadway and the Avenue, the business and fashionable haunts, has any conception of the volcanic elements of vice that are smouldering in unvisited and unseen places. The great fierce beast pursues and finds his prey night after night; and yet he slays so silently that few are aware of his dangerous presence. But in that dreary garret, in that noisome cellar, in that gilded lazar-house, the beast lies, half serpent, half tiger, coiled, crouching, ready for the deadly spring. Go you there, and you will start before the cruel glitter of his eyes and the savage growl that seems to tear mercy to pieces. . . . He is constantly unsheathing his claws and striking his victim, but noiselessly as death. Only at long intervals does he dare to emerge into the open day and roar defiance to the general peace and public security. Until we kill him outright, until the Metropolis is purified, he may awake us at midnight with his mingled hiss and roar, and strike and strangle us in the arms of Love, and on the very breast of Peace."

A girl pushing a baby in a stroller walked up to Grosbeck. "Could you give me a couple of dollars?" she asked him. "I need baby food. He hasn't been fed . . . I don't know . . . maybe a day now."

She was blonde and dirty. Her nails were black. She wore blue denim pants with a red flower at the crotch. Her hair was tangled, her face smudged; blemishes bloomed on her cheekbones like the mountains of the moon. She had no breasts to speak of beneath her striped jersey. The baby was plump, plump and quiet. *Nafke . . . Shikse . . . Trafe.* Me and my reflexes, thought Grosbeck; Grosbeck the Hasid, Grosbeck the Just. All of a sudden.

He said: "Why? Why should I give you a couple of dollars for baby food? Baby food, my ass. You're high right now." Still, the juices rose in his body and anticipation tickled his groin.

"Don't hassle me, mister," said the girl. "Nobody's forcing you to give me anything. I just thought . . ."

"You thought what?" Grosbeck demanded.

"Look," said the girl. "I got a welfare check coming in three days. I just ran out, that's all."

"You ran out," said Grosbeck. "You spent it all on . . . you know goddamned well what you spent it on."

"Mister," said the girl, "you do your thing, I do mine." Her eyes, a light brown, stared off into some distance Grosbeck couldn't find. Whatever she was doing, she was doing it by rote.

"I'll ball you," she said.

"Do you realize," said Grosbeck, "I'm old enough to be your father?"

The girl focused her eyes on him. "So?" she asked.

"All right," said Grosbeck, "I'll do this much for you. I'll buy the baby food and I'll see to it that the kid gets fed."

"Any way you like it, mister," said the girl. "We'll go over to my place. Get a bottle of milk, too, while you're at it. I know a place that's open near where I live. You can even feed the kid if you like. . . . And I'll ball you."

Throughout this exchange, the expression on the girl's face did not alter. Grosbeck was offended at her thin chest, at her indifference. Did he dare to eat a peach? Would the mermaids sing for him? Some mermaid.

"Come on," he said. "Don't tell me where you live. I know. Avenue C. Right? Fifth Street? Sixth? Seventh?"

The girl looked at him.

"Around Tompkins Square?" he persisted. "Did you know there was a public market there a hundred years ago?" Who gave a shit?

"I'm hungry," he said. "You want a hot dog?"

"No," she said. "You go ahead. I'll wait outside." She bent down to the child. He was asleep, dribbling. Grosbeck struggled with pity and hunger. He was overcome by both, excused himself, bought two frankfurters, carefully covering them with mustard and sauerkraut, plucked half a dozen paper napkins from a container and joined the girl on the sidewalk again.

"Want one?" he asked.

"No," she said. "Just the baby food."

"I think," he said, "we better take a cab. I'd just as soon not walk around there."

He hailed a cab at the corner, eating one frankfurter, waving the other at the driver. He had some trouble getting the girl, the baby and the stroller into the cab. The driver looked at what he had picked up and shook his head. He was an elderly man. Grosbeck wished that he had been one of the young ones.

"You can drop us off at Avenue B and Ninth Street," said the girl. And to Grosbeck, "There's a grocery store near the corner." The driver nodded and drove. In the cab, Grosbeck ate his frankfurters. He got sauerkraut on his hands and mustard on his face. The child woke up and made noises.

Grosbeck rubbed his hands on his pants. What was he

doing? Who cleans hands on pants? He had napkins. But he had put his obligation to the child above that to his pants and he placed a clean hand on the child's head. The mustard on his face could wait. No, it couldn't. He wiped his face with the paper napkins, tried to stuff them into an ashtray, found the ashtrays screwed shut; tried to throw them out a window, found they could not be opened; threw the napkins on the floor of the cab.

The driver dropped them off and Grosbeck paid him and counted his money. A dollar for the frankfurters, two dollars for the cab. He had nine left. That would buy the baby food and get him a cab home. In the grocery store, the Puerto Rican owner sold him jars of strained beef, strained carrots, puddings. Jason, Jason, I will feed you. Eat, Jason. Eat, God damn it. A quart of milk. Four dollars. Five left.

The girl led him to a tenement a block away, one of a row which had had some pretensions when it was put up at the height of the great immigration. It still had its high stoop, its wrought-iron balusters and railings on marble steps. It had Italianate pretensions, a red-brick face, brownstone posts, lintels and sills. The glass fanlight in the arch of the entrance was long gone, replaced by a piece of plywood on which had been spraypainted, "Jesus, Mary and Joseph loves you. Efrom sucks cock."

The girl took the baby out of the stroller. Grosbeck shifted the bag of groceries to his left hand and picked up the stroller with his right and the party mounted the steps to a hallway as narrow as Grosbeck had expected it to be. It had been much altered, painted a mean institutional green, gouged to the plaster with messages unfinished and incoherent. The hallway was lighted with three bulbs around which cages had been placed . . . not shades . . . cages . . . not to catch or hold rats . . . but to make sure that the bulbs would be kept burning against the daily destruction of the mad.

"Where to?" asked Grosbeck.

"Down the end," said the girl.

"You have a toilet," Grosbeck said positively. "A bathtub. Indoors, not out in the back. In the hall; one on every floor." He added: "Hot water, when the landlord gets around to it." He was about to give her an exegesis on the housing laws of New York City between 1875 and 1920 when he heard a scream. "It's nothing," said the girl. The baby, on her arm, cocked his head. He could not yet speak, but for him it was nothing, too. The scream did not reverberate in the hallway; it was not repeated, yet it lay fixed above Grosbeck's head, palpable as the cold illuminating-gas brackets on the stamped-tin ceiling.

At the door of the apartment, the girl pulled a key on a string out of her jersey and bent to open the door. "Come on in," she said. Pieces of plaster in the corners of the room; exposed lath; marks on the walls. A crib plucked, Grosbeck guessed, from the streets. A mattress over which had been thrown a sheet printed in some kind of repetitive pattern meant, presumably, to be Indian. A refrigerator standing cockeyed on the splintered floor. A gas stove. The electric-light fixture in the ceiling, a green-enamel shade around it.

She put the baby in the crib. Grosbeck handed her the bag of groceries. She took out a jar of strained beef and a jar of strained apricots, filled a pan with water, lighted the gas stove, found a bottle to put the milk in and put all three in the pan, put the pan on the stove and heated her son's breakfast.

"What's your name?" asked Grosbeck.

"Catherine," she said.

71

"Catherine what?" he asked.

"Catherine . . . Catherine . . ." She pushed her hair to the side of her face. "Catherine Tarlow. Is that some sort of big deal?"

"Where's your husband? Have you got a husband? Or a boy friend?"

The girl felt the bottle and the jars and turned off the light on the stove.

"Mister," she said, "you really are an old dude. What difference does it make? Would it make any difference to you . . . or me . . . if I knew your name? Or if you're married . . . which you are . . . or where you come from . . . or what you do? Cool it, will you? There's nothing you won't get you're not going to get. You want to feed the kid?" She found a spoon and handed it to him. It was dirty and Grosbeck washed it.

The child ate. Grosbeck was very attentive to it, wiping the spoon over the lips, dipping it in the jars, trying to establish a rhythm that would satisfy the child. The child's cheeks became orange with apricot. "You got a towel?" Grosbeck asked the girl. She handed him a roll of paper towel. The caricature of domesticity disturbed him, but he wet a sheet of the towel and wiped the child's face, picked him up and held him in his arms, rocking him, and then put him back in the crib. The baby slept.

Grosbeck and the girl talked. Into, she said. Bummer. Ripoff. Where it lives. Bad trip. Groovy. Far out. Out of sight. My old man. Hip. Like-I mean-you know-oh-wow. What does that mean? Why, it's the way it is. Get my head together.

She showed him a postcard. It was the photograph of an old man named Mehor Baba. He was an Indian saint. Sure. Would you buy a second-hand life style from this man?

There is a Mehor Baba society. He had a huge mustache. The mustache was combed, the hair slicked back. Back to Brylcreem. Mehor Baby. That's what it's all about. Under the portrait of Mehor Baba was printed, "Smile. Be happy."

"You mind if I turn on the television?"

"Not at all."

"I don't know why, but it gets only one channel."

"I don't care. I don't watch much, anyway."

The face that came up on the set had a beard. It talked, between flickers and shadows, of ecumenism. Ecumenism. On Avenue B.

The girl excused herself.

"Where are you going?" Grosbeck asked.

"You got to be kidding," said the girl. "I got to tinkle."

"Tinkle!" said Grosbeck. "Who taught you that? I thought tinkle went out with fraternity pins."

The girl left the room. Presently, there was a rush of water, a choke in the bowl and then the only sound in the apartment the voice of the beard talking about Chicanos and blacks and Indians. Sunday morning television. Grosbeck thought it ironic that the only channel that could be received on this television set was the educational station.

When the girl returned, she was naked. On her left thigh was a tattoo, blue and blurred, of a butterfly. On her left breast, an envelope caught in the lip of a mailbox, was a dagger pointing at the nipple. Above her crotch was a face, all mouth and teeth, like the face above the entrance to an amusement park.

The ecumenist continued to mumble on the television set, interrupted by crackles. The girl seated herself on a chair. "It's yours," she said. "Come and get it."

Grosbeck was struck as much by the lack of emotion in himself as in the girl. "I don't know," he said. "What do

73

you like?" He was acutely aware of the lack of bulge in his pants.

"Anything you want," she said.

"When you went to the bathroom," Grosbeck asked, "what else did you do? Did you take anything? Ups? Downs? Heroin?"

For the first time since he had seen her, the girl laughed. Laughed and bent over, sitting naked in the chair. "Not for you, Pop," she said. "You need anything?"

Yes, thought Grosbeck. At my age, a great deal, and I don't think you can give it to me. A train of excuses ran through his head. He shifted in his chair and pulled at the creases in his pants above the knees. How silly. Settling down for a concert at Philharmonic Hall. Had he been wearing a suit, he could have felt for his glasses to read the program, turn the pages quickly before the lights went down. Instead of the hush in the concert hall, there was only the voice of the ecumenist delivering his scraps of humanistic gibberish.

The girl put an arm over the back of her chair, crossed her legs and laughed again, laughed so hard that she started to cough; coughed so hard that she had to close her eyes and pound on her chest with a fist. "Oh, shit, mister," she said, when she opened her eyes. "You are too much."

"What do you mean?" asked Grosbeck.

"What did you expect?"

"I don't know," he said. He had not expected the Rue des Moulins. He had not expected Valparaiso, the Reeperbahn, New Orleans, St. Louis, Greene Street, thick heels, striped stockings, huge buttocks, melting looks, gilt chairs, mirrored walls, the clop-clop of horses outside, seduction, a measured progression. He had expected none of these, but he had hoped for something in the last third of the twentieth century.

Instead, a baby snoring in a crib, a television set featuring a homosexual liberal Episcopalian with turnaround collar, cracked walls and an implacable young girl sitting naked before him, incapable of grasping what it was he was after, and, in her ignorance, laughing at him. Whatever was left inside Grosbeck's pants nodded in sympathy and withdrew quietly between his thighs.

"I am . . . I have a tendency . . . to be literary," Grosbeck said idiotically.

"You can't get it up," said the girl.

"No," he said. "It's not that. It's just . . . just . . ." he ended, lamely, "You don't understand. No reason why you should."

Middle age and the weight of a thousand thousand written fantasies settled more firmly on his shoulders. His pants grew too big for him; his shoes were the wrong size; he was drinking coffee in a cafeteria and pushing mashed potatoes around on a plate with a spoon. There was a rattling of crockery, the hiss of a steam table, eyes full of rheum sitting across the table, watching him clean the potatoes away from his dentures with a forefinger, rinsing with the gray coffee. There were cataracts in his eyes, a cane by his side, arthritic lumps on his fingers, wisps of green-white hair at the back of his head, a sore on his temple.

"You want to try?" asked the girl. She got up from the chair and walked over to the bed. There was dirt on her ankles, her knees were bony, her shinbones and ribs announced the onset of malnutrition. She lay on the bed and moved, mechanically, like a Salvation Army tambourine soliciting alms.

"Make up your mind," she said sharply. "Come here."

Grosbeck obeyed, approached the bed and was manipulated like a calf in a roping contest.

"Mister," said the girl, "you just don't want to get laid this morning. You bit off something bigger than you could chew?" That made her laugh again. "Hey. How about that?"

"Go home," she said. "Get some breakfast. You don't belong here!" She looked around, leaning on an elbow, and then back at Grosbeck. "I don't know who does, but you sure as hell don't. Why didn't you just give me the stuff for the kid and go home. That's all I wanted. This isn't for you."

Grosbeck nodded and pulled up the zipper on his pants, felt for the cab fare in his pocket, looked at the child, at the girl, at the walls, at the open door of the toilet, at the ruined floor, at the postcard of the grinning guru lying on the table, at his foolish self so clearly limned in his mind.

The ecumenist finished. There was a moment of silence. Then, music: "Onward Christian Soldiers."

The magnificent strains filled the room. "Marching as to war." The authenticity of what he was listening to astounded Grosbeck. It was slightly off key. "With the Cross of Jesus, going on before." General Booth marched through Whitechapel. Behind him the band . . . cornets, trombones, flügelhorn, alto horn, baritone horn, euphonium, tuba, banging tambourines. . . . Before him the flag . . . Blood and Fire . . . blue, gold and red . . . and behind, the ragged ranks of the poor.

Grosbeck was saved. He wept, standing before the girl on the bed, until the music had ended. He wiped his eyes with both hands, bade the girl take care of herself, went through the door, stumbled over a brick lying in the hallway and got into the hot, bright street. It was nine o'clock in the morning. His skin smarted from the dried tears.

It was impossible to find a cab in this part of town and he

took a bus, returning home, shriven by the music of a man who found Jews unacceptable in polite society. He had saved cab fare and risked nothing, only humiliation. On the corner on which he lived, there was a flower store. He bought a single rose and would not permit the florist to wrap it. He picked up the newspapers, put them on a table and presented the rose to Madeline. She accepted it, put it to her face, and asked Grosbeck whether he would like eggs Benedict for breakfast, and he said, "Yes . . . yes . . . yes."

Eggs Benedict. The sound of the words was analogous to the music of Sir Arthur Sullivan, promising wafer and wine, the chanting of cantors. The words eliminated for him the dreadful hour on Avenue B, the hollow in his pants, the retreat at the Khyber Pass. What Sir Arthur had promised him in the miserable chapel on Avenue B, Madeline would deliver in the cathedral on Sixth. Eggs Benedict. And seraphic delights after that, undreamed of on Avenue B. Jason had a Boy Scout hike that day. *Carpe diem.* Grosbeck's stomach rumbled. He excused himself, went into the bathroom and swallowed three tablets of Maalox. Everything would be as beautifully arranged now as in a painting by Puvis de Chavannes.

Fortunately for his precarious sanity, Grosbeck had the gift of all great political thinkers and rednecks . . . the gift of elision . . . of omitting this and including that . . . so that what remained was a consistent world. His trouble, however, was that he could not make things stick very long.

Further, he was unalterably prejudiced in favor of the dead, as opposed to the quick. So, he could hate young white women with tattoos and babies, who took drugs and made fun of him, and yet yearn for a Greene Street whore buried a hundred years in a Potters' Field; harbor a sneaking admiration for Paris Singer or James Hazen Hyde and despise Baleen and Shalit. Engels, examining the factories of Manchester for Marx while running his father's business, fitted in with Grosbeck's notions of revolution.

And since he could not sustain elision or overcome his prejudice for the dead; since his ideas of contemporaneity were to be found only in libraries or sold at auction, inevitably he was at odds with the facts of life. And he was hungry. The frankfurters had done nothing for him.

Madeline said, "I need eggs."

Grosbeck said, "If you're going to make eggs Benedict, why don't you have eggs?"

Madeline said, "Harvey, only you are perfect. Only you have eggs when you need eggs."

Grosbeck said, "You're making something out of nothing. I thought you did all the shopping yesterday."

Madeline said, "Forgive me. The servant has failed. I know my place. It won't happen again. I'm sure both of your other wives had eggs all the time."

Grosbeck said, "You're rising off the ground again. What else have you got? We don't have to have eggs Benedict."

Madeline said, "Oh, yes, we do. The servant got out of line. The servant begs your pardon. She grovels, sir. What else has she done wrong this time?" She tore off her nightgown . . . tore it off . . . and made an inventory of her clothes in the closet. "I've had it with you," she said, and bit her thumb.

Grosbeck said, "Have you? This, too, shall pass. All I said

was how does it happen you don't have eggs. That was it. Not they've blown up the White House. I love you."

Madeline said, "You don't love anybody. You don't even love you."

Grosbeck said, "Your talent for feeling sorry for yourself is equaled only by the size of your ass. They're both outsize. I married you for your ass. And, I'm the only one in this house has any right to feel sorry for himself."

Madeline said, "I'm leaving. Make your own fucking eggs Benedict."

Grosbeck said, "I'm shocked at your language. I wouldn't have believed it possible of you."

Madeline said, "Oh, no? Half the time you demand it of me. The rest of the time it's an aesthetic offense. If it fits in with what we're doing . . ." She rotated her pelvis at him. "That's fine. But not at this hour of the day, and in this year of Our Lord, not when we're talking about breakfast. I don't know what kind of dream world you live in, but the world has moved on."

She pulled a suitcase out of the closet. "I'm getting out of here," she said. "I don't have to take this."

Grosbeck said, "Take what? All I said was why don't you have eggs." He grabbed for the suitcase and the two of them fought over it. They panted like baboons fighting over a stalk of bananas, stumbling around the room and knocking things over. A stale joke, thought Grosbeck: The situation is critical, but not serious. He said it aloud and she threw the suitcase back into the bottom of the closet.

Madeline said, "I've got nowhere to go. It's true. All you did ask was why don't we have eggs. We don't because I didn't look. But you make it sound like a crime. I don't know how you manage to do it, but you do. I'll get eggs. Can you wait, Oh Lord and Master? It'll take me five minutes."

Grosbeck said, "Madeline, you're all that stands between me and the Bowery."

Madeline said, "Don't dramatize. I understand the rose. I appreciate it. I love you for it. But there are times I can't keep up with you. . . ."

"You can't keep up with *me?*" Grosbeck was genuinely incredulous. "Me?" His myopia was awesome. If there were to be a domestic quarrel, it should be on the order of the breakfast scene in *The Life of the Late Mr. Jonathan Wild the Great.* Nothing less than Fielding suited Grosbeck. Epigrams. Slaps. The breaking of crockery. Flight and pursuit. The tearing of clothes. Sweet surrender and hilarity. Cold mutton afterward and a bottle of claret. Instead, this. If there were to be a fight, let it be in rounded periods, not this laundry list of complaints. He felt put upon and dropped the matter.

"I'll go with you," he said.

Madeline said, "Don't bother. Just get Jason up and out of the house. Give him a couple of pieces of toast, cream cheese and strawberry jam and a glass of milk. I'll be right back."

Grosbeck said, "Your wish is my command."

Madeline turned at the door. "Just see to it that he has something to eat, puts on all his clothes and leaves."

Grosbeck said, "You sure you got all *your* clothes?"

Madeline shut the door hard.

Grosbeck tickled the boy awake. "Leave me alone," said Jason.

"You've got to get out of here," Grosbeck said. "You're due at that hike in half an hour."

"I don't want to go."

"Get up, or I'll kill you."

"Kill me."

"You'll kill me first. Give me a kiss."

"Ah, come on, Pa," said Jason. But he offered his cheek reluctantly and let it be kissed.

"I suppose you wouldn't consider taking a shower."

"I had one Friday."

"Brush your teeth?"

"Why?"

"Brush your teeth."

"Balls."

"Oh. A man of parts."

The boy went off and did a minimum of the things Grosbeck would have liked him to do. He came back in dungarees and a shirt, his sneakers untied and his hair uncombed. Grosbeck settled for the fact that he wasn't naked.

"How come no eggs?"

"Your mother's out getting eggs. Or hadn't you noticed she's not here."

"I thought she was still asleep."

"Well, she isn't. Where you going today?"

"Jamaica Bay. The Wildlife Refuge. We're going to take pictures of birds again."

"You got your camera? Film?"

"Pa, for Christ's sake . . ."

"You *do* forget."

"What's this here in the bag . . . right at my feet."

Grosbeck opened the bag. "A camera. No film."

"It's in my room." The boy got the film, dropped it in the bag and said, "Satisfied?"

"Look," said Grosbeck. "You don't take pictures without film. What if you got out there and found you didn't have any?"

"Someone always has an extra roll."

Grosbeck gave up. "Go," he said. "Go with God. But go. What time will you be back?"

"I don't know," said the boy. "Today."

"Thank you," said Grosbeck. "We'll leave a lamp in the window."

"What's for dinner?"

"You want Chinese? If you get back early enough?"

"Oh, wow!"

"'Oh, wow!' You, too. LikeImeanyouknow."

"Pa, cut it out." Jason picked up the bag. "Now, you're mad."

"Like I mean you know I'm not mad," said Grosbeck. "Kiss me, you fool. And get out of here."

"Pa," said the boy, "half the time I don't know what you're talking about and half you don't know what you're talking about." He stood in the door, the camera bag around his neck, his pockets bulging with junk.

Music swelled in Grosbeck's head. He detected an aureole about the boy's head, felt tears behind his eyes again and waited for the vision to disappear. The door closed and he was alone.

Silence.

Grosbeck separated the newspaper into parts and lay down on the couch to await Madeline's return. Nothing new. South Vietnamese troops, supported by B-52 bombers, had done whatever it was the American command in Saigon announced. ("We really creamed them this time," said Captain Stu Buzzell, upon landing at Udorn, Thailand. "It was really beautiful." It was really beautiful, said young Mussolini after a bombing mission over Ethiopia. It was like watching the petals of a rose open.)

He gave up the front page and began looking for his favorite reading. He was not long in finding it:

"Long Beach, Calif.—A sociology student who for a research project worked as a waitress in a bar showing hardcore pornography says the atmosphere was 'like a church filled with reverence. We were supposed to keep the jukebox playing all the time,' Helen Terwilliger, a sociology student at Los Angeles City College, told the American Anthropological Association. 'But when it stopped you suddenly realized the place was just like a church. And the clientele were very reverent to what they were watching. There was a quality of awe in their attitude to the films.'"

The quotation was breathtaking, and, in its inattention to grammar, very like Middle English.

"Carbondale, Ill.—A graduate zoology researcher at Southern Illinois University has received a research grant to find out if quail talk to each other before they are born. Donald Darnton received a grant of $197 from the United States Government, it was announced. He will attempt to find out if clicking sounds heard from quail eggs is a form of communication. He will place some eggs in isolation and observe them in relation to the mother's brooding call."

In view of the difficulty of getting a telephone information operator, Grosbeck found such research egregious.

Since it was Sunday, Grosbeck sought out the latest on theology and found it above a four-line poem by a constant contributor. There was much homely wisdom to be found in these poems but he devoted his attention to today's homily:

"In one of the Bible's most famous passages, St. Paul lists those virtues everyone should strive to attain.

"They are Love, Faith and Hope.

"Few will dispute his emphasis on the importance of Love and Faith. But what of the third member of this triad. Hope?

83

Can it really be regarded as a virtue . . . that is, a trait of character people ought consciously to cultivate?

"Many people, when they stop to think about it, are surprised to find Hope spoken of as a positive moral obligation. They are inclined to feel it's largely a question of a person's natural disposition, or the circumstances in which he finds himself, whether he views the future with Hope or fear.

"But Paul is in good company when he insists that we have a duty to be hopeful, even in bleak or ominous circumstances. Through the ages, many other philosophers and poets have attached high value to Hope, particularly the unquenchable kind of Hope that causes men and women to keep trying even in the face of great adversity."

What? What's that? What did he say?

Silence.

Grosbeck considered the duty to be hopeful.

※

If Grosbeck had no metaphor by which to live, he did have presentiments and nourished them until they were borne out by events. If they were not, that was no impediment. The world would still come to an end. Thesis; antithesis; but no synthesis. *That* was where Hegel fell on his face. No synthesis. Grosbeck had squatted on his hams and rattled knucklebones on the ground and knew better than Hegel. The universe would explode. Call *that* a synthesis if you felt like it. Grosbeck was disappointed at the Lord's insistence on putting off Judgment Day, but always hopeful. He would disintegrate, crying, "I told you so," and the finger he pointed at disbelievers would fly, wagging, into space.

He lay on the couch, sated by the newspapers. The building made noises: the slap of shrouds, a windlass turning, the shifting of dunnage deep in the hold. No, no, the bang of the incinerator door and someone shuffling away down the hall in slippers. The engineer's children shook the ceiling with their maypole dances; the walls shuddered under the assault of a truck moving over a roadway of Standard Granite Block. The serpent in the Kollner lithograph of Barnum's American Museum coiled and uncoiled; in Central Park, the skaters turned and turned on the winter lake; Frederic Rondel's freighter under full sail moved in moonlight through the Upper Bay past Fort Jay and the pilot and his men rowed out to meet it. Forever.

There was a scream in the hall.

Madeline.

Grosbeck was off the couch and out the door.

Madeline stood with her back to the closed elevator door, her mouth open, talking, soundless, one hand outstretched with money in it, the other palm up, halting traffic. At her feet was a torn paper bag, around it a puddle of broken eggs. This dubious lake, these doubtful shores, separated Madeline from a small black man with a shaved head and a knife in his left hand.

The conventionality of his appearance was shocking: seersucker suit, shirt, tie, cordovan shoes. But the fly of his pants was open and he had a knife and he was moving it in small circles at the level of Madeline's face across the puddle of broken eggs. "Talk to me," he wheedled. "Later for the money. Talk, talk." The level of the voice was normal; whatever intensity was in it was the result of annoyance that his shoes might be soiled by the puddle.

85

"Your pants are open," said Madeline. She screamed again.

The knife stopped revolving and dipped a little, trembling in the thin-boned fist. With his other hand, the man pulled closed the zipper on his pants. "Lousy bitch," he said. "I don't want any part of you. Anybody can forget." He seemed anxious to explain but angered by the destruction of the symmetry of his performance, by the oversight. He brought up the knife again.

Grosbeck was afraid. He was, as he had said so often, a born coward, but this time it was no living-room joke. Yet, he advanced down the hall. He loved Madeline. That's right! He loved Madeline and he shouted as he moved in a voice he had not heard before, a trumpet that resounded in the hall, with which he summoned up everything he choked down in the subways and in the office.

"You dirty, fucking nigger bastard. If I get my hands on you, I'll kill you. I'll tear your heart out. I'll cut off your balls with that knife, you cocksucking junkie son of a bitch." Grosbeck's little paunch shook with effort. Coon, smoke, shine, spade. Spick, spook, gook, sheenie, kike. Guinea, wop, polack, bohunk, hunkie, mick. The epithets were as archaic as Grosbeck's tastes. Only the week before, the Landmarks Preservation Commission had given up its genteel struggle to save a limestone French Renaissance mansion on Upper Fifth Avenue, once occupied by people who would have ordered Grosbeck's grandparents to the delivery entrance. Never mind that.

For Grosbeck, this was equally the doing of the building speculators, the pinch-faced *goyim* on the commission (yes, and their smoothly sculptured reform-Jewish colleagues), the mayor, Wall Street, the bankers and the man with the knife. No one would have believed what was coming out of his mouth. "You destroyed this city," he shouted at the mugger. "You, you cancer, and everything like you." *And* the cops who weren't there; dial 911 and get a fart on the phone. "And now I'm going to destroy you." It was Madeline who would feel the knife, but it was Grosbeck who would restore the city, pull down the skyscrapers, put back the St. Nicholas Hotel, bring back the horsecar and expunge the present. There would be small wooden barrels of gingersnaps in tiny A&P stores and the smell of coffee being ground by hand in red machines.

The knife in the hand of the mugger stopped turning.

When Grosbeck was within five feet of him, he withdrew it and put it in a breast pocket as formally as though he were returning a cigarette case there. And fled through a door to the stairway next to the elevator. Madeline slid to the floor and sat in the puddle of broken eggs, tears running down her face, sounds coming out of her chest, unhurt, the money still in her hand. "Thank you," she whispered to Grosbeck. "You're out of your mind." "Oh, really?" asked Grosbeck. He was offended, but he kissed her and helped her to her feet. Doors opened in the hallway. People came out, padded up the hall and down, commiserated, looked at each other, followed the Grosbecks down the hall (Grosbeck had an arm around his wife's waist, and, since she was taller than he, he seemed to be leaning on her) and gathered before the door of their apartment. Grosbeck gently pushed Madeline into the apartment, raised a hand to the neighbors as though he were blessing them and shut the door in their faces. He took time to note that one of them, a young man, was (a) naked and (b) flaccid. And he admired him for this unconscious physiological piece of tact.

Grosbeck led his wife to the couch and made her lie down. He removed her shoes. He soothed her face with touches. He said first that he would make coffee and then that he would call the police. "Coffee!" said Madeline. She was incredulous. "The police!" She turned her face away and Grosbeck tugged it back. "Thank you, Harvey," said Madeline. "I love you. You really are my hero." "I didn't think I had it in me, Madeline," he said. "Where in hell did it come from?" he wondered. "Harvey," said Madeline. "It happened to me, not you. Remember? Me." He had stepped on her lines. She had once acted in amateur theatrical productions; Grosbeck was upstaging her.

The tableau was ineffable, a veritable Rogers group: a middle-aged man seated at his wife's side; she, supine, holding his hand; no trellised vines, no cows ruminating just out of eyeshot; only Darby and Joan in an elevator apartment.

"Get me the Kaopectate, Harvey, would you?" asked Madeline faintly.

"The what?" asked Grosbeck.

"Kaopectate," said Madeline. "This whole thing is giving me the runs."

Jesus, Mary and Joseph, Grosbeck thought. The Rogers group fell apart.

"Sure," he said, and brought it to her with a spoon.

She drank out of the bottle. That's not in character, thought Grosbeck, but, oh, well, what the hell, it must have been pretty rough. He was magnanimous. "Tell me about it," he said, putting the bottle on the coffee table.

Madeline wiped her lips with the back of a hand. That wasn't characteristic, either. Whatever happened to Lady Mary, jogging sidesaddle through the West Riding? Idiot. Grosbeck reproached himself for expecting Trollope when what the city was serving up was sordid and dangerous; in Manhattan, a fox did not run blindly from coverts to nip at a horse's leg and then flee over a stone wall, the hounds in full cry after him.

Grosbeck patted Madeline's leg. Still pretty good, he thought. "Tell me," he repeated.

Madeline told him: The man followed her through the lobby door. She hadn't paid much attention. He got on the elevator with her and started in when the door closed. Her viscera were clumps of dough; thought left her; she was unable to fix on any detail of the man, which would restore her to reason; the knife was all; she did not want another scar on her belly to add to the one which had been put there to permit Jason to be born; the possibility of rape did not excite or disgust her; the thought of death did not enter her head; there was no time for intellectual exercises, only a highly generalized discomfort. No, no, she simply could not reconstruct exactly how she felt . . . only that there was a deafening noise in her ears, punctuated by crackling; that she was as repelled by the puddle of broken eggs as the mugger; and that, finally, Harvey was there. The bowels of Grosbeck's compassion were much moved by what *he* had done.

"What'll you do about breakfast, Harvey?" asked Madeline.

"Fuck breakfast," said Grosbeck. "What you need is a drink. Then, coffee. Then, I'm going to call the cops. I'll take you out later, buy you a big breakfast, pick up some flowers, then, maybe we'll go to a movie in the afternoon."

"Oh, Harvey," said Madeline. "I couldn't. I just want to stay here. And please don't call the police. I don't want another scene."

"What do you mean, you don't want another scene?" asked Grosbeck. "Don't you think they ought to be told, at least?"

"You don't tell, Harvey," said Madeline. "You scream. Let's just wait awhile until I calm down and then we'll go out and have breakfast. That's a lovely idea."

"God damn it," shouted Grosbeck. "What the hell are you talking about? What are you going to do? Lie around and have the goddamned vapors? It wouldn't be right to open your goddamned rosebud mouth and complain to anyone? I suppose if he'd stuck that lousy knife into you, you'd have taken it out, wiped it off and handed it back to him."

"No, Harvey," said Madeline. "It's not that. It's just that calling the police won't do any good. We both know that, and all you'll do is get abusive."

"You're fucking well right I'll get abusive, if that's what you call it," said Grosbeck. "In triplicate. With a copy to that shithead from Yale down in City Hall." He called the police emergency number.

"Harvey," said Madeline. "How many times have you told *me* it doesn't do any good?" A thought struck her. Possibly, she could divert him. "Harvey?" she asked. "Do you remember when they were all big men with red faces and wore white gloves and had big bellies? Be nice, Harvey. Please don't fight with them."

Harvey handed Madeline a small glass of brandy. A crystal glass, naturally. The coffee was done and he set that down before her. She sipped a little brandy, drank a little coffee and got a little drunk, waiting for the police to arrive.

"There's something else, Harvey," said Madeline.

"What, what," he said. "About the cops? You're not going to put me off that way."

"Not the police, Harvey. Something else. I recall now when we got on the elevator, I pressed the button for our floor and *he* pressed Six. It just occurred to me."

"What occurred to you? Nothing occurred to me."

Madeline drew herself up on the couch; was that possible for a frightened lady who was a little drunk? Grosbeck supposed so.

"Not everything occurs to you first, Harvey," said Madeline. "There *are* other people to whom things occur, sometimes first, sometimes simultaneously. It's called independent discovery."

"Madeline," said Grosbeck, "just tell me what it is that occurred to you first and not to me."

"Harvey, what made that man press Six? If he were after me alone, he wouldn't have pressed any button."

"Madeline, I don't *know* what made that bastard press Six and right now I don't much care." He stopped. "Wait a minute," he went on. "What are you trying to say in your goddamned oblique way?"

"Catafesta lives on that floor, Harvey."

"Yes, Madeline, and so do, I don't know, a dozen other people."

"Harvey, I said Catafesta lives on that floor. We know what he does and the people who are forever going up to the sixth."

The stubbornness of Grosbeck was impressive and infuriating. "A lot of people go up to the sixth, Madeline," he said. "Some in rags, some in jags and some in velvet gown. I mean, some in rag and some in jag and some in drag. Hark,

hark, the dogs do bark, the beggars are coming to town. Are you saying this jigaboo had something to do with Catafesta?"

"That's right, Harvey."

"Well . . ." said Grosbeck. He resisted the connection. "I still don't believe it." He looked toward the door. "When in the name of God are those cops going to get here? I don't know where they got that race of midgets they've got now," said Grosbeck. "Midgets with sideburns and dandruff. I never thought I'd live to be taller than a New York City cop. And dirty and lazy and they all live on Long Island, the lousy, crooked bastards. No cop ever was a bargain," Grosbeck went on, "but the only times you and I ever see one working is when he's picking up from Perazzo once a week."

The banality of his complaints was not lost on Grosbeck. Even so, he would have continued, but just then the doorbell rang. The ring was followed by two heavy knocks on the door.

"That's them," said Grosbeck. "Only a cop rings the bell and then knocks on the door. I suppose they'll have their guns out. Maybe they think I'm double-parked at a hydrant. That used to mean the electric chair."

"Harvey," said Madeline, "I think I'll go into the bedroom and lie down."

"No you don't," said Grosbeck at the door. "*You* got mugged, not me. *You've* got to talk to them."

"Then *let* me talk to them, Harvey," said Madeline. "You go into the bedroom."

Grosbeck looked over his shoulder at her. "You're out of your mind," he said and opened the door.

"You Mister Grosbeck?" asked the sergeant. "What's the trouble?" He was a small man; the lumps of his armament stuck out all over him and his tunic was open. His partner was a huge patrolman. It should, at least, have been the other way around. And *his* tunic was closed.

"Oh, nothing, nothing at all, Sergeant," said Grosbeck. "It's good of the two of you to drop around. Matter of fact, you're just in time for breakfast."

Mutt and Jeff looked at each other.

"Mister Grosbeck," said the big patrolman. "You don't have to be hard-nosed about it. We got a report of a disturbance in this apartment." He looked at his watch. "Eight minutes ago. That's not bad time."

Madeline attempted to get up and walk out of the room. Grosbeck pushed her back on the couch.

"Come in, come, gentlemen," Grosbeck said. "Have a chair, have a drink, have something to eat. My wife will take care of you as soon as she stops shaking."

"Harvey," said Madeline. "*You're* making me shake."

"I wouldn't want either of you on your feet too long," Grosbeck went on. "It's probably years since either of you got off your ass . . . except to stand over a barbecue in Nassau County. My wife and I were feeling a little lonely this morning and we thought it would be nice to have a couple of public servants in. I hate to think I broke up your morning nap."

"Mister Grosbeck," said the sergeant. "I was born in Flatbush and I live in the house where I was born. I don't think there's any need to talk like that." He was neither angry nor defensive. He simply couldn't have cared less. Or, as the Neanderthals said these days, he could care less. Didn't anyone have any idea what the hell he was saying any more? But (trembling with hatred), back to our muttons.

"How about you, officer?" Grosbeck asked the patrolman. "You another exemplary citizen of New York? I'd hate to

93

hang one minute for every payment you've made on that nice little mortgage in that dandy little Levittown in the sky."

"Mister Grosbeck," said the patrolman. "What are you going to prove if I don't live in New York City? No, I don't live in New York, but if there's been some kind of trouble here our job is to help you."

"Help me!" said Grosbeck. "Help me? You don't even know what happened? They didn't even bother to tell you?"

"All we know is we got a call to come here," said the sergeant. "Suppose you tell us what it's all about." He reached under his tunic and pulled out one of those narrow, thick, leather-covered notebooks they all carried, held together with a rubber band a half inch wide.

"My wife got mugged," said Grosbeck. "On a Sunday morning. In the building in which we live. By some bastard with a knife. Black, light black. I ran out the door and he ran away. Happens all the time."

The sergeant wet a pencil with the tip of his tongue and flipped open the cover of the notebook.

"Either of you able to tell me what the perpetrator looked like?"

The perpetrator. Police jargon. The subject. The assailant. The victim. On or about August the fifteenth. In the vicinity of the premises at. At about 9:30 A.M. in the morning. The tiny pedant in Grosbeck jumped up. "Nine-thirty A.M. is enough, Sergeant," he said. The sergeant glanced up from his painful transcribing. "Never mind, Sergeant," said Grosbeck. "But do you really have to move your lips while you write?" Still no reaction. Subject was observed attempting.

Madeline described the man, described him in such precise detail that Grosbeck left off his loathing of the police for a moment, left off binding up the wounds of syntax and looked at Madeline speculatively.

"There was something familiar about him," she said. "I know, I *think* I know I've seen him before. Here. Right in this building. Maybe that's why I didn't pay too much attention to him when he followed me into the elevator."

"You say you seen him before?" asked the sergeant.

"Yes," said Madeline. "I'm sure of it now. I think he used to come here quite often to see somebody."

Both policemen came to attention for the first time, ludicrously, like the comic and the house tenor on a burlesque stage at the passage of the stripper from stage left to stage right.

The sergeant cleared his throat. "What makes you think so?" he asked Madeline. "What would he be doing here?"

Something in the tone of the sergeant's voice caught Grosbeck's attention.

Then, then, one of the few times in his life of petty self-absorption, of magniloquent attitudinizing (in anyone else, Grosbeck admitted reluctantly, the word would have been bullshitting), Grosbeck understood what was going on around him. It was not so much that he was stupid as drugged on print and paint and pictures and the mistaken conclusions from them that were inevitable.

The sergeant didn't want to be told.

The sergeant didn't want said aloud something that he already knew.

M. Catafesta. Apartment 6-R.

A protocol of accommodation, of silences and of responses existed today just as rigid as in any Victorian romance . . . and for much the same reason . . . money. Money was the portmanteau word for it all: power, money, brutality, insidious and dangerous alliance.

Money was involved here. How much was, right now, unimportant, but what had happened was that Madeline and he had, in one of those accidents the tidy Marxist simply swept under the rug, been dragged into a risky concatenation of alarums and excursions.

The collage of rumor, gossip and evidence which, half unconsciously, Grosbeck had been collecting in the years he had lived in the building, in the neighborhood, rushed into a picture: the light coming up in the television tube, the image coming into sharp focus. And shouted at him: Fool, fool, fool. Look out. Back off. Get away. Shut up. No, he told himself. No. Stubbornly. That sort of thing doesn't happen to people like us. It doesn't fit in. But it did. The blood in the elevator. The man upstairs with the wife and the dog. And the perpetrator. Perazzo? Maybe, but probably not. He does what he does, but with some other man somewhere else.

He heard Madeline again. "I believe, I really believe," she was saying, "it had to do with drugs, heroin, I don't know what . . . that he came here to see a man who lives on the sixth floor . . . that he was a junkie. And a small-time dealer, and he was here to get his supply. Couldn't it be that was why he was here so often? Is that possible, Sergeant?"

Madeline, keep quiet.

"Ahhh, ummm, anything's possible, Mrs. Grosbeck," said the sergeant. He snapped the rubber band around the notebook and put away his pen. His partner looked at the pictures on the wall.

"You got to realize, Mrs. Grosbeck," said the sergeant confidentially, a man squeezing out a revelation. "Uh, it's not all like you see in the movies or read in the papers. This is a low-crime precinct, the figures show it, that's why we got less cars on the street down here. And a dealer in this house?" He shook his head. "Sure, you're upset. I don't blame you."

"*You* don't blame *her*, Sergeant?" asked Grosbeck. "She's not guilty of anything? We needed *you* to come here and tell us that? You give me a new respect for the police, Sergeant. She's not to blame for getting mugged, but if she'd got stabbed you'd have pulled her in. Right?"

Careful.

What was essential now was not to let the police know that *he* knew. Possibly, it was not too late. These two were not stupid. They were venal, they were callous and they were cunning, these animals, but they were not omniscient. He had begun in genuine anger. He would contrive more. He would divert them. They would, he hoped, be fooled and go away satisfied. For once, his big mouth would serve him. Perhaps. Grosbeck's pessimism, pervasive, lifelong, nagged at him. But he must. Better a live dog than a dead lion. Consistency might be the hobgoblin of a small mind, but a small mind was better than no mind at all to be small with. He would rather they put him down for a crank than get him killed.

"Let me tell you something, you two," said Grosbeck. "You're no damned good. You're no good now, you never were any good. You're all alike. I've been in the newspaper business thirty years and I never met a cop I liked. I've always wondered what kept you from knocking down little old ladies crossing the street." (How did that come out?) "What a fine pair of male Caucasians you are."

He gave them a brief history of police corruption: Dr. Parkhurst, Satan's Circus, the Lexow Investigation, Magistrate Vitale, Judge Seabury, Jimmie Walker, Bill O'Dwyer, John Harlan Amen, Tom Dewey, Abe Reles and the Half Moon Hotel, Lepke and Gurrah (Lepke and Mendy Weiss going to the electric chair: Lepke furious, Mendy Weiss, the big fat *momser,* crying as they strapped him in, "God and Governor Dewey know I'm innocent," whatever he had to say further shut off by the black strap across his mouth); Pittsburgh Phil Strauss, Frank (The Dasher) Abbandando, Pretty Amberg, Harry Gross, the Knapp Commission; side trips into Joe the Boss and Salvatore Maranzano, a murder a week on Kenmare Street during Prohibition, up Centre one block from Police Headquarters. (When the shocks were administered, the prisoner leaned forward in the electric chair as though he were being attentive to a light conversation. The arms, bound to the armrests of the chair, could not move, but the fingers could and they curled around the ends, as though the prisoner, interested in what was being said, could not restrain his small physical movements. And when the current was turned off, the body leaned back . . . a pause in the conversation. And when it was determined that the number of shocks was sufficient and the light foam had leaked out of the mouth, the doctor stepped up to the patient in the chair. He ripped open the shirt . . . there was no need to open it . . . and the white buttons fell to the floor and danced on the rubber mat beneath the chair. And the doctor turned to the spectators, seated silently in the golden-oak church pews, and said, quite casually, "This man is dead." Next.)

"I saw you ride sailors down on horseback during the big seamen's strike in 1936," Grosbeck raved. And more and more. And on and on. They must be kept away from this morning. Had he done it? Would he know? "Oh, you're very big at busting heads," he said. "Very big. Big on towaways. Big on knocking off some two-bit whore on Forty-ninth Street. How many pimps paid for that house out on the Island?"

"Mr. Grosbeck," said the sergeant coldly, "do you think that's the kind of language to use in front of your wife, a lady?"

"Go fuck yourself," said Grosbeck.

"All right, Mr. Grosbeck," said the sergeant. "You got your nuts off and we got things to do. We'll do what we can and you can come over to the stationhouse and look at some mug shots. If you can find the time. A lot of *you* people come on very strong, but we don't get very much out of you but mouth. Like I say, we'll try, but don't expect too much. *We* don't. I hear a lot about community relations and cooperation, but I don't see a lot of it. Ahhh, forget it. . . ."

The sergeant opened the door, let the patrolman out, and, as he walked out himself, looked over his shoulder at Grosbeck and said, not bitterly, not with any sense of grievance, but only quietly and contemptuously:

"You old son of a bitch."

❖

"Harvey, what have you done," asked Madeline. It was a statement, not a question.

"Madeline," he answered, "what did you do?" It was no less a statement. "You told them something you shouldn't have. They *know*, or I'm afraid they know. I hope I fooled them, but I doubt it."

"Aren't you exaggerating, Harvey?"

"No, I'm not. This is no *roman policier*. This isn't history. This is the real thing. Those cops are our enemies. We have

99

interfered with the orderly course of business. I'm scared shitless."

He got up. "Madeline, I've got to go to the can. I swear to God," he said in exasperation, "I'll die incontinent. Back in a minute." He went off to the toilet and thought while his insides emptied themselves out, leaving behind only the worm of fear. He returned to the living room, the worm fatter and longer.

"Five will get you ten," Grosbeck said to Madeline, "the cops have already been on the phone with the man upstairs. They can lay hands on your friend in the elevator in five minutes. And they will. He'll never show his face in this building again. Mr. Catafesta will see to that because Mr. Catafesta doesn't need that kind of trouble in his business. Neither do the cops. You were right. I wish you hadn't been for our sake.

"It's easy to see what happened. The guy's an addict *and* a dealer. Just as you said, he was making a pickup. I don't know too much about junkies, but he must have been strung out badly this time and who knows what goes through their heads then? He did what he did to you and he'll never do it again. Not here. But *they're* not through with *us*. Not Catafesta, not the cops. It's not your fault, Madeline; it's nobody's fault; these things come out of left field now. They happen. Jesus, what do we do now?"

Madeline sat up on the couch. "Harvey," she said, "I *would* like some breakfast. I *would* like you to take me out and get me some flowers and go to a movie. That's what we do now."

The room was stifling in the August heat.

"I'll turn on the air conditioners and it'll be nice and cool when we get back. Look, what possible difference can it make to them if we know. We don't bother them. They won't bother us. We don't count." She stroked his worried face. "And tonight, we'll take Jason with us and get some Chinese food. It'll be a lovely day. And tomorrow, you'll get back to the real thing. Baleen and Shalit. They're more of a menace to peace and security than these people."

"Madeline," said Grosbeck, "you're wrong. Wrong, wrong, wrong."

"Harvey," said Madeline, "you've been wrong, too, in your time." She smiled. "Oh, not often, of course. But you did say we'd all be down the drain by now. That was every day for the last ten years, wasn't it, Harvey?" she asked, with love. "And here we are, aren't we, Harvey?"

"You aren't listening to me, Madeline."

"I always listen, Harvey. You don't always hear. We're of absolutely no account to those people."

"You going to play earth goddess with me today, Madeline? You going to be the mother of us all?"

"Yes, I am, Harvey. I don't feel like cringing before anyone today, Harvey. I want my breakfast and everything else you promised me."

"Madeline, you know McFarland? The big rewriteman, the one who works the late shift, the one with the broken nose, used to be in the Marines? Tough? Right? Fucking-A-Right McFarland?"

"Yes. I happen to like him."

"Forget that for a minute. Old McFarland gets off work at two o'clock in the morning. And you want to know what this good old boy from Deaf Smith County, Texas, does these days? Big as he is? Killed a dozen gooks at the Inchon Reservoir? Well, when he leaves the office, he puts on an act in the street. He talks to himself. In a good, loud voice. He pretends he's crazy. He jerks his head and he throws his left leg to the side every three steps.

"And he sings. Like this: 'Do your balls hang low?/ Do they dangle to and fro?/ Can you tie 'em in a knot?/ Can you tie 'em in a bow?/ Can you sling 'em on your shoulder, like a European soldier?/ Can you sing this little ditty while your balls hang low?' All the way to the Port Authority bus terminal. He's been jumped, you see, and he's figured out that if he does these bizarre things they'll let him alone. And so far, they have. But that's no guarantee for the future. Some of it's organized, some of it isn't, but there gets to be more of it every day.

"McFarland is pragmatic, even phlegmatic. An ex-Marine, a war veteran. Killed when he had to. But that was in a war in which, right or wrong, there was an enemy who could be defined, identified. But it's not that way in New York. Not any more. The whole lousy city is the Five Points. Worse . . . nothing makes sense any more and McFarland has grasped that. He discovered it long before I did. It took me until this morning."

"Then, he's smarter than you are, Harvey?"

"That's neither here nor there, Madeline. He might be. But he doesn't have his feet firmly planted in the nineteenth century, like you and me."

"Foursquare and flatfooted, Harvey?"

"Look, Madeline," said Grosbeck. "There's room in this house for only one comedian and I'm it. That noise you hear is me leaving New York."

"Any time you say, Harvey. A-n-n-n-y time. I'm yr. obdt. servt."

"That takes time, Madeline."

"Sure, it takes time, Harvey. So far, it's taken all your life."

"Madeline, cut it out, will you? How long do you think it will take for them to get at us. And, may I remind you,

Jason? Do you really think they won't chase us out to the suburbs. Hell, they already live there."

"Haven't you had enough of this, Harvey?"

"I've had enough of everything but my life with you, Madeline."

"You *do* know how to make love to a lady, Harvey."

"Madeline, this kind of talk went out with Pinero."

"You started it, Harvey. And I love it. It makes me feel better."

"Well, it doesn't make *me* feel better. Not right now. I told you I'm scared. I think you are, too."

"I am, Harvey."

"Yes, but not as scared as I am."

"That's probably true, but I don't have the same kind of fevered imagination you have. Either of us can get killed in the streets any time. I don't deny that. But I'll tell you again: Organized crime isn't very much interested in us. You may find that unpleasant to believe; it may diminish you in your own eyes, but that is the fact of the matter."

Grosbeck and his wife were in a panic. The faster they talked to each other, the worse they felt and fed the worm. The paintings did not help the panic. The books did not mitigate what had been committed upon Jason:

A dirty faggot with his cock out, holding Jason by the hair and forcing him to his knees; the cops sneering at Grosbeck. The cops continued to take their bribes, the faggots to mince and rape and hold hands and giggle and rattle their silver chains and polish their leather, brush their teeth, comb their hair and spray themselves with deodorants.

The junkies in the doorways of the raddled tenements grew sick and vicious. Some died on the splintered stairways; others went out to kill . . . an army with orders which were not to be disobeyed . . . blood in their eyes, blood in their mouths, blood on the streets, the lurid light playing on them as they marched forth. Jason. Madeline.

Help us, oh Lord. Deliver us in Thy infinite mercy. Balls.

The men responsible for all this continued to make it possible for it to happen. (Grosbeck was torn between the conspiracy theory of history and the Marxist and settled for a convenient combination of the two.) Enough, enough of this watered-down philosophical discourse. Grosbeck should have known there was a real world to be dealt with when Jason was wounded. He had refused to contemplate it, very likely because, however much he loved him, it was Jason who had been the victim and not he, Grosbeck. Grosbeck, your mind is twisted. You are guilty, Grosbeck; you are condemned to die. You did not love Jason enough. He was not flesh of your flesh, bone of your bone, only an abstraction given birth to by Madeline, a child to whom you counted out love in absent-minded portions. You did not see him; only yourself. And now, you do not see Madeline; only yourself. *She* was attacked; *you* will be punished. That is the sum of it.

Such drama.

"You do think we should go, Madeline, don't you?"

"Yes."

He was still perverse. "How do you like the idea of living up in Connecticut, say? How would you like to *relate* to, be *relevant* with, adjust your *life style* to . . . I'll vomit if I ever catch either of us using those words in earnest . . . all those great liberals who broke their asses to get out of the city so they wouldn't have to drink polluted martinis in Manhattan?

"The enlightened ex-radicals who make a very fine living writing *ademonai kademonai* for the same torch of truth for which I work. Or the ad agencies. Or television. They're poison, I tell you."

"Rhetoric, Harvey, rhetoric. The rhetoric you've been feeding yourself ever since we met. Long before we met. That's *your life style.*"

"Thank you, Madeline. You used to like it well enough."

"I still do, Harvey. But it's time to be practical. I'm sorry if I said life style. But it's time to be practical. You don't *live* in the city any more, anyway. You simply occupy a tiny place in it and run on a track and come back here nights and read about a city that went out of existence seventy-five years ago. You can do all that somewhere else, too, and never know the difference."

"Practical, Madeline? All right. Jason'd be on acid in fifteen minutes; I'd be on that train every day with my stinking little attaché case sitting next to those intellectual cops and you'd be running in a car pool with all those cunts and their marriage contracts."

"Keep it up, Harvey."

"In two weeks, we'd be baying at the moon. In a month, I'd be living across the street from the paper. In six months, we'd be divorced and in a year I'd be dead."

"In a year, *you'd* be dead, Harvey. *You.* Not me. Not Jason. *You.* Poor Harvey."

"I'm sorry, sweetheart. You're right."

"You haven't learned anything, have you, Harvey?"

"Yes, Madeline, I think I have."

"What? Tell me quickly."

Well, what? What had occurred between a thousand acts of violence read about and savored and two experienced, not even by himself (Jason, Madeline) to teach Grosbeck anything? There was a connection between the enlightened brutality of Baleen and that of the man in the elevator. The cash nexus. My God, he had invented the telephone again.

Baleen. Gangrene, cancer. Long drawn out. The grave.

A hole in the guts. Swiftly. The grave.

"It's time for me to climb out of the grave, Madeline."

"I don't know what you're talking about."

"Yes, you do. You always do. I know we've got to make a move."

"What kind of move, Harvey? You're the man of the house."

"I haven't figured it out yet. It's been so long since I had to. Let me crawl around awhile."

"No, Harvey. Not on the basis of past performance. You've got the both of us afraid for our lives. I'm infected, too, and you've got to do something."

"All *right*, Judge Lynch. Give me a couple hours. You said you wanted breakfast and a movie. Let's have them."

Grosbeck's respect and admiration for his wife grew and grew, but it would have been futile to report that to her at this juncture . . . not (in the paper language of space engineers) "at this point in time." The "window" (another one) wasn't there. Put it down in a note for the Book of Reflections; pull it out later and put it in a nosegay. Her mind was otherwise occupied.

Two ashtrays were filled with cigarette ends. An aquatint of the Great Fire of 1835 hung slightly askew above Madeline's head and a tiny, grotesque ivory *netsuke*, a fat-faced man who seemed to be devouring his own leg, had been turned completely around. Nothing had touched either of these objects, nothing human, but consternation is a powerful force. It had dimmed the lights, slanted the picture, moved the grotesque and lent the ivory a yellow cast it had not had before.

The room was hot because Madeline, in her agitation, had not turned on the air conditioner. Whatever small amount of alcohol she had drunk had burned away and she now sat alert on the couch. Grosbeck withdrew to a corner of the room. It would have been painful to touch her or be touched by her. Because both of them were afraid. And the smell of that was overpowering, driving out the familiar smells: food and perfume and bedding and dust and books disintegrating in their shelves, the dank odor of chlorine and disinfectants.

Look to your sphincter, Grosbeck. Make a juju. Horseshit. No magic . . . black, white, green or purple . . . will exorcise a murderer on the sixth floor, the police who work for him, the anonymous figures scuttling in and out of the building, ready to pinch the breath out of his and Madeline's bodies with their claws. A coven of two was not enough.

"How do you feel, Madeline?"

"Queasy," she said. "You convinced me. I hear a snuffling at the door. The beast is here."

"No." But, reluctantly, he got up and looked over his shoulder at her and went to the door. He opened it. Nothing, of course, but the effort had been monumental.

"That's the first step, Harvey."

❖

Noon. "You said you wanted breakfast, didn't you, Madeline? Let's go out. We can talk about it going upstreet, sitting down, across a table, in some secluded rendezvous, over a bagel, under the weather, *de temps en temps. Ni moi non plus. Nihil obstat.* Roger that. Hold one. Right on. Right off. Kiss my ass in Macy's window. Do I not bleed?"

Madeline was not listening. Mme. Sans-Gêne had other

fish to fry. She got up, squeezed his hand, passed by him, tidied herself, made him pat his pockets to make sure he had everything he needed, and got him to lock up.

How far away from, how long ago, Avenue B.

He had had no sleep for more than twenty-four hours. He had, the afternoon before, staged his titillating operetta, with alcohol, tobacco, costumes and a cast of two skilled in the requirements of the play from long familiarity and inclination. He had presumed to play the fool most of the night, thereafter, reading absurdities out of books. That had not been enough. He could not sleep and he had wanted more. Avenue B. He had been humiliated and repelled there and been rescued by religious music written by a man who had, obviously, never intended it for such a purpose. Not enough.

And then, he had, at one remove (through Madeline) been slapped by circumstance out of his puerility.

That was more than enough.

What would the chief rabbi of Vilna have made of that? So, Life isn't like a bottle!

Can I be overwrought? he asked himself on the way to a restaurant.

Still, he and Madeline held hands for blocks. They sweated salt into each other's hands. But it was a hot day. No more than that? Were they accustomed to holding hands on the street in any weather? They were not. Did anyone look at them strangely, whether for holding hands at their age or, knowledgeably, knowing what had happened? Or, not at all?

Grosbeck could not say. He would not ask Madeline. He did not know what Madeline thought, and, right now, he did not want to know. He would put her off again, not for very long, because it was his life now, as well as hers. He would have to furnish her with an answer. And himself. And Jason.

On this walk up to Eighth Street, he did not wear sunglasses and he did not keep his eyes to himself. He looked into the faces of people passing by and over his shoulder. Lay figures in the street. Good morning. Walk to the left to avoid pieces of glass. To the right to give passage to a group of boys with a basketball. Nobody among them. Slow down, Harvey. Stumble on the ribs and handle and black cotton of a broken umbrella. Sorry. The restaurant. Paper place mats on the counter. Orange juice. Bacon and eggs. Side order of hashed brown. None for you, Madeline? Oh, come on. Bloody mary, maybe? Do the both of us some good. Coffee. A second cup. Another cigarette. *Le Dejeuner sur l'herbe.* Manet, go home.

"Talk to me, Harvey." Her voice had an odd, high pitch, yet muffled and constrained at the same time. It was not the voice she used over breakfast.

He told her about a wealthy skinflint, who, in 1882, demanded five thousand dollars for a piece of property he owned on Lexington Avenue . . . a hundred and four feet somewhere in the eighties. A builder wanted to put up a row of houses in the side street and all that was missing was the skinflint's piece of property to complete the lot . . . no more than five feet wide from the avenue in. The builder wouldn't pay more than a thousand.

The miser refused to sell at that price. The builder put up his houses, anyway. You know what the old bastard did? He built a house five feet wide on his strip. Five feet wide! That's the way they thought in those days. You've got to admire him. Special furniture had to be made for it. You couldn't pass anyone on the stairs. Only one to a room in the whole house. And that's the way he lived with his family.

For years. It's gone. The builder's houses are gone now, too. The old man was going to shut off the light from the builder's windows. Whatever's there now shuts off the light from everything. I haven't been around there in a while. Hell, it was gone before I was born, anyway. Did you know there used to be a miniature steam railroad in Central Park? On the Fifth Avenue side?

"Harvey."

He felt nauseated. "Tonight," he said. "I swear to you. After Jason's gone to bed. Let's take a walk."

Madeline assented. But they must continue to hold hands on the street. Where to? Chelsea? Clinton? San Juan Hill? Red Hook? Not today. Not for all the long, amazing front yards, flowers and shrubbery and wrought-iron railings (lumpy with coat after coat of black enamel to cover the rust which had flaked away the iron). Not for all the lovely tangle of rusted cable and steamships of Erie Basin. East of Park Row, north of the Brooklyn Bridge, to the two-story, red-brick double house with slanting roof and dormers on Madison Street, standing between two housing projects. All right. Chrystie, Forsythe, Eldridge, Orchard, Suffolk, Norfolk, Essex. Sheriff. Attorney. Ridge. Columbia and Pitt and Henry and Gouverneur and Montgomery. (Scammell was long gone, although it was still to be found on old street platts.) Jackson, Lewis, Cherry, Pike.

Acanthus. Akroteria. Palmette. Ogee. Running dog. Trefoil. Quatrefoil. Thisgal. Egg and dart. Egg and leaf. Foliate tracery and plate. Gadroon. Greek Key. Anthemion. Bead and reel. Campaniform. Gorge. Gable. Crocket. Lunette. Guilloche. Quoin. Parget. Tympanum. Finial. Meander. Drip molding. Fret. Mutin. Nosing. Scroll, cartouche, cabuchon and swastika. Ah! And the first cemetery of Congregation Shearith Israel (the Sephardim, like the Roman Catholics, tried to preserve) and the Mariner's church, a classic in brownstone.

Most of it . . . not all . . . but most of it was gone . . . and what there was to be seen of ornament was cast in cement. The carvers, the Englishmen (phthisic and drawn, dying at an early age), and the robust Italians who followed them . . . all gone. Besides, it was easier and cheaper to make molds and cast. It looked fancy, anyway, and what immigrant Yidel was there to complain if it were not done by hand? It was a *mitzvah* to find anything at all, carved *or* cast.

Every time they walked here, they found something more had been torn down or had fallen down and they mourned, these two disengaged fools, then plucked a pickle out of a barrel on Hester Street, a bialystoker roll out of a bakery on Essex, a piece of smoked whitefish out of an appetizing store on Rivington. They took communion out of the daily habits of their grandparents, the loaves and fishes of immigrant Jews. They were comforted, but only briefly.

The day wore on. It was seven o'clock. Then eight. Then, fear pushed its way up through their throats and they decided they must go home. Jason would have returned from his bird walk.

He had. And he was hungry. Before Madeline prepared dinner (on second thought, no Chinese), she took Grosbeck into another room and told him that he would have to tell Jason what had happened that morning. "I don't think we ought to," he said. "I don't mean everything," said Madeline. "Just that I was attacked, that I didn't get hurt and that he'll have to be careful."

Grosbeck did as he was told, seated the boy in the living room, did not smoke (as though to underscore the seriousness of what he was about to say) and told Jason. Neither lightly, nor hysterically. He thought his tone was about right.

Jason took off his hiking shoes as he listened and his socks. They smelled. He wiped his forehead with the back of his forearm. What a darling boy. He was politely attentive. And when Grosbeck had finished, he said this:

"What's the big deal, Pa? Somebody rips me off every day at school. What do you think I walk around with my pockets hanging out for?"

Grosbeck bent his head in grief, forbore from clasping his son in his arms, and the family sat down to dinner.

Eleven o'clock. Jason went to bed. The telephone rang. Madeline answered and said, "Hello," several times, and "Who is this?" And hung up.

"There was nobody there," she said.

"Relax," said Grosbeck. "That wouldn't be the first time. It could have been a wrong number. It could have been one of your breathers." But he put down the magazine he had been reading. "We both used to get calls like that."

"What makes you think they were for you, too?"

Grosbeck laughed. His wife was capable of gallows humor.

"All I mean, Madeline, is sometimes I used to answer the phone. He breathes for us all, doesn't he?"

"It's been months," said Madeline.

"Nobody said anything?"

"I would have told you. But not even breathing this time.

Whoever it was must have covered the phone with his hand."

"That's happened before."

"Yes, but why tonight?"

Grosbeck did something ridiculous. He got up, pushed aside the heavy gold-cloth portieres and looked out the window. "Nobody there," he said.

"What did you do that for?"

"I don't know."

"What did you expect to see?"

"Nothing, I suppose."

"Then, why did you do it?"

"Madeline, please, it was nothing but a stupid reflex." He was annoyed at the pedestrian tone of the exchange.

"Is there something you haven't told me?"

"'Is there something you haven't told me?'" he mimicked. "You talk like one of those medical things on television. A rare case of loose dentures, which can be cured only by the love of a good woman and regular injections of guano which can be purchased, without prescription, at your drug counter." He was so frightened; so was Madeline.

"That's enough, Harvey," said Madeline.

"I know it is," said Grosbeck.

"You've convinced me that what happened this morning was no accident," said Madeline, "and now you have got to do something about it."

"Nobody knows that better than I do, Madeline," said Grosbeck. "But what?" He was in the position of a man who, having had fed to him the statistics of disaster for years, suddenly discovers that the computer has whirred, whirled, stuttered, chattered and flung at his feet the card saying, "You, you, you."

"There must be someone you can talk to."

"Who, Perazzo? Some corporation lawyer at the paper? The cops? The cops! How about Catafesta himself?" He mocked himself. "I hardly know the man." The disillusion which had corroded Grosbeck all these years had had an effect on him which he had not anticipated. It had left his intestines in a state of disorder . . . tiny thrills and pains in his abdomen . . . the result of all those little men downing tools in the interstices and curves of the *gederim* . . . squirting caustics on the red, gray and green walls, instead of emollients; refusing to do their stipulated jobs. They were demanding a new contract.

Grosbeck's notions of biology were medieval. They were much like those colored oilcloth histories of the world once used in some grammar schools: Twenty-five feet long and two and a half feet wide on wooden rollers; tracing the fantasies of some charlatan Protestant divine, with a careless Boston printer, from the Creation to the opening of Africa, in long, circumstantial red lines; with illustrations of the Seven, or Nine or Eleven wonders of the world; together with the Foremost Families of the Day; the Presidents of the United States to Rutherford B. Hayes; the Supreme Monuments of the Great Cities; and, at the very end of the rollers, the optimistic Sun of the Future . . . in red, grinning . . . America the Beautiful . . . Forever . . . God, swiped from Michelangelo, fingering his beard on an amethyst throne. In times of stress, Grosbeck's thinking antedated even his biology . . . by thousands of years. He squatted on his hams in a clearing before Stonehenge, peering through the morning fog, his face, belly, loins and back daubed with blue. He recited runes and invoked magic. He said to Madeline, in a whisper, "Throw the Tarot."

"What did you say, Harvey? You? You of all people. You

astonish me. You almost take my mind off what's happened. Are you that afraid?"

"Yes."

"Harvey, I beg you, be practical."

"*You* think it's practical; you've told me so often enough."

"And you have sneered at it every time I told you so. No."

"Please," asked Grosbeck. "There isn't much else makes sense out there and maybe this will."

"Do you realize what you're saying?"

"I don't feel coherent, Madeline, and we both need something to get hold of." He scratched his neck. "There's something I ought to tell you. I . . . I have a pain in my chest and I'm having difficulty breathing. I swear it. I've tried the locks on the doors over and over tonight. You've seen me do it. You've got to."

He walked about the living room. He turned on all the lights. He felt himself a dwarf. He poured himself a drink and at once was nauseated. And he waited for Madeline to answer.

"Harvey," she said, "you know that I don't like to read the Tarot any more; that I have never done it for you or for anyone else in the family. I regard the Tarot as . . . I can't quite put it into words . . . as something outside myself, over which I have no control. I believe in what the cards tell. I have done it for money and I have done it for charity and for strangers and once in a while for friends, and the cards have said terrible things. I didn't say them. The cards did."

Madeline on the couch, Grosbeck walking about the room. The lights dimmer than they should have been. Impossible. Silence where there should have been sound. But they were talking. Conversation did not erase the quiet. Their voices merely invaded it. Their voices were the voices of attendants in a morgue, hollow, the other sounds the opening of slots in the steel and stone walls and bodies being slid out for identification. Or, the definitive noise in the death house: "This man is dead."

Grosbeck fell to his knees. "Do the Tarot for me, Madeline," he asked again. "I don't give a damn what they show as long as they show something." He added, half in earnest shame, half in mockery of the bathetic language people do use every day: "I can't stand this uncertainty."

She looked at him sadly. "I forgive you, Harvey."

"Forgive my ass," he said angrily.

"You're not sober."

"I'm sick. Do it."

Madeline lowered her head and thought. She looked up and said, "All right. Come inside. I'll throw the cards on the bed."

"And you won't hold anything back?"

"It is impossible to."

Grosbeck followed his wife into the bedroom. There was a silver bowl on her dresser and several packs of Tarot cards in it. She picked the oldest one from it, a pack she had bought in a thrift shop many years ago.

"Wait," she told Grosbeck.

"Wait for what?"

"Just wait."

She took off her clothes, made up her face and combed her hair. She stepped back from the mirror and contemplated her body. So did Grosbeck, but this was no time for diversions. She found a long white robe of thin cotton in the closet and put it on.

Grosbeck, impatient, incredulous, looked at her. "What in hell are you doing?" he asked. "You want me to put on a silk jock and a leather vest? A jade talisman? Braid my hair and blow some hash? Uppers, downers, inners, outers? I don't want a production, I want to find out something."

Madeline paid no attention. She sat down on the bed opposite Grosbeck, picked up the Tarot pack, removed the wide rubber band that held it together and started to talk.

"I have been reading the cards for twenty-one years," she said. "And every year, it gets more frightening, because I feel as though I'm getting closer and closer to some kind of truth I don't want to know about. Maybe that's the kind of truth I'm going to find out tonight. Maybe my worst fears will be revealed by the next pack I lay."

Grand Guignol. Nevertheless, Grosbeck was half persuaded.

"Tarot is the truth behind the veil," Madeline said. "What happens to our souls when we are alive . . . what happens to our souls after we die . . . when the veil is torn away. Nobody wants to know that."

"*I* do," said Grosbeck. "You need more light?"

Madeline shook her head.

"The cards joke with you," she said. "They talk with you. And they tease you. Those three things. *And,* they let you know if you're lying. They tell you your fate. They tantalize you if you're too eager for an answer."

Madeline arranged herself on the bed, the cards before her.

"Go on," said Grosbeck. "Start. What do you do first?"

"The first thing I do," she said, "is find your face card. In your case, it is the Knight of Pentacles, because you fit his description in personality and coloring." She was no longer talking to Grosbeck. "You could have been the Knight of Swords, or the Knight of Cups or the Knight of Wands. Any one of the four suits of the Lesser Arcana."

The deck was so old and had been used so often that some

of the cards had fallen apart and been pasted together again with Scotch tape. The colors had faded from the bright blue armor of the Knight of Pentacles. The black had been fingered out of the heavy, slow body of his horse, the ink gone out of the end of his lance.

"You always use the left hand to throw the cards."

"Why?"

"Out of respect. It has to do with the Arabs, because they ate with their right hand and handled their private parts with the left hand. They do the things that require respect with the left hand. That is the way they deal with the arcane."

Grosbeck wondered how much of this had been known to the Algerian printer in the eastern end of Paris who had operated the flatbed press on which these cards had been printed, or whether he cared, or how many hundreds of sets of this particular pack had been run off, put together and sold in mysterious little stores to people for whom they became the equivalent either of an evening's entertainment, like Parcheesi or word games, or the entrance to the universe or to the three hundred and sixty-five rooms beneath the streets, from one end of Paris to the other, constructed in the time of Villon, forgotten in the days of Haussmann, now nothing but legend, the keys gone, no lights in them, not even a candle, the connecting passageways blocked in piles of fallen stone.

"Be allusive," Grosbeck demanded. "Be concrete. Save me. Why am I the Knight of Pentacles?"

"The reason you are in Pentacles is that Pentacle men are dark and they are either merchants, lawyers or professors. They are men of the head."

"Some head."

"Now, if I were doing a stranger, I might use the Magician, because the Magician covers all men. The Magician represents the Holy Figure Eight. It is above the head of the Magician and it never ends. It is called The Endless Cord. It is like a serpent devouring its own tail. It means eternity. That's the Magician."

Madeline showed him another card. "This is the High Priestess. She covers all women. She holds the Torah in her lap. She wears a cross around her neck, because she embodies all religion. On her head are the Upper and the Lower Crowns of Egypt. And at her feet is the Moon of the Turk."

Grosbeck wanted to be bored. He hadn't the remotest idea of what his wife was talking about, but he was caught up by her strange attitude.

"I'm doing a face card because I love you," said Madeline. "For a doctor, I might choose Cups. Cups are giving. Doctors are giving. In Wands, you'd be an athlete, because Wands are the symbol of virility."

"I'm no Wand, am I?" asked Grosbeck. "I hadn't heard any complaints lately. You used to get it four times a year. Now, it's up to six, plus national holidays, contingent only on your mood. For a Pentacle, I do pretty good." He knew he had said the wrong thing.

Madeline pushed the cards aside. Grosbeck rose hastily from the corner of the bed, ran into the bathroom and vomited. When he returned, Madeline was sitting on her side of the bed, her face in her hands. "I'm sorry," said Grosbeck. "I promise you, no more. Not another word. Go on."

Madeline, her face still covered by her hands, shook her head. How strange. She really meant all this. He didn't. Or, he did. Grosbeck pulled her hands down. "You must know by now," he said, "that I'm not kidding. I don't know what the hell I'll do if you don't read those cards. I'll go out in the streets and let them finish me off."

"Put your arms around me, Harvey. Do that first." Grosbeck embraced his wife and was tempted to forget the whole thing. She pulled away from him.

"Now," she said, "we will go on. If you were in Swords, you'd be a military man or a senator or a bad person. Swords are difficult, because most people in Swords are hostile. They always want to do things in a cutthroat manner and hurt other people."

Grosbeck restrained himself, thought of Boule cabinets in *hôtels particuliers,* of badly lighted German movies and ambiguous figures entering and leaving rooms, of mandrake in leather hatboxes . . . all the paraphernalia and mumbo jumbo he had always regarded as nothing more than entertainment. But Madeline was beyond even being serious and electric light did nothing to dispel the atmosphere she had created.

"In reverse," she said, "when a card turns upside down, it's someone who wants to hurt you . . . man or woman."

Grosbeck knew it was futile to ask questions.

"The most important part," Madeline went on, "is that

when a man is young, his arcanum is the King. He is a King. As he gets older, he becomes a Knight. It's the very opposite with a woman. In the Tribe, a man loses virility. A woman gains virility as she grows older. She's a Page when young, but she becomes a Queen when she's old."

Upper case, lower case.

"Why?" asked Grosbeck.

"That might have to do with the Chinese aspect of Tarot," Madeline said. She had explained nothing, but Grosbeck knew better than to press her. "Forty is the cutoff point . . . maybe thirty-five. Maybe, it's because one time at that age people were considered old."

"Uh huh," said Grosbeck.

"The deck must be laid three times, because three is a mystical number."

"Why three?"

"Three is the mystical number of Tarot. And the deck must be shuffled seven times before you do somebody else. Seven is a mystical number, too."

Sure, said Grosbeck to himself. And one, two, four, five, six, eight, nine and a hundred and eighty-six thousand miles a second.

"Do you realize what I am doing?" asked Madeline. "I'm stealing your soul."

"It's yours for a groat," said Grosbeck and leaned across the bed to kiss her. She pushed him away and shuffled the cards.

"Four times in one direction," she said. "Three times in the opposite." He was alone.

"That is, if the cards are all upright, with the heads at the top, then you must reverse the cards three times so that some are upside down. Because the cards have a meaning also when they are reversed. The meaning, when the cards

121

are right side up, is that the aspects are good. When they are upside down, the aspects are either negative or questionable. They are no longer clear, because, you see, they are no longer straightforward. Sometimes, there's a mitigating circumstance if a card is upside down. It makes a bad card less bad, but it also makes a good card less good."

Gibberish.

"You must put your hand on the face card and make a wish. That makes the card yours." Grosbeck did so and felt awkward as though he had fallen trying to vault a gymnasium horse.

"Cut the cards into three piles. With your left hand. Out of respect. As I told you." He did that.

"Now, cut the deck in half.

"Now, close the deck.

"Pile one half on the other.

"Now, I'm going to throw the deck, which means spreading the cards out, face down. With *my* left hand.

"From now on, I will not touch your face card. Because it is *your* face card and it will influence what happens next. You will speak through the cards to me. If I touch the cards, it will interfere with the message from you and all the spirits influencing you at this time, all the aspects. Pick a card. Face down."

Grosbeck did so.

"This card lies *on* you. It's the closest influence to you at this time. Pick another card.

"This card *crosses* you. It is the mitigating circumstance of the closest influence. Meaning, whatever is happening to you that is the most important, this card will intensify or lessen its importance.

"Pick another card. This card lies *above* you. This is your wish in whatever is happening. This is what you wish will happen. Pick again. This card lies *behind* you. That is the way the Celtic cross is laid out."

The image of dark, fat gypsies sitting in curtained storefronts rose abruptly in Grosbeck's mind, the women all looking as though their brassieres had not quite been fastened beneath their chemical-satin blouses, the men skulking in corners, their codpieces awry, looking to steal.

"Pick me another card. This card lies *below* you. This is the basis of the matter, what actually is going on."

"Damn it, Madeline," said Grosbeck. "You haven't told me anything yet."

"Please. Pick me another card. Either I'm reading your cards or not. I cannot stand your impatience."

Grosbeck wondered whom his wife was talking to. But he did as he was told.

"This is what is happening immediately. In front of you. But, it's only a passing phase. Pick me another card."

Grosbeck sucked at his teeth and, with his tongue, extracted a fragment of food from between a cap and a tooth that was fast going. Further intimation of mortality. He put two fingers into his mouth, removed the food and flicked it into an ashtray. Outside the apartment, he heard the siren of a police car and, following it, the hoarse urgency of a fire truck. Cuddle up and don't be blue. All your fears are foolish fancies, baby. Can't you see that I'm in love with you?

"This is your House." The voice had become implacable, separated from the body. "Whatever is going on in your House.

"Pick me another card. This is beside you; the influence of others on you.

"Pick me another card. These are your hopes and fears."

"What *are* my hopes and fears?" Grosbeck asked.

"I'll tell you when I read the deck.

"Pick one last card. And pick carefully. Think."

Grosbeck hesitated. He lifted a hand toward the cards spread out like a fan. It was all he could do to make himself select one and put it before Madeline. He heard sounds from the tomb, a rat scrabbling behind the arras.

"I got it," he said reluctantly.

"This is your destiny."

Grosbeck began to tingle.

Not yet, though. "It has to be done two more times," said Madeline. "You didn't end in a Major Arcanum."

"Oh, Jesus, sweetheart," Grosbeck whined. "Can't you just go ahead?"

"No, I can't. Pick two more times."

"What do you mean I didn't end in a Major Arcanum?"

"The Major Arcana deal with the important things in life. First of all, you must understand that the entire subject is called 'The Doctrine Behind the Veil.' The Tarot embodies the symbolic presentation of universal ideas. It has to do with all the major mystic interests, including Cabalism, Alchemy, Rosicrucianism and Craft Masonry."

"You mean those silly men in their white leather aprons?"

"In other words, it embodies all secret literature."

"What's a secret these days . . . other than the day and time one of us is going to get it?"

"The Secret Doctrine has been presented in the following Books," Madeline continued. "The Book of Thoth; the Mutus Liber; the Folio of Mangetus; and the Book of Lambspring."

"Never mind," said Grosbeck. "Just go on."

"There must be a Major Arcanum, if you expect to get a real answer. If it comes out a Minor Arcanum, your question has not been answered. I *have* to do it two more times.

What's more, a very funny thing is happening. The cards are telling me all about what you're doing. The cards don't lie. Cut three times. Close the deck. Cut the deck. Close the deck again.

"This time, you came out in a Major Arcanum. Ha ha ha ha ha. Oh, boy, are these cards funny."

"All *right*. Go *ahead*."

"On you is . . . let's get it exact. We might as well."

"I can't go get a drink, can I?"

"I don't care. Bring me one, too."

Grosbeck brought back the drinks. They both drank too much, quickly.

"I shouldn't have done that," said Madeline. "I should stay cold sober. It's too late now. And it can't make any difference, anyway." One by one, she turned the cards over.

"*On* you is flight," she said. "A change of residence; emigration; alienation.

"*Across* you is hard work and craftsmanship and excellence.

"*Above* you is a desire to be noble and honorable."

Since when?

"*Below* you is a feeling of being caught in a terrible trap."

Yes.

"*Behind* you is a stab in the back."

Yes.

"*Before* you are truth, loyalty and imperfections."

Sure.

"*In* your House is Justice, meaning you will get what you deserve."

Such as?

"*Beside* you are boredom and weariness, but that has to do with other people and imaginary problems; as if the wine of the world had caused you satiety. But, since you're a wastrel, you don't care. You're surrounded with discontent with your environment. Your hopes and fears."

There was one card left to be read.

"This is the last," said Madeline. "Your destiny." Grosbeck turned it over.

"It is The Tower," said Madeline. She trembled.

"What's the matter?" Grosbeck asked. He grasped her arm. "What's wrong?"

"It's The Tower," said Madeline.

Grosbeck looked at the card. It was, indeed, a tower. From the left-hand corner of the card came a bolt of lightning. It had broken off the crenelated top of the tower. Fire burned in the ruins. Two men fell from the crenelations. One lay crushed in the moat. The other fell, fell, fell through eternity to die with him. They had stood guard over something at the top of the tower, halberds in hand, when, out of the West, the lightning had issued from the mouth of the Sun, taking them all unaware.

The card had the Roman numeral XVI at the top, the words *La Maison de Dieu* at the bottom.

"What does it mean?" asked Grosbeck.

"Disaster," said Madeline.

"Disaster?" asked Grosbeck. "Why? Why?"

"I don't know. They are *your* cards. *You* picked them. *You* told *me*, not I *you*. Your relation with someone will bring you disaster."

"Death?"

"No. Not death."

"How do you know?"

"All the other cards. Disaster is mitigated."

"That's it, then?"

"Yes."

Disaster. But not death. Disaster mitigated. Not death. What did she know or could those cards know? Why *not* death as disaster? He had assumed an importance he had not foreseen and certainly did not want and for all the wrong reasons. The court plaster had been ripped from the quiet wound and with it the crusted scab; the nails had screeched as the slats were pried up from the wooden crate and the packing had been pulled aside to reveal the homunculus within. (A coffin?)

The irony! What it had taken to do it was neither reason nor logic nor wisdom nor experience. Only this mucilaginous farrago of nonsense. Grosbeck had regained a metaphor: It was that in the midst of death we are, indeed, in the midst of death; that the hurts of daily life are a joke, a fly whisk, Baleen nothing, Shalit nothing. Death, death is all that really counts; not even unemployment. How to circumvent death? How to push away the sergeant and Catafesta?

Grosbeck, the child, toeing inward, walked, in knickerbockers, toward the public school past the parochial school on a Bronx street . . . frame houses on one side, the remnants of Liberty Gardens from the First World War on the other . . . houses inhabited by the red-faced Irish children who beat him regularly from kindergarten through 7-A and took his birthday wristwatch. Sheenie. He could not have known they were as doubtful of what they could do to him as he was certain. (Nor, forty-odd years later, did he doubt the puissance of Catafesta and the sergeant.)

They were all smaller than he. But they had decided to hit first and faster: that was the way they lived. They did not let themselves gauge pain or consequences. They did not particularly want the cheap wristwatch. (The black vermin had not wanted Madeline; she was simply in his way.) They had let *him* decide that he was the isolated enemy, and, since he had so decided, they had beaten him. That was the death of childhood, from which he had risen miraculously, day after day, until his parents took him out of the neighborhood, until it no longer was necessary to stand wailing up from the sidewalk that Gerald O'Loughlin, a wizened runt half his size, was picking on him, and his father, trumpeting down from the window, "Fight him back; don't be a coward," and his mother shrilling, "Edwin, Edwin, let him come upstairs."

Other deaths followed, in other neighborhoods, but the hair grew in his groin, in his legs, nostrils, on his chest and arms and face, and he learned that he was as afraid of Jews as he was of the Irish. But his tongue came to life and he fought with that. Bite your tongue. He did not bite his tongue when he should have and the result, so long afterward, was notes from Baleen and warnings from Shalit. The tongue attracted girls and women, making his fingers speak fumblingly on the top-floor landings of apartment houses.

Mrs. Frisch. "Harvey, do you know anything about radios? Your father tells me you're very clever with such things." The pubescent Grosbeck could not put the garbage on the dumbwaiter without spilling some of it down the shaft. "I can't seem to get the dials right on the superheterodyne. It lights up, but all I get is static. Come upstairs. Maybe you can do something with it." The red-haired Mrs. Frisch. And the pot-bellied Mr. Frisch, the furrier. Furriers are not home at three o'clock in the afternoon to fix radios.

"Forget it, Harvey," said Mrs. Frisch. "Has anyone ever told you you're a very good-looking boy?" Menstrual smells, onions and pot roast. Mrs. Frisch hankered after Harvey's cherry. She was very explicit. Tillie the Toiler. Toots and Casper. The pages flipped rapidly to make a movie. Mrs. Frisch did not neck, pet or muzzle. For her, even then, the dust of history lay on those words. She sat Harvey down on the overstuffed velvet couch, and, with one hand, opened the buttons on the fly of his second pair of long pants. With the other, she opened the front of her dress. She was very adept and she sighed and giggled as she worked.

Beneath the dress, she had on an incredible arrangement of ropes and cables and structures, but she had no trouble making them come off, all the while kissing Harvey and exclaiming softly over the thing she had in her hand: a French housewife critically examining a *baguette* at the *boulangerie*. Soon nothing was left on her but the red hair, above and below, and, on the good white flesh, the red lines left by the complicated siding she had just removed. The birth of two children, hardly younger than Harvey, had not damaged her breasts. She put Harvey's hands to them. They were so big . . . so . . . so . . . impressive. "Squeeze," she demanded. "Hard. But not too hard. And take your things off."

Harvey obeyed.

"You're very big for a boy your age, Harvey," said Mrs. Frisch. "Did you know that?"

"Yes, Mrs. Frisch," said Harvey. "Somebody told me that." The tongue he could not control wagged some more. "But only from the outside."

"You're naughty, Harvey."

"Also," he said, "I guess I've been able to tell myself, from the way it feels. Sometimes, I look at it in a mirror and I've seen the other boys in the locker room at school."

"Lovely, lovely, Harvey. I can't bear to let it go and I just want to kiss it and kiss it; both at once. I bet nobody ever did *that* to you before."

"No, Mrs. Frisch, but I've read about it."

"You know I'm going to do it to you, Harvey, don't you?"

"Are you, Mrs. Frisch? It's getting late."

She squeezed with pleasure. "Dottie and June are having supper with a friend from school," she said, "and Mr. Frisch has to go to Brooklyn . . . right after work. You know about Mr. Frisch, don't you, Harvey?"

"No, Mrs. Frisch, I don't."

"Well, Harvey, he has his moments, too," said Mrs. Frisch. "But let's not talk about that. Let's not talk at all. Let's . . . *do* something to me, you little bastard, prick, fuck!"

The words impressed Harvey as much as had Mrs. Frisch's big knockers. He was committed to words and the tongue at an early age, admiring of free expression. But he had no idea that women ever talked that way.

Mrs. Frisch was very busy by now. She released Harvey for the time being, leaned back on the couch, kicking off her shoes as she lay down, put one hand behind her head (the pins had come out of her hair and it flowed, nicely, almost to her shoulders) and the other, fingers applied knowledgeably, between her outspread legs. She was enjoying herself to the utmost; at the right time, she would enjoy Harvey, too.

So greedy, that woman; so greedy.

She trilled and tittered and talked . . . dirty words over and over . . . the same ones . . . Basic English . . . she was no professor. She let go and grasped at Harvey, obligingly sitting up to get her hands on him. She pulled him down on her and kissed him again and again, saying, "M-u-u-u-h" and "M-u-u-u-h." She said, "I can't get enough of you, you little *vonce.*"

"Me neither, Mrs. Frisch," whispered Harvey. "But I guess you figured out now I'm no cockroach."

"No, darling," she said. She said? She crooned. "Darling." She let his hands alone now because they had learned quickly and they walked around on her, poking and stroking and joking; sampling and sliding and stopping; and going and coming and resting. *Zul Zein Mit Glick.*

The effect of Harvey's hands on Mrs. Frisch was powerful: She had anticipated everything he might do, for he was not the first boy she had conducted over this terrain, this delicious, perilous landscape, lifting his arm when he stumbled, helping him over hummocks, stiffening his resolve. She was guiding him around the rim of the crater into which he might have fallen and been consumed (the tour into the smoking volcano was part of the picnic, but like any consummate guide, Mrs. Frisch knew that it had to be taken in easy stages), when Harvey paused and said something.

"Mrs. Frisch," he said, "remember, you said you were going to kiss it?"

For once in her Jewish-picaresque-Bronx-careful-careless life, she was surprised. The little cockroach had surprised her. A thrill went through her body; she was suffused with it; she stiffened like an epileptic and keened; fell away from him and bumped about, fingers busy in herself, imposing a severe strain on the stuffing of the couch, alone with herself and came and came and came. She had won the door prize, the extra added attraction.

"Oh," she said, when her body had done with her and she

was sufficiently revived to sit up. "I did, didn't I, Harvey? How could I have forgotten? I've been bad to you, haven't I? Let me make it up to you, my darling; oh, let me do it."

She grasped Harvey firmly by the arms and pushed him back on his side of the couch. With one hand, she brushed back her hair, with the other, she took hold of his rod and his staff, bent her head down and took it in her mouth. She revolved her head about it; then she kept her head still and ran her tongue around it. But, for all the unexpectedness of what Harvey had said to her, she was a self-possessed woman and she wanted her money's worth. She drew back for a moment, still holding daintily on to Harvey, and said, "Harvey, if I make you come this way, you might not want to fuck me after that. I don't want to waste it. Not the first time."

Harvey had no opinions. Mrs. Frisch, torn with doubt, beset with appetite, tried to make up her mind. When it came right down to it, she was a generous woman, and so she came right down to it again with her mouth and went at Harvey as though he were an ice-cream cone filled with caviar. She did things to him with her mouth he would try to have other women duplicate decades later; he estimated the percentage of their success, in the light of hindsight, at no more than thirty to forty. On the other hand, of course, he might just be hankering after the past, as he did in everything else.

At the moment when, it seemed to Harvey, he would burst in her mouth and do serious damage to himself, besides covering her with blood, she drove a badly manicured forefinger up his backside, shouting as she did so, the shout muffled by the obstruction in her throat. The virgin flooded her mouth and she swallowed as though she were never going to drink again.

Later, they sat at either end of the couch. Mrs. Frisch offered Harvey a ham and cheese sandwich. Harvey refused. "I don't want to spoil my appetite, Mrs. Frisch," he said. He accepted a glass of orange juice from the icebox.

"So, you've lost your cherry, Harvey," said Mrs. Frisch. "In a way, I'm sorry it had to happen that way. I'm not very practical."

"I still feel pretty good, Mrs. Frisch."

"Do you, Harvey?"

"Oh, sure," he said. "I liked it."

"I know you did, Harvey," said Mrs. Frisch. "I did, too, more than you'll ever know. But I feel so selfish. You didn't mind not having it the other way the first time? I'm such a pig."

Harvey shook his head. Mrs. Frisch looked away from Harvey's eyes and then down at him and saw that it *was* all right . . . that if he had had any kind of disappointment, his body was concealing it manfully. In some dim way, she had read the history of the race accurately and found room somewhere in it for the footnote of her own predilections. The thrill went through her again and this time she was tactful enough not to withdraw from Harvey. Instead, she drew him in and fucked him thoroughly, leaving him wet and hungry. He departed her after dark and walked down two flights of stairs to his parents' apartment. He did not thank Mrs. Frisch, although it would have been appropriate, and she did not kiss him again; it was unnecessary. They met again and again until the Frisch family moved to Manhattan . . . *terra incognita* . . . Mr. Frisch having moved up in the fur business.

Grosbeck swept the cards together and tried to tear up the pack. He was not strong enough to do it. It had been years since he had torn up anything more substantial than a solicitation for a magazine subscription or a coupon addressed to "Occupant," promising five cents off on a plastic bottle of underarm deodorant. The green veins on the back of his hands stood out prominently, a cartoon of strength denied by the stringy tendrils of muscle beneath the soft forearms.

His body was petulant and wayward in middle age; he had not taken very good care of it, and his mind was both weak and petulant. In a cell of La Santé prison, a week ago, a murderer named Claude Buffet had written, and Grosbeck had memorized it:

"In two or three minutes, I will be nothing but an inanimate object. Until today, I have not considered the different ways to die. Too late. Now, I have no more time. The blade that is to end my life was cast and sharpened long ago. The executioner should give the martyr the right to see the approach of his own death by placing him on his back, his head facing upward in order to see the blade fall on his neck. But, no. I am going to die with my head down, facing the basket that will catch my head. I will have, in a last vision, the right only to see the spot where my head is to fall, not the right to see what it is that is going to kill me. In my thoughts, I already see it drop toward my neck. With what pleasure the executioner will see it slip beneath his eyes to my neck."

Morbid. Morbid. Come back from Manhattan, Mrs. Frisch, and succor me. Succor. Suck. Stop that. Grosbeck, unlike Buffet, did not know who his executioner would be, but that there would be one and that his head would fall, he did not doubt. Where it would fall was beside the point; so was the finicking business of whether he would see the blade. Grosbeck did not approve of aesthetics in death. He was no *fin de siècle* French novelist cataloguing the thousand delicate cuts of a knife by which a coolie was put to death in a back alley of Shanghai, the blood running ever so delicately, the victim expiring after hours of informed incisions without a sound, collapsing almost imperceptibly in the ropes which held him. Grosbeck did not want to die.

He must take counsel.

None was to be had from Madeline any longer tonight. She had exhausted herself in the Tarot. She took the cards out of his hand. The expression in her eyes, at his effort to tear them up, was one almost of mischief. She tore the cards up herself, one by one, and threw them in a wastebasket. "See, Harvey," she said. "See how easy it is? There's a way around everything."

Mrs. Elbert Hubbard. "You think so, don't you. What about that roiling around in my guts? How do I live with that?"

"Our guts, Harvey. I always have to remind you of that."

"Let's get some sleep, Madeline. That's enough for one night. There's someone in the office I can ask some questions. He's got connections downtown and maybe he can do something."

He got into his pajamas. "I can't sleep," he announced.

Madeline treated him like Jason. She saw to the air conditioning, smoothed the sheets, propped herself up on the bed as he lay next to her and stroked his forehead and cheek. He was not ashamed, only afraid.

And he fell asleep. Nor did he dream. And, as he discovered the next morning, Madeline did not sleep. He awoke at the right time and wanted his breakfast. Madeline did not look well and did not want even coffee. Jason got up, ate his breakfast and went off to summer day camp. Grosbeck read the papers over breakfast, got ready to go to work and made no reference to the night before. Sufficient unto the night before is the evil thereof. He performed an act of humanity: He, for one of the few times he could remember, said nothing, although he ingested fright with the bacon and nausea with the coffee.

All he said to Madeline as he left was, "Leave it to me," and thought, If anything ever were left entirely to me, my family would be on welfare and I'd be rattling a tin cup in the subway and three Puerto Ricans would kick the shit out of me somewhere between Fourteenth Street and One Hundred and Twenty-fifth Street and I'd wind up in Harlem Hospital where the emergency room would be closed down because of a staff strike, and they wouldn't have to operate on me, because, whatever it was, was going to fall off anyway. Ha ha. Madeline, why in hell did this have to happen.

He kissed his wife. She closed the door firmly behind him. He took the elevator to the lobby, walked out into the street, felt the heat, put aside his index of complaints about the city and crossed over to take the bus uptown. The ride was classic: Between the Lower Village and Eighth Street, the Italian women, young and old, still in the particular kind of purdah their husbands and fathers had put them in for so many years;

Between Eighth Street and Fourteenth, trash, old farts in conservative clothing like Grosbeck's, intent on getting to Rockefeller Center with as little contact as possible with anyone else. They were commuters who, it was difficult to credit, still lived in the city, immured in tall apartment buildings;

Blacks with eyes which glared; children on their way to Central Park; young Village women and old, anomalous, out of whom all character had been washed because, he supposed, they were *not* in purdah, like the Italian women, but nobody had yet told them what to be;

All kinds of ragtag and bobtail about which Grosbeck refused to speculate because he could not categorize them.

Four blocks to a light; five if the going were good. On the streets, people hurried, despite the intense heat of the hot summer day.

Index the sights:

The women's prison at Greenwich Avenue, the dingy sirens, unseen, calling down from the barred windows with the Art Deco lintels (what pretentious idiot had been permitted to do that?), to their scruffy little men on the sidewalks;

The Jefferson Market Courthouse next to that, a crazy *olla podrida* of red and white, which looked as though it had been planned by Ludwig of Bavaria; the gray cupola on the southwest corner of Fourteenth Street;

Nothing noteworthy between there and Seventeenth Street (some might disagree);

From there to Twenty-third, the solemn piles, on both sides of the avenue, of what had been the finest department stores in New York . . . Siegel-Cooper ("Meet Me at the Fountain"), Hugh O'Neill, Stern Brothers, Arnold Constable;

From Twenty-third north, The Corner, all that remained of Koster & Bial's Music Hall, the name carved in winsome script in a light-brown sandstone, halfway up the building, the tin pediment proclaiming, indistinctly, the name (in it, the basement room in which so much champagne was opened and the corks driven into the wall, oaths sworn and legs fondled beneath petticoats, still existed, but now boxed hardware and piles of kitchen utensils were stacked from floor to ceiling; farewell, Champagne Room, hail Hardware!);

Then, broken rows of modest, nondescript two- and three-story buildings, once part of the Tenderloin, now the offices of sewing-machine wholesalers; some of them had marble fronts still . . . a miracle;

Then, the flower market, which was beautiful and in which the small trucks, double- and triple-parked, slowed down traffic to one block to a light;

Twenty-eighth Street, Tin Pan Alley; Thirtieth Street, southeast corner, the Haymarket; Herald Square, Horace Greeley greened in his armchair, his mouth shut; the bell ringers off the lost, arcaded building which had housed the New York *Herald*, per the design of Stanford White, the Hoe presses in the windows; forget Macy's; a mysterious old hotel at Thirty-eighth, in which people still lived (who?); a loft with the broad window painted over and advertising; "Photography . . . Live Models . . . We supply cameras";

Then, Forty-second Street and the walk across, west, to the paper, through the blasted heath of dirty movies and dirty-book shops and furtive doorways inviting furtive men (not all furtive, Grosbeck knew, some vulpine). No one remembered that Bridgie Webber once ran a gambling joint on the northwest corner of Forty-second Street and Sixth Avenue and that, there, had been planned the murder of Herman Rosenthal, which led to the death of Lieutenant Becker in the electric chair. (Murdered by the state of New

York.) Remembered? No one knew or cared or realized that, not so long ago, traffic had been two-way on the side streets, else the getaway car couldn't have made a U-turn in front of the Metropole on Forty-third.

It was pointless to remember these bits of ceramic, glazed over by time, glazed like Staffordshire shepherdesses and so become quaint. Pointless to remember because now the police stole heroin from Police Headquarters and were the close allies of people like Catafesta. Mine own drug dealer, thought Grosbeck. He did not want to be another Herman Rosenthal, getting in the way of the police and murderers of his own time. It was one thing to read about Beansie Rosenthal, it was another thing to be Beansie. Why did the pernicious, foul brotherhood between the police and criminals, and, ultimately, the best people, come as such a surprise to every new generation? The only thing new about it to Grosbeck was the possibility of his demise.

Today, he and everyone on the bus was distracted by a talker. They showed up every now and then on the buses . . . like this one . . . little, possessed men with mutilated heads and shining eyes, piles of soiled, week-old newspapers under their arms, and, between their legs, a shopping bag out of which the corners of rags showed.

This talker, like most of the others, challenged people around him, disputed their politics (which they had not stated), their sexual habits (which obviously were not immediately manifest), what they ate (shrewd guesses could be made there), invited debate. (No takers.) Eyes were averted, skirts pulled aside, trousers pinched upward between thumb and forefinger, all in a ceremonial effort to avoid whatever this mad innocent might demand. *Noli me tangere.* The talkers were almost never drunk or drugged. (There were others who were that.) They never made any trouble; only noise. (It was the others who made the trouble.)

Today, the talker talked incessantly. As a rule, Grosbeck did not listen to them, but today, he was looking for oracles. Madeline had been the first; he wanted more. (I attend the services of all the major religions. It may not help me, but it can't do me any harm. And, you never can tell.)

This talker had a big, harsh voice, far out of proportion to his crumpled package of a body and he said something to which Grosbeck listened.

"I'm very fearful of the human race," said the man. He was wearing a heavy overcoat on this summer day, and, as he talked, a copy of the Sacramento *Bee* (a month old) fell from under his arm. The talker picked it up and continued:

"They're out to get me."

True.

"There's no freedom of speech for lunatics."

Again, true.

"They're out to get me."

Indeed! *Moi aussi.*

"Where are we?" And, with a final, broken cry of despair, softened by the diesel engines of the bus:

"What city is this?"

That was not the way Grosbeck wanted to get to the office.

Clack. Clack. Clack. Ding, ding. The cable-car driver plunged the lever down and the claw grabbed gingerly at the running cable beneath the ground. The car went around

Dead Man's Curve in Union Square and all aboard, willy-nilly, leaned backward or fell forward with it. The curve must have been at least a hundred and ten degrees. In the heat, the passengers pressed closely on one another, the smell of bodies rising from the tubes of alpaca and linen and muslin they wore. Hands grasped at hats (yellowing panamas and straws; masses of taffeta flowers); other hands reached down in the press and strove for secret things.

"Do you break your corset steels?" inquired a car card. "Do they rust? If so, replace them with 'Waloha' and your boning troubles will end." The fragrance of Oussani's Milooki Egyptian cigarettes, cork tip, and the blunt odor of bad cigars on the outside platforms. In seconds, turning had been accomplished and the car was on its way up Broadway. No crackpots, no mad prophets. Fares, please.

Ding, ding. Clack. Clack. Clack. It was only the bells on the wire-service machines. Eighty words a minute. Twenty-four hours a day. The machines stopped only to gather breath and hum. Then, they spewed forth more.

Johnny Tully, the reporter Grosbeck wanted to talk to, would not be in for another two hours. In the mornings, the big city room of the newspaper was taken up by the inside people. There were chores for all, from Baleen and Shalit, down through Miss Adeline Gannon, through the editors, who, like Grosbeck, sawed away at their fiddles throughout the day, rehearsing the symphony that would be the news-paper at ten o'clock at night.

The obscenity of what he did daily bore heavily on Gros-beck, but he had taken the king's shilling and must bite the bullet. There was a balance to be maintained. One tip the wrong way, one genuinely revolutionary gesture, and the car (his car) overturned, and he was crushed beneath the heaps of bodies. But, at the same time, one piece of conciliation too many to the Baleens and the Shalits and the truce he had reached with himself was at an end and he was out in the street, wiping car windows at traffic lights on the Bowery.

That had been the case until now. Now, there was another element, a realer one: Catafesta and the police, hands joined, treading about the maypole of his body while the mayor clapped his hands rhythmically to their steps and his cabinet applauded arhythmically and in boredom and the junkies ran under, in and out, the linked arms and the gray, chromed Cadillac body wagon from Frank Campbell's awaited him, three attendants in black tailcoats and striped pants standing by, their arms folded impassively.

He wished John Tully would show up early for a change. But Tully did not; did not know, could not know, Grosbeck's need. And so, Grosbeck started on the day's work . . . the cables to be answered, the wire copy to be read, the stories to be assigned. He read on and on . . . and marked . . . and placed exclamation points here and question marks there. To all appearances, he was the following: Rational. Detached. Amused. Serious. Responsible. Anyone passing his desk could see that. He had the bank deposits and withdrawals to prove it. The attendance record. The length of service. The clothes. Despite everything, he belonged. No matter the tongue. Regard the clothes. But now, there was the grisly prospect, as they put it, of early retirement; he would spend the golden years six feet under. Grosbeck looked up at the clock. Still an hour to go before Tully would be in.

He ran across another epistle from Saint Seymour the Sanctimonious, the wire-service God lover and minister to millions.

God damn you, Saint Seymour. Hurry, Saint John Tully.

Grosbeck was not built for adversity. Put it this way: Grosbeck was not Bartleby, the Scrivener. He did not say to Baleen and Shalit, "I would prefer not to. . . ." Nor, "Fuck you." Not to them. And not to what he faced. He broke out only when a series of quick, mean calculations let him think he could get away with it. He revenged himself on *Untermenschen,* a wild boar in a chicken yard, with Missy Gannon and other anonymouses. And always with the tongue; never, never did he forget the beatings in the Bronx. And, up to the weekend, he had supposed he could go on indefinitely that way, relying on discretion to save him from those above and the pacific humanity or indifference of those below. (Only sticks and stones could break their bones; so long as no bones were broken, they would only be wounded in the heart and they could dismiss him as an unpleasant eccentric to be put up with and ignored. Therein lay *their* triumph over *him.* Or, they could indulge him with a laugh. That was worse than being ignored.)

A young man walked up to Grosbeck's desk and approached him diffidently. No question he had been ushered in properly, or he would not have been there. When the moon was full, so newspapermen said, the unbalanced visited the newspaper by the score. They heard voices in their heads or there were radio broadcasts in their teeth or they knew of a plot to kill the President or they were about to be killed themselves or a neighbor's dog planned to bite a pound out of their asses. They were screened by the security guards downstairs and turned away or, every now and then, dragged away. But, it sometimes fell to Grosbeck to deal with people whose business with the newspaper was deemed legitimate, although not necessarily important, and they were sent to him to be disposed of. Here was a chicken sent to Grosbeck, the boar. He snuffled in anticipation and pawed the floor. It would pass the time until Tully walked into the city room.

The young man was tall, thin, wore glasses with thin metal rims and was dressed altogether unexceptionably . . . unexceptionably as Grosbeck judged these things.

"Mr. Grosbeck?" he said. "I'm Peter Fahnestock. I believe you've had some mail from me regarding the conference." Mr. Fahnestock's was the presumption of the self-absorbed. Grosbeck, of course, was just as self-absorbed, but he did not presume to think that the world had a xeroxed copy of his toilet habits and had committed it to memory.

"Conference?" he asked. He had something in mind for the young man. "What conference was that?"

"Why," said the young man, "the conference on 'Learning Through Transcendental Meditation,' up in Attleboro. I sent you an agenda and I called your managing editor's secretary about it."

"Ah, yes," said Grosbeck. "I believe I did see something about it. Something about this Maharishi you've got up there in the woods and how he's going to get the world straightened around while the birds twitter in the arboreal hush."

Mehor Baba all over again. But this time no postcard, no tattoos on unappetizing flesh, no baby. Even a Brooks Brothers suit. He was annoyed by the inconsistency.

"Aimee Semple McPherson in saffron-colored drag, eh, Mr. Fahnestock?" Grosbeck asked. "Eats brown rice as though it were pheasant under glass and cleans out his bowels just thinking about it. Brown rice'd clean me out, too, Mr. Fahnestock, except it'd come out the other end. Whitens the teeth, too, brightens the days and shows The Way and The Truth. Nothing like him ever before, was there?"

144

"Haven't you ever envisioned the possibility of revelation, Mr. Grosbeck?" asked the young man.

Have I not. Hurry up, Tully.

"Yes," said Grosbeck, "I have. I have all the days of my years. I regret to have to inform you that where some of my contemporaries found it in alcohol and some of yours in whatever chemical you happen to favor at the moment, none of it lasted longer than was necessary to produce a hangover. But, I take advantage of you.

"You're young. I'm old. I'm old. You're young. Did you know that there's a comedian who made a whole act of those few words, managed to string it out for ten minutes? There's revelation for you, there's the riddle of the universe answered."

The young man gestured vaguely at Grosbeck. Grosbeck held up a warning hand and half rose from his chair.

"So," he said, "you and the rest of you are going to do it the easy way, on the cheap. Sit on your asses and meditate the shit out of things until you've . . . and I use the phrase you love so well . . . got it all together. Or is it, alternatively, got your heads together? I've got a little story to tell you."

He settled back comfortably in his chair and rubbed his palms together. He had remembered something about the Maharishi.

The young man managed to get in a word edgewise. "All I wanted to tell you, Mr. Grosbeck," he said, "was this . . . that there is to be a meeting between the Maharishi and the head of the Army War College. He's black, as you no doubt know."

"Which one is black?" Grosbeck asked.

"Why," said the young man, "you know very well. General Barnes."

Grosbeck knew.

"I mean," said Fahnestock, "what he and the Maharishi plan to do is meditate together and then determine what, if anything, can be done to adapt the methods of 'Learning Through Transcendental Meditation' to the military. It's not impossible, you know. There are many ways to peace."

Grosbeck contemplated Fahnestock, the Young. "As I said," he told him, "I've got a little story to tell you. About a month ago, you may or may not know . . . you might have been busy meditating . . . we ran a piece about your Maharishi and his academy. It seems that the author . . . and we've dealt with him since, despite my ungrudging admiration for him . . . took a few liberties with the Maharishi. God knows, they were innocent enough; he was a freelancer, a staff man wouldn't have done it. We run a lot of free-lance pieces on Sunday and we don't always check them as thoroughly as we might. One reason is not many people see fit to question the paper.

"Well, he put in a few things just to cover up the fact that he hadn't exactly seen the Maharishi's academy. He'd simply done a little home *passementerie*. Nothing malicious. Possibly a little ironic. There should be room somewhere in the world these days for irony. Not so?" Grosbeck enunciated his words with the clarity of a Berlitz teacher trying to work over a stockbroker for a quick trip to St. Tropez.

"Well," he went on, "apparently, there isn't much room in the Maharishi's world for irony. You know what he did? He unfolded his legs . . . you never saw the lotus position come unstuck so fast . . . got into his Cadillac and ran down to Boston from Attleboro, screaming for a lawyer. O-o-o-m. His ratty little holiness had been offended. What's more, the piece could have cost his crummy little academy some donations. There's always North American Rockwell looking to build extrasensory perception into its missiles."

Young Fahnestock looked away. "I know," he said. "We advised him to. We felt there had been certain misapprehensions. . . ." He was about to say more, but Grosbeck wouldn't let him.

"Misapprehensions," said Grosbeck. He waved a finger at the young man. "How does it happen that a man of the Maharishi's spiritual dimensions would either know or care that there had been any misapprehensions?"

"He really doesn't have a Cadillac," the young man replied.

"Shee-ut," said Grosbeck. "Why would he care enough to find the address of an expensive firm of Boston lawyers and get down to Tremont Street as fast as wheels could get him there. And get the lawyers to send the paper a letter the length of the Bhagavad Gita? What possible retribution was there to be exacted from some poor wretch of a writer with a sense of humor whose sole objective was enough money to keep him in rent for another month?"

No answers, naturally. Even upon first acquaintance, people had learned to let Grosbeck rave; it was either that or punch him.

"Mr. Fahnestock," Grosbeck asked, "has it ever occurred to you to wonder about the juxtaposition of the Army War College and true holiness? What do they have in common? Proximately? Did you expect . . . did you really expect . . . that napalm, 155 millimeter, fragmentation bombs, defoliants, dead children, dead people, dead land would evanesce, to be replaced by iced tea and straw fans, through the emollient offices of transcendental meditation? Now, did you, God damn it!"

Grosbeck did not raise his voice, but neither did he wait for an answer.

"Mr. Fahnestock, what do you know? Very little, I suspect,

147

or you wouldn't be fluttering about my head with your foul Christ on a crutch. I don't have the time and you have neither the patience nor the background to cast back and count up all the rotten little tinpot saviors who have infested the earth. And I have yet to see the real article.

"I would like to point out something to you. Neither Christ nor Buddha had a lawyer. They didn't see any need to correct anyone's misapprehensions via the exertions of some Boston shyster. Christ died for us all, I suppose; I don't remember whether Buddha fell out of a tree. But neither of them took a dime for what he did. Christ drove the money changers out of the temple. Etc., etc., etc.

"But, as for you, I am Pilate. I wash my hands of you for your ignorance, for your presumption, for your essential laziness, for your refusal to learn that it has all been done before . . . with what results I need not tell you because you know already that the world is in a sorry state. I wash my hands of you also because of your venality and I make no case for my own.

"It would make some sense to me . . . I'm not saying you'd be right, but it would make sense . . . if you had read Marx, say, for openers. If you went on from there to fight the cops or throw bombs or shut down Washington, or whatever, I could understand it. I don't say I would like it, but I could understand it. I understand it when a big corporation steals a billion dollars and I understand it when a general tells lies.

"I could even understand it if you decided, the hell with the whole thing, I'll just goof until they pick me up. But, no, that's not for you. You've got to be a fake mystic in a discipline you know nothing about and which is not applicable to you at all. And, moreover, a discipline you've learned from a fraud so palpable that he can be smelled for miles and to the heavens. Only, you try to tell me it's frankincense and myrrh."

Grosbeck paused . . . but not for very long.

"I despise you, my son," he said. "You're a lousy press agent for a brazen thief. Go get your fucking *lakh* of rupees somewhere else. Get the hell out of here, Mr. Fahnestock. You have exhausted my patience and my rhetoric." Grosbeck was lying. No one had ever exhausted his rhetoric.

"You do have recourse, naturally. You can always, like your mentor, complain to my boss. Or get your lawyers to do it. You can do that and it probably would get results. But, it would be a cheap triumph. As cheap as mine over you.

"Do you understand what I have just said? I hope that somehow I have reached you." He pointed to an exit. "Get out, will you. I have work to do."

And Tully to talk to. The clock had moved around to the time when Tully *must* come in and already young Mr. Fahnestock was going out of Grosbeck's mind.

Fahnestock gathered up his papers. God knows what he was thinking, but even a moron would have known that Grosbeck was not the man to apply to. He left.

"God bless you, you little camel," Grosbeck whispered at his back. "I doubt He will. It's going to take every last nickel your old man owns to get you through the eye of that needle."

In walked Tully. Five minutes late. The way the world was going, that was early.

Grosbeck was monomaniacal on the subject of promptness. It was his way of excusing the general slipshodness with which he ran his life. If one were on time, it did not matter what one was on time for; it was one of the reasons he found for admiring television: It was always on time. Sainthood was attainable sidereally; one ascended to the stars with the Gregorian calendar in the left hand, a Hamilton railroad watch (with heavy gold chain and Masonic seals) in the other, to sit at the foot of God.

God sat on His throne, regarding an enormous binnacle, and, above it, an enormous chronometer, steering the universe through the universe, eternally on time. At His feet sat those who had been no more than thirty seconds late for anything in their lives. (God is forgiving; in His infinite mercy, a thirty-second lapse either way is acceptable.) The blessed prompt. A loud tick was all that broke the silence of space.

Long since consigned to Hell were those who had been late, the uncountable billions of souls who, in one language or another, had said (and been damned for it), "Sorry to be late." Surely among the damned must be those Negroes who lived by what was called C.P.T. . . . Colored Peoples' Time. A bright young sociologist had done a monograph on C.P.T., in which he had observed, with keen perception, that C.P.T. was a subtle form of black rebellion; that if the white man were determined to make a shuffler out of the black man, well, then, the black man would oblige him by being late. So, perhaps, all those Negroes who had lived and died on C.P.T. weren't in Hell, just in a separate Heaven of their own. Separate but equal, having attained it with all deliberate speed.

It was a peculiar kind of theology, the result of which was that Grosbeck and Madeline often showed up on time at dinner parties to find that their hosts were in deshabille and annoyed at their presence; leaving Madeline to look stonily at her husband and Grosbeck to drum his fingers on a coffee table first, then to get drunk and, finally, to get tendentious over dinner.

Grosbeck admired John Tully for many reasons. Like Grosbeck he had been born in New York. High Bridge. In a frame house! And lived his boyhood in Hell's Kitchen, two blocks south of San Juan Hill and its blacks. Tully had grown up among the knob-faced Irish who went to early Mass on Sundays, having clubbed the Negroes to the north of them unmercifully the night before, fuddled on growler after growler of beer or boilermakers. Forgive me, Father, for I have sinned. Tully used to say to Grosbeck: "It's a wonder the bastards didn't choke on the wine and throw up the Host."

Tully was thin, somewhat above medium height, cultivated in the areas Grosbeck thought it imperative to be cultivated in (that is, he was acquainted with the novels of Baron Corvo and was fond of the city still and had a sense of its lost magnificence); a fine reporter who knew a great deal more about the things he reported on than he ever committed to paper. He was not just a reporter. He was a fixer for the publisher and the managing editor, a producer of accommodations, such as helping the circulation manager prevail on the police to let the newspaper's trucks run the wrong way up one-way streets at edition times.

While he was several years younger than Grosbeck and his hair was still dark (a black Irishman), he was Grosbeck's kind of anachronism. His speech, delivered out of the corner of his mouth in an accent to be found only in Manhattan, tended to be orotund. He had been raised in a parochial school at a time when the sisters could still rap a pupil on the knuckles with a heavy blackboard pointer. (There was no Human Rights Commission to interfere.) He was a graduate of Fordham University. (Rose Hill.) And he had the good taste to inhabit one of the remaining houses in Chelsea near the General Theological Seminary.

Grosbeck was delighted by that. He was delighted, also, by the fact that there were cuffs on Tully's trousers; three buttons on his suit jackets; Peal shoes on his feet; a Cavanagh hat on his head; a fly-front Chesterfield with velvet collar on his back in bad weather. Tully had a sharp nose, high cheekbones, a pointed chin and good teeth. Altogether, he was satisfying to look at, to listen to and, if Grosbeck were lucky, to be the savior of an aging, irascible Jewish snob.

Dandy John Tully. The fact that *anyone*, today, could be called Dandy John! Grosbeck often considered buying him a bowler, but Tully was one of the few people he did not intrude on, and besides he didn't know his head size.

Grosbeck got up from his desk and walked across the city room to Tully. Other times, he would have stayed at his desk and waited for Tully to wander by. Then, he would have put down whatever he was doing and said something as obscure as he could think of, confident that Tully's cock-eyed sensibilities would bring a reply in kind: two royalists playing court tennis while the nobility diddled with themselves in the *dedans*. It was college humor raised to the level of two men who had accumulated thousands of pointless yet apposite facts and displayed them like Armenian rug dealers.

These exchanges were, for Grosbeck, one of the few proofs of universality; at the same time, they excluded almost everyone else. The paradox was a nice one and delicate and it was not lost on either man. They cultivated it, while, quite self-consciously, staying clear of each other. In a time when people confessed the most vulgar details of their lives to others (none of them able to hear anyone else or to make sense out of what was being said), Tully and Grosbeck observed a marvelous punctilio: You spare me your *mishegaas,* I'll spare you my blather. Please don't bother to communicate one-to-one, eyeball-to-eyeball. Don't call us, we'll call you.

Tully's back was to Grosbeck. He was in the midst of a conversation with the three men who ran the city desk . . . housekeeping details . . . an assignment for the day. Grosbeck tapped him on the shoulder. Tully turned around and said, "Why, Harv, what are you doing all the way over here? I had no idea you'd gone in for physical exercise. Look out, dear man, for tachycardia, defibrillation, enosis of the enharmonic tetrachord."

"Dandy," said Grosbeck, "you got a minute?"

Tully's eyes opened a little. "Hold one," he said (Grosbeck was amused when Tully used language of that kind; Grosbeck did it himself and the two men enjoyed the contempt both felt for it; but Grosbeck had no time to be amused right now), and turned back to the city desk.

"It's important, John," said Grosbeck, importuning Tully. Tully gave him his attention. "I need some advice *and* I need help. And, it's about time to eat. They've got the gin-mill number on the desk. Have you got time?"

"What's bothering you? You don't usually dither, you berate."

"John, I can't fool with *rondelles* today," said Grosbeck. "Let's get out of here. I think I'm going to be killed."

"You, Harvey? Killed? What for? Nobody even gets contempt of court any more for splitting infinitives."

Grosbeck took Tully by the arm. All-wool worsted tropical. At least two hundred and a quarter. Even with all his years on the paper, Tully didn't make that kind of money. He was to be applauded.

"I'm not kidding," Grosbeck said. "I don't want to talk about it here. And not in the elevator, either. We can get a table in the back across the street."

"All right, Harvey," Tully said thoughtfully. "You've convinced me." He looked at Grosbeck. "I thought at first it was one of your usual murky flaps. But, I've never seen you so upset before. Noisy or furious or making a pain in the ass of yourself over not very much. But not quiet and nervous. No, sir. I take your word for it."

Grosbeck went back to his desk for his jacket and the two men left the building for a restaurant across the street, making their way doggedly through the human filth eddying about them in the heat. The bits of mica in the sidewalks jabbed light into Grosbeck's eyes and he hurried himself and Tully into the restaurant.

The restaurant was blessedly dark, cool and dank at all times of the year. The man who owned it was a cranky German from Minneapolis who, for years, had refused to have a television set in the place or a jukebox. He had learned to pay off the police (there was a little bandy-legged horse cop who made the rounds on the block once a week . . . up one side and down the other . . . collecting), and, eventually, he learned to pay off the gangsters.

There was a television set over the bar now and the German turned it up only when a policeman or a hoodlum was scheduled to come in. If a customer asked to watch a football game, the owner told him the set was out of order and that the repairman wouldn't be in for a week. Nobody ever played the jukebox they made him put in and the owner got around that, for pay-off purposes, by filling it with quarters once a week.

The fittings of the restaurant were not special in any way, neither old nor valuable, but they were heavy and one could sit at a table in comfort. The food served was substantial and good. And the owner charged a good price for it. He had to do that, too: There were pay-offs all the way from the Gansevoort meat market to the Bronx produce market and all the way around through linen and bar supplies. Rather than serve crap, the German took his chances and raised prices. The men on the newspaper were happy to pay, even the printers and the pressmen who patronized the place in their cotton aprons and square hats made of paper from day-old editions of the paper.

Marriages had been made in the restaurant and ended at the bar. There were long, long dribbling conversations ended at four o'clock in the morning on weekdays and three o'clock in the morning on Sundays. (Blue law.) Men had plotted in that bar to get away from it all and some of them had. Others had wept in front of women and been paid no attention to. Women had slapped men and men, women. Now and then, a customer slid off a stool onto the red Spanish tiles the owner had found somewhere. Women felt safe in this restaurant, and, domestic creatures that they were, marveled that it existed in the very storm's eye of so much depravity.

This restaurant had accrued to itself a feeling of sentiment. People were pleased by it. There were fights, every now and then, but so old-fashioned, and nothing like the warfare that went on outside. A drunken newspaperman or a belligerent advertising man could suffer not much more than a black eye, a torn shirt and the depression of being denied admittance for three days.

The secret of the restaurant, Grosbeck believed (he had expounded on it), was that it was a link with the past. "Yes," he would say, "I know it's not that old." Nor was it. It had not even been a speakeasy; it contained no poorly colored reproductions of sporting prints, no mementos of wood back of the bar or even a bar mirror of any proportions; no baloney pictures of the proprietor squaring off with a lightweight prizefighter, the glossy framed at the five-and-ten and the glass flyblown. The restaurant clasped hands with the past only because of its German owner, who had grown up believing in solidity. He had transported that solidity to this block, which, sooner or later, would blow up, taking with it the owner and Grosbeck and all who ate and drank in the restaurant. The Landmarks Preservation Commission would never commemorate the place. The bar was not made of mahogany and it wasn't very long and the tables and chairs would not have been coveted either for the Good Design Collection of the Museum of Modern Art or the American Wing of the Metropolitan Museum of Art. No, the Landmarks Commission would not commemorate it because it would not have the wit or *sagesse* to do so.

Tully ordered knackwurst and dark beer.

Grosbeck ordered a double scotch, straight and warm.

"That's not your style, Harvey," said Tully. "Not at one o'clock in the afternoon. And not without ice and soda."

"I know," Grosbeck said. "Dying isn't my style, either."

Steam rose from the hot table at the end of the bar. The two waiters, in black jackets and pants and white aprons, worked quickly and unobtrusively. The place was crowded, but everyone was served when he asked to be served. When a table emptied, it was cleaned at once. The waiters were paragons, tall, strong young men, who, as people used to say, looked as though they were right off the boat . . . scraped off the boat.

They worked very hard and the customers tipped them very well. If they kept their distance, that was their decision and not that of the people who ate there. They seemed not to expect anything, and, as a result, they got everything. Grosbeck used to speculate that they both had large bank accounts, doctorates of philosophy, cattle ranches in Montana, three Bugattis in running order and safety-deposit boxes stuffed with British consols. In fact, they were homosexuals who lived together no more than three blocks from Grosbeck in the Village and who nodded distantly at him on weekend afternoons, when, by chance, he ran into them shopping on Bleecker Street.

It was obvious to Grosbeck that the restaurant owner's prejudices were diffuse enough so that he would not let anything so insubstantial as an employee's sexual habits to stand in the way so long as the man did a good day's work and didn't lallygag in the toilet soliciting anybody.

"All right, Grosbeck," said Tully after they were served. "Let's get at it." He took a bite of knackwurst, added a forkful of sauerkraut and wiped his lips with a linen napkin. (The napkins were another thing about the restaurant.)

"What's on your mind? I say mind when what I really mean is that bundle of hysteria from which you draw so many false conclusions."

"Not this time," said Grosbeck. He told Tully about the mugging of Madeline; the summoning of the police; what Madeline had let slip about the connection between the mugger and Catafesta, the dealer on the sixth floor; about how he had tried, by raging at the cops, to make them think he knew nothing about the connection; about the reaction of the sergeant; the last words the sergeant had spoken as the two policemen left the apartment: "You old son of a bitch." He said nothing about Madeline throwing the Tarot.

"John," Grosbeck went on, "you know enough about this city to realize that what I've told you isn't farfetched, that they won't tolerate any interference. I'm no Jake Lingle and this isn't Chicago during Prohibition; it's much worse. I know what they're doing and they know that I know and I'm badly frightened. I'm too young to die. I'll be too young to die at a hundred and fifty. Keep me alive."

He drank his scotch quickly and it went to his head.

"Do I exaggerate?" he asked. "Right outside this door it goes on day in and day out. You see it all the time."

"Yes," said Tully, "I see it. Are you comparing yourself with that police-blotter stuff?"

"No, worse," said Grosbeck. "Most of them . . . not all, but most . . . die for no reason at all. I don't mean for no reason at all, but for reasons that don't concern us. Or they didn't use to. But I'm up against an *organization*. More and more, I've come to think we all are. It doesn't matter any longer what the organization is called, either, big business, crime. It's all *la même chose*. You know my shorthand. Put it this way: My life is in the hands of a collection agency and they're going to get what they think I owe them. What I owe them is my life. Big business is going to foreclose me.

"Look, why I came to you is, forgive me, that we are both of a certain class, a class with some privileges, some means of getting around restrictions and rules. But now I'm not talking about fixing parking tickets or settling an income-tax dun."

Grosbeck was near to blubbering in the middle of the afternoon.

"You know these people . . . on both sides . . . the cops *and* the others. My one hope is that you can say something to them. Tell them I meant no harm. To be quite frank with you, I would kill *them* if I could, but we both know I can't. So, tell them to forget it, that I'll forget it, that I overstepped, that I'll never do it again."

"Harvey!" said Tully. He was shocked . . . and moved. "Control yourself." And he did something Grosbeck found so percipient. He reached a hand across the table and took Grosbeck lightly by the wrist. Just for a second. Grosbeck knew he had been right to like this man. Of course. Tully would not ever do that again in his life to Grosbeck. Understood. But, he *had* done it this time and Grosbeck was overwhelmed. He had intended to order another drink, but he did not. Instead, he sat opposite Tully, calm and, for succeeding minutes, purged of the lightness in his head, the burning in his face, the indescribable turmoil in his chest and belly.

"It does happen, Harvey," said Tully. "I tell you this reluctantly. For two reasons. I never want to admit it to myself, although I know better, and I didn't want to say it to you because you're in no condition for that. But, there it is.

"I don't know the particular cops you're talking about, but I do know the precinct. And I know of the guy in your house. I've seen him around. He doesn't get in the papers much. He's been arrested and I think he even did some time twenty years ago for something on the docks. Shylocking. Six for five. I see he hasn't even moved out of the neighborhood. You're only three blocks from the river, aren't you?"

Grosbeck nodded.

"He's medium big. He doesn't carry a gun. He doesn't have to. Tell you what I'll do. I'll go downtown and poke around. And I'll see a few people. On both sides. I'll tell them what you told me. Not the *way* you told me: That's personal. I think they'll go for it. Maybe something else will occur to me. In fact, I know damned well it will. And try not to worry too much." Tully smiled faintly. "I might as well not bother to tell you that. You worry every time you can't get an information operator. Or, rather, you lose your temper.

"A last word on the subject: This time, don't lose your temper. For any reason."

Grosbeck nodded vehemently.

"I think you'd better have something to eat, Harvey," said Tully.

"I don't think I can, Dandy," said Grosbeck. "But, I thank you."

"Come on, Grosbeck, eat something. You can't go back across the street the way you are now. You're loaded. You get in enough trouble around that place without doing it drunk."

Tully held up a finger and one of the waiters came over. "Give my friend a plate of roast beef, please," he said. "One vegetable, anything you've got. No potatoes. And, an end cut, if you have it. He's been eating too much rare meat." The waiter looked at Grosbeck indulgently. "And a pot of coffee for the both of us."

When the waiter came back with the food, Tully said to Grosbeck, "I'm going to talk for a while, Harvey. About my grandfather. On my father's side. He was a New Yorker. Like us. And then, you're going back to work and I'm going somewhere else."

Inexplicably, Grosbeck got angry. "For Christ's sake, John," he said, "don't treat me like a child."

"Harvey," said Tully, "shut up."

He finished his knackwurst, poured himself a cup of coffee and pointed a finger at Grosbeck's plate. "Eat, *mein kind*," he said kindly. And Grosbeck started to.

"My grandfather, Tom Tully, was born in New York, Harvey," said Tully. "In the same frame house in High Bridge where I was born. The Irish . . . oh, not just the Irish, everybody, I suppose . . . didn't have their children in hospitals then with the husband gawking in the delivery room. *His* father came over after the potato famine. I don't know what possessed the family to move downtown, but, I guess, in some mystic way, they felt they weren't really New Yorkers living in High Bridge. No, that can't be right. What prob-

161

ably happened is they went broke during the panic of Twenty-one and *had* to give up the house."

Grosbeck found he had an appetite.

"Tom was a prizefighter," said Tully. "A crowd-pleasing young contender from Manhattan's West Side at a hundred and thirty-five and a quarter pounds. I've still got a photograph of him at fighting weight. Sepia. The shorts are too long, he's clean-shaven and his hair is slicked back. He was built beautifully . . . legs not too long, waist not too short, the shoulders just right and the arms. None of your thyroidal apes. He looked like a fighter should look. Benny Leonard looked like that years later. Tom didn't have any fake name, either, just Tom Tully. In the picture, he's wearing one of those silk sashes around his waist. I suppose some photographer talked him into wearing it for the picture, because he didn't go in for that sort of thing.

"He belonged to the old Pioneer A. C. and he actually did fight once in the old Garden. Stanford White's Garden. To me, the old Garden always smelled of horses and hay. I guess that was because the only times I went there as a kid were when the circus was in town. Evelyn Nesbit and Harry Thaw were before my time."

"Is that possible, Dandy?" asked Grosbeck. "I thought you covered the shooting. You sure *talk* old enough."

Tully said, "You are feeling a little better, Harvey. To go on: Tom never got to be anything more than a crowd-pleasing young contender from Manhattan's West Side. But he was hungry and he needed the money . . . he married young . . . and by the time the picture was taken his nose was mashed to the left. I think he had about seventy-five fights before he got out and went on the cops."

"On the cops," said Grosbeck. "I can smell something coming."

"There's no moral to this story, Harvey," said Tully. "I'm not pulling any parables out of my pocket."

"I don't care," said Grosbeck. "But leave the parables for the heavy thinkers. Go on. I like your grandfather."

"As a young man," said Tully, "he was thin and picky and fast. Fastidious."

"Like you, Dandy," said Grosbeck.

Tully nodded unself-consciously.

"He drank some beer on Saturday nights with his wife. They had eight children. One of them got killed by a car and another died of diphtheria. He finished the second year of high school . . . Incarnation . . . over near Tenth Avenue and Forty-eighth . . . it's gone . . . and when he got through fighting he knew he'd have to find something to do. Harvey, are you listening?"

"Yes," said Grosbeck. "Don't I always, to you? And eating, too."

"Actually, he got through fighting because my grandmother wanted him to. He probably could have gone on for another couple of years, but he never would have gone anywhere. There were too many really good ones around. Anyway, he went on the cops."

"No parables, eh, Dandy?" asked Grosbeck. "No moral?"

"Hear me out, Harvey," said Tully. "And have a cup of coffee." People were beginning to drift out of the restaurant. It was getting past lunchtime.

"Tom went on the cops, I don't have to tell you, because there wasn't much else he could have done outside of work for the gas company or be a bricklayer or a hod carrier or dig ditches. Speaking of the gas company, we lived about a block away from the big gas tank at Fifty-ninth and Tenth. The women used to take their babies to sit on benches all around the tank. There was a superstition that the gas was good for infants. Did you ever hear of anything like that?"

"Yes," said Grosbeck. "What makes you think Jews are any the less superstitious than the Irish?"

"Going with the gas company wasn't for my grandfather," Tully continued. "He'd got a little interested in politics because there were always a couple of minor Tammany lobbygows coming to see him fight. They'd be taken there by the precinct captains who lived in Tom's neighborhood and he'd rung doorbells for them at election time and delivered turkeys and coal at Christmas. So, he didn't have much trouble getting in.

"He really was a hell of a cop. No hypocrite. He took. In those days, it was stuss games, saloons, Bleecker Street whores and so on. Would you believe he once even helped a squad knock off one of Richard Canfield's gambling joints? That didn't happen often, only on orders from above, when Canfield got more than ordinarily haughty."

"Which Canfield place, John?" asked Grosbeck. "I'll bet I know. The one next to the last Delmonico's . . . northeast corner of Forty-fourth and Fifth; Canfield in the building next door to the east. Right?"

"Yes," said Tully. "I knew you'd know. You've always behaved as though you were ninety years old. That was the one and after the raid was over the squad got invited into the kitchen at Delmonico's for a meal. I'm sorry I can't tell you what they had to eat, but you can bet your ass it wasn't broken funeral meats."

"Hah," said Grosbeck.

"Tom took his cut, as I say, and he gave the rest to the sergeant who got his and gave what was left to the captain and where the rest went is only a matter of name and rank. That's the way it went. No different from now. But, there was more to Tom than that. He was no Johnny Broderick parading up and down Broadway. There wasn't that kind of flash in him. But, he did take on Monk Eastman once down on the lower East Side when he was mustering out of the Elizabeth Street stationhouse.

"Monk Eastman was what they call these days, an animal. Like Abe Reles to come. A killer. Remember what Eastman did in the First World War? He was a killer in New York City and he was a killer in the Army in Europe. In fact, if I remember right, they let him out of jail to go into the Army. Probably hoped he'd be killed. He wasn't. He killed his quota of Germans . . . it didn't make much difference to him whom he killed. And he got decorated, came home and early in the Twenties, they found him dead in a gutter with a couple of bullet holes in him.

"But, to go back. Tom once beat the shit out of Eastman on Delancey Street because Eastman was on one of his crazy tears and beating up a woman. Tom did it in full uniform, too, and laid his night stick down on the sidewalk before he did it. First, he took Eastman's gun away from him. Then, he held Eastman off with one arm and pushed the woman into a doorway with the other. Then, he went to work on Eastman. He put him away with a short left hook and a right that came up from the sidewalk. That's the way Tom used to tell the story and he was telling the truth. Truth was all sorts of things to him, Harvey. Beating up Monk Eastman *and* taking."

"You're maudlin, John," said Grosbeck. "Far worse than I am."

"About the same," said Grosbeck. "Tom was so proud of that uniform, you wouldn't believe it. The badge got shined every day. The black shoes you could see your face in. The pants were pressed, the tunic was pressed, the winter overcoat. My grandmother ironed them. You'll not overlook the fact, either, that in those days the cops paid for their own uniforms. He even saddle-soaped the visor they had on those stiff, funny-looking caps."

"The good old days, Dandy," said Grosbeck. "What you mean is the old days that were good for some people."

"Forget that, Harvey. I guess I am getting to something in a roundabout way."

"I was sure you would, John. But it's two-thirty."

"It's better to see you frantic over that than the other thing, Harvey," said Tully. "Tom went to Mass every Sunday. He raised his kids strictly. I am the son of one of them. He drank nothing but beer. As the years went by, he slowed down and got heavier, but he was still just as picky and the only boss he acknowledged outside of the captain was his wife. My grandfather was a real typical flatfoot."

"So?"

"I'm getting there, Harvey. He took, as I say, but he didn't get to be a millionaire. Today, a cop like that is known as a 'grass eater.' Live and let live. The really big thieves are called 'meat eaters.'"

"I know," said Grosbeck. "I read the papers, too."

"Well, Harvey, he lived to be seventy-eight. He died over in Hell's Kitchen where he still lived after he retired. After he put in his papers and took his pension, he used to go to the Polo Grounds two, three times a week when the Giants were in town and yell at McGraw. If you were a Giant fan in those days, you were an aristocrat. You might not be rich, but you were an aristocrat. The Yankees were new money and the Dodgers were too unspeakable to contemplate. There's folklore for you.

"Tom used to sit in the fifty-cent bleachers with a lot of other old-timers and he got more tan in his last years than he ever did on the force because most of the time he worked nights. He brown-bagged it with one of my grandmother's meat sandwiches and he bought a beer or two and he'd come home with a light sweat on his forehead and just a little bit mulled. The trip downtown on the Ninth Avenue El didn't exactly contribute to the peace of his stomach. Not when it rounded that incredible high curve at One Hundred and Tenth Street."

"Please, John," said Grosbeck. "It is getting late."

"I'm trying to make a point, Harvey," said Tully. "In all those years . . . on the force and after . . . Tom never felt he'd done anything wrong. On the contrary, he was absolutely certain that everything he'd done was right. And it was right because everyone before him had done it . . . ever since there was an organized police department and headquarters was down on Mulberry Street. And everybody after him would do it. Just so you didn't take too much, it was all right. And when he died, he died in peace, sitting in a wicker armchair in the apartment on a late spring day. I was there. The windows in the living room were open a little to let in the spring air and the cotton curtains bellied and it was a good day.

"He was sitting in that chair with that red-and-green carpet runner under it so the good rug wouldn't get worn. He never said a word, no last-minute doubts, much less confessions. He died unshriven, Harvey. The father wasn't there to give him Extreme Unction, last Communion, but the priest took me aside and said to me, 'John, I very much doubt that man will be in Purgatory very long.' They held a four-day wake for him. Then, they buried him out of Transfiguration and that was it."

Tully stopped. Then, deprecatingly, he added: "Sounds soft, doesn't it, Harvey?"

Grosbeck merely gestured.

"Well, it isn't, Harvey. Tom was a victim."

"Oh, Jesus, John, is that what you've been leading up to? A victim! Whose victim? A victim of what? He died gaining weight, didn't he? And he left his widow enough to live on and send a couple of kids through parochial school and college. Some victim."

Tully was patient. "You know very well what I mean, Harvey. He stole because he had to. He also did his job. So does most everybody else. I don't say everybody. Most everybody. They must, they must, they must. You're no different. You steal what you can off your income taxes, expense accounts, Christmas gifts from press agents. More, if you could get away with it."

"You really think it's the same thing, John."

"You're no different, Harvey. And your hatred and fear of the cops is one of the few forms of snobbery in you I don't hold with. So the cops don't live in Hell's Kitchen any more. They live out of town. They're the same cops."

"I don't agree, John. There *is* quite a qualitative difference."

"They can be reached, Harvey, just as Tom could . . . in a human way, just as much as by money."

"Do you really believe that, Dandy?" asked Grosbeck. "Support your local police? With *your* experience."

"Yes and no, Harvey," said Tully. "For your sake, for the sake of both of us, I am going to think yes. You try, too. Pretend it is so, if you can't believe it. Say to yourself, 'Not all cops and not all priests are mother-fuckers.' I can't speak for your drug dealer. But they all depend on one another, and, maybe, because of that, something can be worked out."

Grosbeck had finished his food. The drink had worn off and he was despondent and fearful again. He said, "I'll

168

trade you parables, John." He pulled a piece of wire copy out of his pocket.

"This," he said, waving it in Tully's face, "is one of the great rationalizations of the century."

"What is, Harvey?" asked Tully. "I don't know why I'm asking, because you're about to tell me."

"Remember that plane crash in Chile?" asked Grosbeck. "The other day? And the survivors who came out of the mountains?"

"Yes," said Tully.

"Then, this will be instructive. It turns out they kept alive by eating the people who got killed. That's not what's so awful, though, it's the excuse they gave for it."

"And what was the excuse, Harvey?"

Grosbeck unfolded the piece of paper, put on his glasses, and read:

"'We thought,' said one of the survivors, 'if Jesus in His Last Supper distributed His Body and Blood to all His Apostles, He was making it understood that we had to do the same thing: take the body and blood which would then nourish us. And that was an intimate Communion among all of us. It was what helped us to survive.' What I think, John, is that they will survive and the way they'll do it is on my body and blood. No capital letters, please."

"That's cheap and easy and glib, Harvey," said Tully. "And not worthy of you." He rubbed his chin and looked at Grosbeck again. "I'm sorry," he said. "And you've got to get back to work."

Grosbeck put away his piece of paper, insisted on paying for lunch and followed Tully into the street. They shook hands in hell. Tully caught a cab and Grosbeck went across the street and upstairs to his desk.

Tully had opened up for Grosbeck the *vision* of Communion . . . stingily, for Grosbeck, unwillingly and thickly smeared with fear . . . but there.

At seven-thirty at night, the tens of thousands of choices that would be the first edition of the newspaper had been made. It was the time of vespers. But, there was no dimming of the hard fluorescent lights on the editorial floor of the newspaper; in the streets, no lamplighter to mark the transition between day and night, no Welsbach mantles to flicker or carbon arcs to flare.

Grosbeck finished his day's work; there would be others to carry it on during the night; the newspaper was like one of those private-detective agencies: "We never sleep" or "Do you want to know?" with a big, unblinking eye over the slogan. He put his glasses in his left-hand inside coat pocket, pushed everything back on the desk. (Tomorrow, what he did not need or want would be swept to one side and into a huge wastebasket.) His apprehensions, his lunch with Tully, the requirements of his work had induced in him a multiplicity of reactions the dimensions of which could not be measured.

Grosbeck said to himself as he pushed back his swivel chair:

For all of seventy-five years of Freud, a hundred of Marx, six thousand of recorded history, the droppings and hen tracks of uncounted biologists and physiologists and neurologists, physicists, sociologists, anthropologists and other kinds of scholars; for all of their asterisks, daggers and dou-

170

ble daggers at the bottom of the page, the billions of yellowed pages, the microfilm, the unreadable computer numbers, I cannot be accounted for. I am not the statistical mean; there is none. They can tell me what time of day I will get up and when I will go where and what it is I will do. They can trace the least drop of blood through my hardening arteries and, presumably, tell me the number of micromillimeters of semen that will dribble out of me; what I will eat, how it will be transformed, the color upon discharge.

They can nail me down to the last dangling ganglion, the smart-ass bastards.

Only, they can't. I am infinite and they cannot embrace infinity. In the end, they cannot account for me.

Tully, save me.

Baleen descended to his chauffeured chariot, passing Grosbeck with a distant nod of disapproval. Once more, Baleen had insured the right of the people to know; could Grosbeck say as much? Shalit entered the sturdy Swedish automobile that would bear him to the suburbs, where, tonight, he would have to dinner the one Negro (black) couple in the neighborhood . . . two martinis each, a pot roast, noodles ("We don't change much, do we?" he would ask the Negroes, apologizing to them for the fact that his Jewish wife couldn't cook collard greens, ham hocks and black-eyed peas), string beans with almonds, a young wine that breathed as though it had bronchitis, strudel, decaffeinated coffee, Courvoisier. ("No, go ahead, I'd rather just have some club soda myself. You can take the boy out of Brooklyn, but you can't take Brooklyn out of the boy." And an anecdote about the seltzer man and the weekly deliveries of a case of seltzer, the bottles to be returned. He would forgive the Negro accountant for not regaling the table with stories of the fun his grandfather had getting lynched in Alabama.)

The reporters, giddy with exertion, went out to eat, perhaps to get drunk, possibly to go home or some other dirty place, as the wits among them said over and over every day. The secretaries shut off the current on their electric typewriters. The copyboys fingered their beards and drank coffee, dreaming of doctorates of philosophy in journalism. Were there such things? The changing of the guard at the newspaper was a slovenly business, an army in retreat without its colors. The high-pitched whine of a metal saw rose through the floor from the composing room. Every few minutes, the floor shook; the presses turned with a groan to receive page plates.

Grosbeck said good night to the rear guard, was acknowledged and composed himself for the trip home on the bus. From tonight on, that trip . . . any trip he would take, anywhere in the city . . . would have a different connotation. He would have to keep his eyes open and his mind alert and not think back to the past.

Riding home on the bus, he could not now luxuriate in reverie. He could not drift, not go back and forth in time. The uniform of the day in the city room was no longer rolled shirtsleeves, ties pulled down and shirttails half out. There were very few men on the copy desk who wore green eyeshades today or wet the tip of a No. 2 soft-lead pencil with the tongue and called out, "Boy!" Richard Harding Davis. The Message to Garcia. Puttees. Lucius Beebe. Stanley Walker. *Young Man of Manhattan* and Richards Vidmer.

Printing House Square. The steam engines that ran the presses for all the newspapers on Park Row. Where were they? In that building at William and Spruce? Theatre Alley. The Tribune Building. The World.

An intoxicating universe.

The Sixth Avenue Elevated locomotives strewing cinders on the walkers below. The Grand Central Hotel. Jim Fisk pistoled by Ned Stokes for the love of Josie Mansfield on the grand stairway of the hotel. Fortuny cloth on the walls and blood on the carpeted risers. (Josie and the Manhattan Opera House; Jim and the Erie grab.) There, in that hotel, the National Baseball League founded.

Was ever such a city.

Now, the junkies spat and vomited in the corridors of the old hotel and the women on welfare cooked over burners in the horrid rooms while their children inserted fingers in the holes in the walls in the hallways.

No.

Paris Singer and James Hazen Hyde (when you stole an insurance company, you simply sailed elegantly off to France until the heat was off; when you died, the newspapers commented only on the fineness of the linen you wore); Evander Berry Wall (the stand-up collar brought to perfection); C. K. G. Billings and the horseback dinner at Sherry's. Bond St. A. Oakey Hall. The Hip Sings and the On Leongs.

Gorgeous jumble. No more.

Now, it was a question of who sat next to you, who observed you from the street. Grosbeck had been yanked back into the present so that he could no longer concentrate on the marble profundities of the Appellate Division courthouse on Madison Square, could not dream he dwelt in marble halls.

File away the special reference.

When the bus stopped for a traffic light, a man looked up from the passenger's seat in a car stopped next to it, directly at Grosbeck. Only for an instant, unquestionably did not see him, gave his attention to the driver. The light changed, everything moved on. The car, the driver, the passenger would never reappear. Guess, Grosbeck, guess. The conspiracy was all about him.

When he arrived at the apartment building, he opened the outside door and Catafesta, the man on the sixth floor, walked out, poodle on leash, wife at side. Catafesta's face was florid and polished, his hair a brown-white pompadour, his eyes those of a basilisk. Grosbeck made way for him; he did not even regard Grosbeck, lowered his head in conventional enactment of a politeness and stepped outside. The wife did not look back; the poodle did not look back; Catafesta presented a blind back. Grosbeck felt the heat of the dying day acutely, but there was nothing untoward about this encounter. The Catafestas normally walked the dog at this hour and Grosbeck passed them at the door at least three times a week.

Grosbeck let himself into the apartment. Madeline awaited him. Jason was there. He asked the questions expected of him. (Madeline could wait until later to hear about the lunch with Tully.) He ate, but he was aware of a strange sensation he could not precisely identify. He had had that same sensation or something like it (it was so hard to tell) on a Saturday morning weeks before the mugging.

He and Jason were accustomed to get haircuts in a barbershop on Hudson Street, a run-down place with three chairs, but only one barber, a man whose life was finished, although he was no more than Grosbeck's age. He was a mournful little Jew from Flatlands in Brooklyn, whose teeth were half gone and who had found senility early or perhaps it was only a disinclination to make sense. The barber's link with the past was a photograph of himself, stuck in a corner of the mirror in front of the barber chairs. It showed him in uniform. He had fought in an infantry battalion in Europe in the Second World War. Nothing remarkable. Just another dogface. But young, erect, a private first class. Nothing was left of that young man, goggling at the camera.

He talked too much, but not about himself; the photograph was there for the world to draw its own conclusions about him. He asked questions of Jason, always the same ones. Was he enjoying his summer vacation, whether he wanted to go back to school, whether he was going to do what his father did. (He didn't know; Grosbeck never told him; and the man was not that inquisitive, anyway; not persistent like that barber in the Pinaud cologne ads, leaning over his shrinking customer, scissors in hand. He was garrulous, but that was all.) Jason put up with the questions; he had developed, at his age, a tact his father appreciated but was, himself, incapable of. Grosbeck compensated for his own impatience by overtipping the barber, who didn't care either way. To him, it was all one. Soon, he would be gone.

And he was. One Saturday morning, Grosbeck looked at Jason and said, "You need a haircut." Jason replied, "Pa, not this week." "I need one, too," said Grosbeck. "You never need one, Pa," said the boy. Both spoke their lines by rote; the lines drew them together and had often been spoken. Any deviation from them would have upset Grosbeck and, temporarily, disconcerted the boy. "Come on now," said Grosbeck. "We go through this every time; let's get it over with." They walked to the barbershop, which was several blocks away, and when they got there they found the door was locked and the place empty. They peered through the window. There was still hair on the floor, in a ring around the one chair the barber used, magazines on the bench against the wall, everything else as it was.

But.

The first thing Grosbeck noticed was that the photograph in the mirror was gone. It was fully a minute before he found the sign in the window, a piece of gray cardboard, one of those stiffeners inserted into freshly laundered shirts. On it had been printed, in blue crayon:

"No More Barbershop Here."

Grosbeck and Jason looked at each other.

Why? Why? Grosbeck demanded to know.

"No haircut today, Pop, I guess," said Jason. There was no malice in the way he said it.

"No," said Grosbeck. "We'll have to find another place. Let it go another week."

Jason said to his father, "Pa, it's not one of your old buildings."

Grosbeck laughed. He had not intended to. But Jason had lifted the grave cerements; the boy's intuitions were flawless.

But "No More Barbershop Here" had been an omen and produced a desolation in him.

Grosbeck was not very good at hiding things at home. Madeline knew what was on his mind, so there was nothing to hide from her. Jason, whose antennae were so sensitive, had to be kept from knowing. Madeline talked at, it seemed, maddening length about a project she was engaged in at her office. She worked for an architect of whom Grosbeck did not approve, but a man who, if his clients did demand awful things of him, still salved his conscience by collecting bits and pieces of the old buildings he so obediently tore down for money. The lousy WASP whore of an architect turned them into chic. Madeline's job was to track down such things and see to it that they were transported to the hideous glass house the architect had built for himself in Connecticut. What she did *was* interesting, but Grosbeck didn't want to hear about it that night. Nor did Madeline want to tell him about it, but she had to.

Grosbeck went to his customary, excessive lengths. His nervous frivolity was wearing. He made up gossip about people in the office. He said, for example, that Perry Phillips, an assistant city editor who sat near him, had been taken to the hospital. "What for?" asked Madeline, who knew the man. "For an autopsy," said Grosbeck. "Harvey!" said Madeline. "Is there anything really wrong with Phillips?" "No," said Grosbeck, "I was just being funny."

He got up after dinner and did imitations both Madeline and Jason had seen many times. He imitated a rooster strutting in a barnyard; by himself, an entire Mardi Gras parade in New Orleans; his suit jacket over his head to convey the idea of the huge papier-mâché heads the paraders wore. He imitated a lighthouse with a revolving light and a lighthouse with a stationary red-and-white light. He sweated and pirouetted. He imitated a Chinese incense burner, inhaling a deep, deep puff on a cigarette and letting the smoke trickle through his teeth, bared in a grimace. They were good imitations; the family had seen them many times before and they still laughed.

It was fine domestic *commedia dell'arte,* but the audience and the performer were not in the mood for it tonight. The laughter, it seemed to Grosbeck, sounded like shards of plate glass falling in a high wind on a cement pavement. Madeline waited to hear about Tully. Jason, his face screwed up to attention, waited to find out anything. Grosbeck waited for the time to pass until Jason could reasonably be ordered off to bed . . . as he had waited for Tully earlier in the day. The time passed. Jason was told to go to bed.

He kissed Jason on the head. Madeline pinched his arm. Jason said, "You don't have to tell me, but there's something going on." "You're half right," said Grosbeck. "I *don't* have to tell you anything and there's nothing going on." The boy said, "I know when you're being funny, Pa." Grosbeck clasped his hands on the table and pursed his lips. "And, Ma," Jason said, "I know when you think he's funny." Madeline did not blink. "So, don't tell me," said Jason. He forgave his parents and went to bed.

Madeline started to clear the table. Grosbeck was afforded a number of views of her fine legs as she moved about and he put out a hand and ran it up under her dress. Jesus! But that wasn't what he was supposed to have on his mind. . . . Oh, no! . . . and withdrew the hand. What the hell, why not? She picked up a bowl and he made her put it down.

"That can wait," he said. "Let it go for once. You're so damned compulsive. You'll put away laundry on the morning of my funeral and straighten a few pictures before climbing into your widow's weeds."

"Harvey," she said, "you're cruel. You're a son of a bitch." She slapped his face and began to cry. "Funeral. Widow's weeds. And the other thing."

"What in hell was that all about?" he asked. She had just told him. For the ten thousandth time in his life, he had done something which, by anyone's standards, was wrong, objectively wrong: He had outraged dignity; he had been guilty, in a situation demanding the utmost seriousness, first of caprice, then of captiousness; not heroic, not debonair. He felt dirty . . . not for having fooled with his wife's legs, but for complaining about her household habits and for the reference to funerals and widows.

He gnawed at a piece of bread. Madeline hit at his hand and the bread fell to the floor. He stood up, seized both her arms and held her hands behind her back.

"Apologies don't do much good," he said. "But, I apologize. I beg your pardon. I don't know what gets into me at times."

Madeline said, "I waited all day to hear from you. I couldn't do my work properly. I didn't call you. I hardly knew what I was shopping for for dinner. I saw things in the streets I've never seen before and whenever I turned around to look more closely there was nothing there."

Grosbeck interrupted. "Me, too," he said.

"Be quiet," Madeline said. "I took a cab home instead of the subway. And now you've got me whimpering and whining."

"You're shouting," said Grosbeck. This kind of thing would be the death of him.

"You stupid little man," said Madeline. She dried her face with a kitchen towel and sat down, her hands in her lap.

Grosbeck cleared his throat. "I apologized, didn't I?"

"Harvey," asked Madeline, "would you like me to open the windows and shriek? I can't take any more of this."

Grosbeck worried the bone. "More of what?" he asked. "All I was trying to do was get you to forget the dishes so I could tell you what Tully had to say." A lie.

"The way you did it, you might as well have . . . Oh, forget it. You're not going to change."

"I have changed, Madeline," said Grosbeck.

"The only change in you, Harvey, is that you think you're going to be killed. And even that didn't stop you. I want it as badly as you do, husband mine, but not now. No. I can't."

"I'm afraid for you, too, Madeline," said Grosbeck. "And Jason. Not for myself alone. And that's not all. Other things. Too complicated to go into right now."

"Harvey, you're about as complicated as a recipe for boiling water. And as likely to change. Now, tell me. I love you, Harvey. Tell me."

"Well," he said, "I had lunch with Tully and I don't have to tell you he's pretty well connected. He's going to talk with the cops and the other people, tell them that I'm harmless and see if they'll settle for that. And if that doesn't work, he's going to think up something. Also, I got a long lecture from him on cop morality. I could have done without it, but I sat still for it. I'll hear from him tomorrow."

He went faithfully into detail, every scrap of what he could remember, what was said, the atmosphere of the restaurant, the street, the handshake, the feeling of communion in despair. He was not the most selective man in the world.

"I forgot one thing," he said when the recital was over. "I ran into Catafesta and his wife going out when I came in. With the dog, as usual."

"Did he say anything?" asked Madeline.

"He didn't even *look* anything," said Grosbeck. "He doesn't have to. He's got all the time in the world and the resources. It's possible he hasn't made up his mind yet. He's got all the time he needs. My time."

Madeline ignored that. "Do you know what interests me, Harvey?" she asked. "The Communion story. You're not a metaphysical man." She took his face in her hands and kissed him. "Have I underestimated you? Can you, have you, changed?"

"You mean, have I found something to believe in. It comes and goes. I get glimmerings I didn't use to get. I suppress them when I can. The phenomenon of getting religion when a man is *in extremis*. Think. Think. The idea of finding some meaning in life at the end of it is a form of grotesquerie I hadn't planned on. I don't like it. I cherish my cowardice. I don't make excuses for it. I would prefer not to put poultices on it. But . . . there it is." He tried to imagine the smash of a bullet, the tearing of a knife.

"Don't be somber, Harvey," said Madeline.

"You want me to do a *tarantella?*"

"Yes," she said. "You did it for Jason. You gave me another inkling of the possibilities in you."

"That's sentimental horseshit. I just explained to you what it is that's happening. I don't like my cowardice adulterated by piety."

"I don't shrink at sentiment," said Madeline. "And my idea of horseshit isn't the same as yours."

"My insurance is paid up," said Grosbeck. "I don't know much about pain. I had my tonsils out when I was a kid and all that stays with me is how much ice cream they let me eat. And the broken arm I got from Milton Michaels, the fights with the kids on the block. But what kind of pain do you feel dying? If it happens quickly, if it's drawn out."

"I don't know," said Madeline. "I can't help you with that. I have to cry again. I can't help that, either." He found it interesting that she could weep without resembling either a drab or a matriarch in mourning. He loved her.

"Tully said I'd hear from him early," said Grosbeck. "After all," he added bitterly, "it can't take long to decide a matter of life and death."

"He's doing his best for you, Harvey."

Grosbeck got up from the table. "I'll do the dishes," he said.

"Don't," said Madeline. "You never get them clean."

"I said I'll do the dishes."

"Let me do them. You have a drink and keep me company."

"We're low on scotch."

"Then drink vodka."

"I don't like it after dinner," said Grosbeck.

"Finish the scotch and you can get more tomorrow."

"Tomorrow." Small talk in a funeral parlor.

He opened a cabinet. "I guess there's enough," he said. He opened the refrigerator. "And there's soda."

"Make do, Harvey."

They both smiled. *Risus sardonicus.* Chimpanzees grinning in a cage. Water flowed in the sink. Ice made small noises in Grosbeck's glass. He sat on a stool in the kitchen. Madeline washed and splashed and wiped. Grosbeck felt the whirl of intoxication come over him and purl in his belly and brain. Madeline finished and dried her hands.

"Now?" asked Grosbeck.

"No," said Madeline.

"Why not?"

"It is not appropriate, Harvey."

"I forgot," he said. The whiskey had hold of him. "Going to bed with you has to be appropriate. Victoria in state, going from Balmoral to Windsor."

"You're not the Prince Regent, Harvey."

"You believe in *organized* license."

"It works best for me, Harvey. I have my rights, too. And I haven't noticed that you're deprived."

"Please."

"I can't bear to be begged, Harvey. I want to be taken."

"You want to be taken so ceremonially. You have to be arranged for in advance, protocols signed, route of the procession laid out. . . . Laid! . . . And every step paced over three times. Outriders in place. The college of heraldry consulted. The carriage wheels greased. Whatever gilt has flaked off replaced. Petals strewn in the way."

"Again, Harvey: No."

"A walk, then?"

"That would be nice. But it *is* late. And I *am* a little nervous about going out after eleven o'clock."

"Fuck it," said Grosbeck. "For now, fuck it, fuck it, fuck it. Let's go."

Madeline teased. "It's still hot out, Harvey. In here, it's air-conditioned."

"Come on," he said. "I'm going to be brave. For fifteen minutes."

"You are, aren't you?"

"I don't know what I'm going to be. But, we're going to take a short walk."

Grosbeck and his wife went for their walk with teeth clenched this time rather than hands clasped.

The streets had lost whatever promise they had had. The remorseless street-grid plan of the early nineteenth century had been an act of remarkable prescience: Those who drafted it had foreseen the monstrous technology to come; indeed, had prayed for it in their counting houses and drafting rooms.

The new city forbade exploration and exclamation; it had no winsome eccentricity. What was left of the old . . . except for tiny pockets here and there . . . exhibits in a museum . . . looked as though it had been shelled and burned . . . blackened, abandoned, gutted . . . mile after mile . . . silent save for the rustle of vermin in the ruins.

And an ominous thing had happened also in conjunction with the fury of change and destruction and new building since the end of the Second World War. The poor no longer could be counted on to be in certain places nor crime to be precisely isolated. Such was their obduracy and disdain for logic that every time some well-meaning fool plotted their place and movement to contain them, they confounded him by breaking out at another hour in another place. They confounded the rich, who solved the problem . . . or so they thought . . . by living in fortresses and traveling in long, locked black cars.

The rich had created this pit and they controlled it by main force; government and the criminal were their necessary, if aberrant, allies; the poor were to be shoveled over and buried (the task of shoveling and burying daily grew more urgent and difficult); government and the criminal more and more got out of hand, but had not yet reached the point of being unmanageable. So long as these mercenaries were well paid, the theory ran, they could be handled.

It was a child's cosmogony Grosbeck had evolved . . . he knew it . . . but like so many babyish things, it was accurate, demonstrable. History did not dispute him and he did not think it would.

Rapine and murder of a secretary on a Park Avenue corner. Stabbing on Madison. Holdup and robbery in broad daylight in Rockefeller Center. On the West Side, an elderly psychoanalyst strapped to the black leather couch he had carried on his back from Vienna to London to America, his tongue lolling blue from his mouth, strangled; the prattle of Jung or Adler ended, the lips drawn back over the irregular, yellow teeth. Seventy-five dollars, change, a small television set taken, and a black leather satchel. What a surprise the intruders were in for! The satchel contained only the old man's lunch and a curiosity: an ancient dildo intended for the private collection of a colleague, its provenance meticulously written out in German on a white tag tied to its end . . . the corpse of lust identified and catalogued.

The two who had finished off the old man were undisciplined: they had not pried the gold fillings from his teeth. *Schlamperei.*

To walk now, day or night, was to reconnoiter in elephant grass and await the enemy.

Even on a battlefield, the diurnal and the nocturnal have fixed rhythms; the light comes up and is snuffed out by the dark, notwithstanding the explosions of shells, the arcing of flares, muzzle flashes, the thrashing about of the wounded. There was always the embarrassment of stubbing a toe on a body in the blackness. Patrols breathed heavily, their heavy metal equipment padded against the chinking of steel, not to give away their position.

Fixed rhythms. The Grosbecks came out into the street. It was beginning to drizzle. As they left, the solid burghers of the apartment house were coming in for the night. The

Grosbecks were greeted civilly by two Italian ladies and their husbands; the doctor who lived on the top floor and was invariably drunk before midnight at a neighborhood bar; and an unattached girl who lived on their floor. She was studying archaeology and smoked a great deal of hashish, delivered to her irregularly by friends returned from Katmandu. The odor filled the hallway as she invoked Ur of the Chaldees.

Before they had crossed the street, a wino from the Bowery came up to the Grosbecks. The winos ranged far and wide these days; change had affected them, too. The Bowery was infested with more complex people: drug addicts, vicious and determined. Time was when the worst that could happen to a wino was that his shoes would be stolen while he slept in a doorway; now, he could lose his shoes and his life, too. It was a wonder how, debilitated as they were, the winos found the strength to walk the distances they did. But they did; the human spirit apparently is inextinguishable.

Madeline was wearing slacks and dark glasses and, over her shoulders, Jason's raincoat. Her black hair was cut short. The wino walked up to her in his tatters. The stubble on his face stuck out like straws. He was classically filthy. He rolled his bloodshot eyes and addressed Madeline: "Would you," he asked, "care to contribute a pittance, a tithe, toward my spectacular delinquency?"

Grosbeck was tickled. The wino had mistaken her for a man. Not only that. For *the* man, the one with the money; he, Grosbeck, being only the elderly, seedy dependent. Further, his way of begging was kingly. "Pittance." "Tithe." "Spectacular delinquency." "Care to contribute." Was there a background there, or, now that he had to beg in middle-class neighborhoods, had he acquired a few sure-fire lines? It was unimportant.

Certainly. Certainly. The graceful sentence had grown out of his squirming to survive to drink and drink (the stomach could not take whiskey any more; a pint of muscatel was enough now); he had engraved in him this one sentence. If there were more, Grosbeck did not want to know; he had been won. Madeline covered her mouth.

"Just a minute," said Grosbeck. He leaned against the building, took off a shoe and removed a dollar from it. "Here," he said. "They may not see your like again." No condescension. Nor did the drunk humble himself to Grosbeck. "Plainly," he said, "you are the one with the exchequer. No reflection on your comrade, none on you." (So he did have more than one sentence.) "And very wise of you to keep it in your shoe. They do sometimes make you take off your shoes, though."

"You shift it around," said Grosbeck. "A little in the shoe tonight, just change in the pocket. We weren't expecting to spend much." The necessity to explain himself to a drunk was absurd; he did not always extend the courtesy to people he worked with or friends.

He added: "Oh, by the way, my comrade is my *wife*."

"How do you do," said the wino. "My eyesight isn't what it was."

"No need to apologize," said Grosbeck. "If you'll excuse us, we've got to go."

"Thank you, again," said the drunk. "On second thought, just thank you. I didn't thank you the first time. Good night," he said. "The air is salubrious, though damp, and you are a gentleman. I salute your wife."

"That's what makes life worth living," Grosbeck said to Madeline as they crossed the street.

"I wish," she said, "you treated our friends half as well."

"They have no appeal," he said. "No what we call in Yiddish, *tom*. They're all so goddamned busy being voguey."

Perazzo was closing up for the night. They spoke to him. He seemed, at first, merely to acknowledge their good night. Then, hesitantly, he asked Grosbeck, "Could I talk to you, Mr. Grosbeck?"

"Of course," said Grosbeck. "That's what we're doing."

"I mean alone," said Perazzo. "Inside the store."

"Jimmy!" said Grosbeck.

"Don't get mad, Mr. Grosbeck."

Panic settled on Grosbeck again. "What do you have to tell me, Jimmy, that Mrs. Grosbeck can't hear?"

"Things get around, Mr. Grosbeck," said Perazzo. "I'll tell you the truth, I shouldn't even be talking to you. You know what I mean."

"No," said Grosbeck. Yes, he did, but he was stubborn and unwilling to abide by ambiguities by which the neighborhood lived when they affected him. Andaman Islanders were fascinating to an anthropologist and so were the people among whom Grosbeck had chosen to live . . . just so long as, like the anthropologist, he had the privilege of staying on the outside and looking. But he wasn't on the outside any more; accident had made him an Andaman Islander. Terror made him realize he had to stop looking, or listening or recording. He had to conform.

Still, he said, "Jimmy, don't beat around the bush."

Perazzo shook his head and looked up at the sky. He looked *through* Madeline; not unkindly, but simply *through* her. He was so Italian, so fixed in generations of custom and attitude. To Perazzo, the woman was irrelevant, a hindrance, a woman; the man was a dumb ox who should have been whipped with stripped tree branches. In his anger, in his adherence to what he believed men should be and do, how they should behave, he took on a dimension Grosbeck would not have attributed to him.

"All right, Mr. Grosbeck," said Perazzo. "If you want. It would have been better if I could of seen you without Mrs. Grosbeck. But what I have to say, I have to say right away, and here she is and we can't do anything about that, can we?" Grosbeck perceived that, in addition to being angry, Perazzo was not free of fear, either.

"Everybody knows what happened to Mrs. Grosbeck," said Perazzo. Grosbeck had deprived him of the right to be oblique and it was a strain. "It was a terrible thing."

"Yes," said Grosbeck. "It wasn't any secret. Half the house showed up in the hall. And the cops. The sons of bitches."

"I wouldn't say that if I was you, Mr. Grosbeck."

"Why not?" asked Grosbeck.

"Don't you know, Mr. Grosbeck?"

"You tell me, Jimmy."

"Do people where you work talk like that, Mr. Grosbeck? Tell each other everything? Right straight out? You know better. Business is business. There's ways of doing things."

Stupid Mr. Grosbeck. He kept right on. "Jimmy," he said, "you don't have much time to tell me what's on your mind . . . that's what you said . . . and I don't have time to go into subtleties."

"I got a good mind . . ." said Perazzo.

"To do what, Jimmy?"

"You don't know the score, do you, Mr. Grosbeck?" His voice, rough and phlegmy, was cold. "I would have thought, a man with education . . . never mind," he said abruptly. "You're in trouble."

Grosbeck got down off his high horse. "I gathered as much, Jimmy," he said. "I'm sorry I talked the way I did."

He reached out to take Perazzo's arm, much as Tully had taken his, but Perazzo moved ever so slightly out of reach. He would not go that far with a stranger who, up to tonight, had behaved himself, if he did not belong, but who now was behaving badly. Perazzo was his own kind of snob.

However, if he would not be touched by Grosbeck, he would tell him one or two things more. And then no more.

"There's ways of talking to people," said Perazzo. "It's not right Mrs. Grosbeck should get mugged in her own building. . . ."

"I had a reason for talking to the cops the way I did, Jimmy."

"Don't tell me, Mr. Grosbeck. I don't want to know."

"Jimmy, can't I at least explain?"

"No, you can't, Mr. Grosbeck. You said things you shouldn't have said to the wrong people. It gets around. They like things quiet. Mrs. Grosbeck won't get hurt again or bothered. That's been taken care of. Nobody wants to see a nice lady annoyed. You should have let it go at that."

"That would have been enough, eh, Jimmy?"

"Yes, it would. I told you there wouldn't be anything like that again, didn't I? And not to anyone else in the building, either. You should of thought ahead."

"I did, Jimmy," said Grosbeck. "I told you I had reasons."

"Whatever they were, they were wrong, and you're in trouble. It could blow over and maybe not. And if you didn't know, now you do, and I got to go. I said all I'm going to say."

"I thank you, Jimmy," said Grosbeck. "Very, very much. If I did wrong . . ."

Perazzo stopped the words with a flap of his skinny arm.

"One last thing, Jimmy. How's Anna?"

"About a week, Mr. Grosbeck," said Perazzo. "Good night.

Good night, Mrs. Grosbeck." He moved off under a street light, out of it into the shadows and off to the widow's bed.

"Let's forget the walk, Madeline," said Grosbeck. Neither of them had paid any attention to the drizzle while talking to Perazzo and they were wet. Grosbeck could not tell how much he was wet from the rain and how much from perspiration.

"He was right, Harvey," said Madeline. "But, he doesn't know you as well as I do. He was harsh. I don't blame him. Those are their rules you broke. And the way he looked at me and what he thinks of me . . . all women. Feudal. He doesn't even know what I look like. I don't care. You have your own kind of feudal ways and I understand both of you. But he was right and you guessed wrong when you did what you did. He went out of his way to tell you. I wouldn't have thought he would. No, I don't want to go for a walk, either. Come home."

"Why wouldn't he?" asked Grosbeck. "What did I ever do to him or anyone else around here?"

"Nothing, Harvey. That's why he said as much as he did. It took a lot for him to do it, too."

They crossed the street in the rain and let themselves into the building. There was no one out, only a single car passed behind them as they crossed, no one in the lobby. Grosbeck pressed the button for the elevator and then stepped back to wait for it.

"That's foolish, Harvey," said Madeline. "Who do you expect will be in that elevator?"

"You moved with me, Madeline," said Grosbeck.

"I'm no better than you, Harvey."

They rose in the elevator, each with an arm around the other's waist. In the apartment, they went to Jason's room.

He was asleep. They went into the living room, not yet ready to go to sleep.

"For a change, I have nothing to say, Madeline," said Grosbeck.

"I can't say, don't be afraid, Harvey," said Madeline. "And I haven't got anything else to say, either. Except . . . except . . . Harvey, *now* let's go to bed. I would really like to."

"I don't want to be crude, Madeline, but I couldn't get it up."

"I'll get it up for you, Harvey."

"I don't want to die, Madeline," said Grosbeck. "I don't. Or you, or Jason." He shivered and sweated and forgot the banality and repetitiveness of what he was saying.

"Let's, Harvey."

"No, I told you. Is that all you can think about?"

"It's all *you* usually think about and you got me to thinking about it, too."

"Here, God damn it," he said. He opened his pants and laid everything out. "Now, will you believe me?"

Madeline inspected the diminished goods, turned them over, played with them, was genuinely interested and absorbed. No sale.

"I told you," he said, closing his pants. "I'm going to call Tully."

"At this hour?"

"He never sleeps," said Grosbeck. "I won't, either, if I don't talk to him." He made Madeline accompany him to the bedroom while he called Tully. No answer. "There's a couple of places he goes nights," said Grosbeck with the receiver in his hand. He called two more numbers. No, no Tully.

"I can't stand this," said Grosbeck.

"Yes, you can, Harvey," said Madeline. "If you don't want to make love, you might as well go to sleep."

"Love! That was your idea of love, Madeline?"

"Yes, it was, Harvey. Yours, too. We're not dead yet."

"I can tell that, Madeline. It's close but no cigar. Right?"

"Yes, right, sweetheart. Right."

She undressed. So did Grosbeck.

"Jesus, God," he said. "I never saw anyone looked like you."

"Thank you, Harvey."

They went to sleep. Not to bed. To sleep.

❖

The telephone rang at four o'clock in the morning. A working day. A girl said, in a low voice, "Leslie" (was she asking for a man or a woman?), got no answer from Grosbeck, laughed provocatively, added, "Ooops," and hung up.

During the day, the telephone company sent out thousands of people who saw to it that connections either were not made or were broken when they were. It talked about peak loads and consumer demands; said metallically, "The number you have dialed is not in service" and "Sorry," when, indeed, one was able to get an operator. Its unending sorrow was equaled only by its unassailability; it was impenetrable and it raised its rates commensurately with the steady deterioration of service. People joked about it or not, but it could not be touched. It was like the sea or foam rubber.

Once, in a restaurant, Grosbeck went to make a telephone

call. The three telephones in the men's room were out of order. It took him two dimes in each to find that out. When he had determined that the phones would not work, he decided to destroy them. He began by attempting to yank a receiver off its wire. Then, he beat the receiver repeatedly against the box. Men came into the toilet, washed their hands or pissed, looked at him, some sympathetically, some noncommittally, and left. Nobody interfered with him and he made no progress. The telephone company had made one technological advance in its history of which Grosbeck had any personal knowledge: It had devised materials which would withstand the kind of puny effort of which he was capable with bare hands. But it had not provided for every contingency; no one could do that, not even the telephone company.

Grosbeck left the men's room with both hands aching; he had ended by beating the telephones with his palms. "Out of order," said Madeline. "That's right," said Grosbeck. "Ah, well," she said, "forget it. It wasn't anything earthshaking you had to say." "Not to you," he said. "But I'm not through yet." "What are you going to do?" "You'll see," he said. "Look, we're just about through dinner, anyway. You have dessert, I'll be right back. We'll have coffee together." Madeline did not go to extremes of that kind, having her own, but she understood people who did and she did not discourage Harvey this time. He took a taxicab home, had the driver wait downstairs (giving him some money while the meter ran so the man wouldn't think he was trying to beat him out of the fare) and went up to get what he had in mind.

It was an iron marlin spike from an old lugger, a sailing vessel the French call a *chasse-marée*, used by Channel smugglers even after steam drove most sailing ships off the seas. The spike was heavy, pointed and not too long for work at close quarters. That, and a hammer, would do. Grosbeck put both in an attaché case and returned to the restaurant. Madeline had finished her coffee. The waiter, in some unwonted spasm of tact, had not brought the check in his absence. "Order another pot of coffee," Grosbeck said. "I won't be long." "How are you going to work it out?" asked Madeline. "You'll see," he said. "I should be only a few minutes."

He went into the men's room again and took out the hammer and spike, hung up his jacket and kicked the attaché case into a corner. At the first telephone, he put the receiver into its cradle upside down, placed the tip of the spike into the receiver and struck the blunt end with the hammer. It took only four blows to split the receiver. The end of it fell off, exposing the tangle of colored wires inside. Then, he put the tip of the spike at the point at which the receiver wire entered the box, braced himself carefully and hammered again. This took longer, but, finally, the wire and its steel-cable covering broke off and he threw them on the floor. Grosbeck was not yet through with the first phone. Into the coin-return slot, the slot that never returned coins, went the spike, pointing up as far as he could get it. He had to hammer from below and that was a little awkward, but it worked. The front of the box fell off. Ultimately, he got to the coin box.

He went on to the second telephone and then to the third. No one paid the slightest attention to him. It was true that he was wearing a business suit, but he had tools in his hand. Perhaps, thought the men who came and went, that was the way telephone-company people worked these days, especially at night in good restaurants. He took two dimes from each coin box, the number he had lost, scooped the rest of the coins out and spilled them on the floor. The job took about fifteen minutes and when he was done he stepped back and looked at his accomplishment. It satisfied him deeply. He put the spike and the hammer back in the attaché case, washed his hands, straightened his tie, put on his jacket and returned to the dining room. "Beautiful," he said to Madeline. "I wish you were a man and could go see for yourself."

The burglar alarm went off in a car parked somewhere down the block. "That's it for the rest of the night," said Grosbeck. "Call the police," said Madeline. "Sure," said Grosbeck. "Oh, sure. Should I try Tully again?" "No," she said. "It can wait until you go to work. Let the man alone." Grosbeck looked out the bedroom window. "I wonder which one it is," he said. "What difference?" asked Madeline. "You couldn't shut it off, anyway." "No," he said, "but I like to know. Not to know drives me crazy."

The burglar alarm raved on at a pitch which never changed, in a monotone solid as the walls of the building pushed up against the windows of the Grosbeck apartment. The siren awakened people. Some stayed in bed and prayed, not for an end to the bawling, for there was no end, but simply for some slight change in pitch. Others opened windows and howled against the street lights for whatever good that did them. There was no respite; the police were sleeping in their squad cars under bridges and in vacant lots behind warehouses.

A man wearing only the pants of his pajamas came out of the apartment house across the street and walked down the block, stopping at each car, ignoring bits of broken glass on the sidewalk, which could have cut his bare feet. He found the car with the defective alarm, tried the doors, which were locked, and then stood back with his hands on his hips. He picked his nose, scratched his chest, which was hairy and strong, peered up and down the block and up at windows in the building across the street and waited. At last, another man, fully dressed, came out of another building and walked up to the car, car keys in hand.

"This yours?" asked the man in pajamas.

"No," said the other man. "I'm stealing it." He spat a cigarette out of his mouth; it showered sparks and fell near the feet of the man in pajamas who jumped back. He opened the door of the car, bent in and shut off the alarm.

"You got any idea what that does to people?" asked the man in pajamas.

"Fuck off," said the other man and started to get into the car. The man in pajamas grabbed him by the back of the jacket and ripped it. The man in the suit punched the man in pajamas in the stomach. The man in pajamas made a sparrowlike noise, then a noise deep in his throat, waved his fists at nothing and fell to the sidewalk. The man in the suit got into the car and drove away. The man in pajamas got up and wiped his mouth. Since the car was gone, he had nothing to shout at, so he peed at the curb, shook off recalcitrant drops, adjusted his pajama pants and walked slowly back to his building.

Lights went out in the windows up and down the block. Dozens and dozens of eardrums throbbed in painful reminiscence. The night was over and the first faint streak of day, false dawn, was there. Justice had not been done. The man in pajamas should have torn out the arms of the man in the suit and pushed his eyeballs into his throat and set the car on fire. But evil had been quick, and righteous anger not enough and Grosbeck was disappointed.

He was about to turn away from the window when a police car rolled slowly down the block.

"Of course," murmured Grosbeck.

"What did you say?" asked Madeline from the bed.

"Nothing," said Grosbeck.

Grosbeck went to work that morning not having slept. He was anxious, constipated and without appetite. He was down to his last pair of clean socks; his underwear was too tight, his pants too loose; the collar of his shirt was beginning to fray; his suit jacket needed pressing. He did not cut himself shaving but he did drop the soap in the shower and he almost fell retrieving it. The bath towel was damp from the night before; Madeline had turned off the air conditioning. He said to her, "You're the only human being I know who lives in a sauna with pictures on the wall."

He sucked on the minutiae of daily life not to taste the large lump of the other thing in his throat. Catafesta, the sergeant and the patrolman marched through his mind. They danced about him in a circle, sinisterly, poking at him with sticks, saying nothing, nodding or shaking their heads. His senses were sharpened excruciatingly, so that at every step he found a false crisis and at every pause a fake dénouement. So far. Looked at from the outside, such a state of mind is undeniably comic. Molière had made hypochondria something to laugh at. But Grosbeck was no longer on the outside and he saw eyes staring at him from the bottom of a coffee cup. He left an hour too early for the office and took a taxicab. On the way uptown, the driver asked him, "You married?" Grosbeck resigned himself. From now on, all his luck would be bad. He said he was.

"Let me ask you a question," said the driver. "I been married for fifteen years. What do I do about my wife?" "How in hell would I know," said Grosbeck in some irritation. "You haven't told me what's wrong." He leaned against the thick plastic shield separating him from the driver, the shield intended to keep the driver from getting killed. All it did was muffle voices from either side, despite the holes in it. He raised his voice. "What's wrong with all of you?" he asked the driver. "Make sense." He decided to be patient, to induce lucidity. "Don't you see," he said, "you've left something out. You can't just go from A to E; you've to give me B, C and D, too. Otherwise, nothing works. What's that word people are so fond of these days? Communicate. We don't communicate." Socrates in tight underwear. He would have liked to hit the driver with Newton's apple. Whatever went up now no longer necessarily came down. But he would try. "Now," he said, "why do you feel you have to do anything about your wife?"

The driver said, "I give her everything she wants. House, washer, dryer. Charge plates all over town. Florida in the winter with a side trip to Nassau." "How do you manage that?" asked Grosbeck. "I got something on the side," said the driver. "Her brother's in the produce business at the Bronx Terminal market and I work for him from three in the morning until I take the cab out. Also, I own the cab. It adds up." I wish it added up for me, thought Grosbeck. I'm supposed to be rich by comparison with this man, and I'm not sure I can buy my way out of getting killed.

"All right," said Grosbeck. "That's out of the way. What's your problem?"

"Well," said the driver, "it strikes me she ain't grateful. She looks restless. You know what I think? I think she's fucking some other guy. Mind you, I don't *know* that for a fact. But she's always home on time, the cooking's been great for six months, and she always looks like she stepped right out of the hairdresser. That's no way for a wife to behave."

"Isn't it?" asked Grosbeck.

"No," said the driver. "Not my wife. I think she's getting a little something on the side."

"Don't you . . . ever?" asked Grosbeck.

"I didn't until the kids came, a boy, two girls," said the driver. "And I don't only once in a while now. Some nymphomaniac, some crazy broad you get in the cab. She hasn't got the fare. How'd you like to take it out in trade? In the back of the cab. Blow job. Then her purse is open and you see she's got plenty of money. But it's my cab and there's nothing lost. Just mileage, gas. But that's not the same thing like with my wife. She just doesn't have any reason to do what she's doing."

"You mean, *if* she's doing." It was his private opinion that the driver wasn't getting anything and that his wife wasn't doing anything. But you never know.

"The thing is," the driver went on, "I got an idea. How would it be if I just told her I knew, gave her the works, cab, house and all, and got out? How would she react to that? It's a switch, isn't it? No getting mad, no fights, nothing. Just give her everything, get out and let her stew. She's taken care of, the kids are taken care of and I go my own way, start all over again. Does she get guilty enough to stop and be grateful and cut it out, or does she go right on with my cab, my house and my dough? Or, do I just keep my mouth shut?"

"But, you don't even *know* that she's doing anything," said Grosbeck.

"That doesn't make any difference," said the driver. "Say she isn't. It's still a hell of an experiment in psychology."

"Oh, my God," said Grosbeck. "Do you tell this to everybody who gets into your cab?"

"A few people," admitted the driver. "If I look in their faces and think they're experienced. You struck me that way. You got that look says to me, 'This guy's been around.' I wouldn't think of telling it to a lady. In the end, it's man to man."

"So I look as though I've been around," said Grosbeck as the cab went the last few blocks to the newspaper. "Thank you. I wish I had an answer for you, but I don't. I've only been halfway around, so the only answer I could give you would be a half-ass one."

"You kidding me?" asked the driver.

"I don't kid," said Grosbeck. "Except when I'm alone or with someone else." That seemed to mollify the driver and he grunted. He could not possibly have listened to what Grosbeck had just said.

"You better try someone else," Grosbeck continued. "Someone you pick up in midtown, not in the Village. You just think people in the Village know more. They don't. Believe me, they don't."

"I didn't expect a real answer," confessed the driver. "But I find it's good for me to get it off my chest. I probably won't go any farther than that. She'll do it, I'll talk and the world goes on." Yours does, thought Grosbeck. I don't know about mine.

He paid the driver and got out of the cab. "There's one thing you've got to remember," he said, leaning in the window. "As I told you, you don't *know* whether she's doing anything." "I haven't forgotten," said the driver. "All I'm saying is, it's smart to be ready for anything." "Yes, it is," said Grosbeck and all his misery settled on him again. He wasn't ready.

❖

Grosbeck, of course, was early and Tully, of course, wasn't in the office yet. How could he be; he did not care. Neither snow nor rain nor heat nor gloom of night stays these couriers from the swift completion of their appointed rounds. Grosbeck had won innumerable small bets on the exact wording of this inexact translation from Herodotus, engraved below the pediment on the General Post Office. Tully was not swift enough for Grosbeck; the gloom was thick; the heat unbearable. He telephoned him at home. "I'm up," said Tully at the other end. "I'll be in in fifteen minutes. It isn't as bad as you think, but it'll take some time to tell it and there are some things you'll have to do and they can't be told over the phone. And not at your desk, either. I'll meet you in the cafeteria."

Grosbeck put the newspapers under his arm, stuffed cables into his jacket pocket and took the elevator up to the cafeteria. It was a large one and there were plenty of empty tables away from other people. He got orange juice and coffee and arranged them, the newspapers and the cables before him as though he were planning a seance, as though there were some cabalistic significance to be found in the fact that the orange juice was at his left, the coffee at his right (cream not yet poured; it would get cold too quickly), the newspapers directly in front of him and the cables on top of the newspapers. The neatness was horrifying, but only Grosbeck thought that. Pity he didn't have an ouija board to dust off.

Tully came into the cafeteria, looked around, saw Grosbeck and came over to the table. Grosbeck got up to greet him and knocked over the orange juice. Instead of saying, "Good morning," he said, "Shit," and left Tully at the table while he went to get paper napkins to mop up. The newspapers and the cables were wet and gray with orange juice. Grosbeck threw the newspapers into a garbage can, patted the cables so that they would dry (those he *did* need), pushed aside the coffee and sat down opposite Tully.

"I won't tease, Harvey," said Tully.

"No, don't, Dandy. Don't even tell me you won't tease. Just tell me."

"It's peculiar," said Tully. "But the way this thing is going to be worked out . . . and it *is* going to be worked out . . . is pretty convoluted. They're a Byzantine lot."

"John," said Grosbeck. "Please."

"Harvey," said Tully, "you have to listen and I have to begin somewhere. Very well. The situation is this: Catafesta is what we call middle management these days. He has his territory, his perquisites, some power. That includes that sergeant, the patrolman and some other cops in the precinct. I'm not going back over what cops are or aren't. The cops don't like the way you talked; Catafesta doesn't like the idea that you and Madeline know anything about him. It's the federal people who bother them, if anyone does, and they don't want them nosing around because of any disturbance you might make. The federals are an unknown quantity. Sometimes they can be reached, sometimes not. They blow hot and they blow cold. Catafesta doesn't want them to blow any way. Neither do the cops."

"And I'm in the way," said Grosbeck. "The noisemaker."

"That's right, Harvey," said Tully. "And there's a way for you to get out of the way. I told you they were circumlocutory people and I must say I was impressed by what they figured out."

"Impress me, John," said Grosbeck. "In a hurry."

"What you've got to do, Harvey, is get very, very middle class. It's the big thing in New York City these days. Get righteous. Make a public outcry. Your wife's been mugged, right? Other people in the neighborhood have been assaulted, isn't that so?" Tully was not seeking replies. He was, in effect, standing at a blackboard, demonstrating a theorem, mad Euclid.

"It's time, Harvey," said Tully, "for you to organize a tenants' patrol in the building to protect yourself and your neighbors. Everybody does it. A block association would be even better, but a tenants' patrol will do."

"I don't believe what you're telling me, John. I hear what you're saying, but . . ."

"You put up a notice in the lobby of your apartment building, Harvey," said Tully. "And you say there will be a meeting at such and such a time to discuss measures . . . measures is the right word . . . to insure the safety of the people who are your neighbors."

"John," said Grosbeck, "what I'm trying to do is deflect attention *away* from me."

"No, no, Harvey, that's not it at all. Your job is to *attract* attention to yourself. The right kind of attention. You're a square, indignant citizen. Square, indignant citizens hit out in all directions. They accuse, they get up petitions, they picket City Hall, they address letters to the captain at the precinct, they write letters to the newspapers that say, 'It is high time . . . ' or 'If the past is any precedent . . .' They hold meetings and pass resolutions. But, what they don't do is get specific. They don't have any real target. They are so general, so entangled in the popular sociology they pick up from magazines and newspapers and television and paperback books; so *unable* to focus on anything, so unwilling *or* unable to investigate that they quickly vitiate any good they might do. And once they've made their gesture they're through. The Catafestas know this, just as our distinguished mayor does and the bankers and the real-estate men and judges and district attorneys and cops. The usufruct of our lovely civilization."

"I'm beginning to see, Dandy," said Grosbeck.

"Yes," said Tully. "You do all these things. You do them loudly and passionately. Door to door, if necessary, ringing doorbells and signing things and holding meetings. And sitting in the lobby nights, good citizens all, to defend yourself. But what you don't do, Harvey . . . ever . . . is get specific. No names, please. And the effect will be dazzling, not to say beneficial. You won't die; you will even get to be some sort of minor celebrity in your building, possibly on the block, in the neighborhood.

"Harvey, you will become, for the purpose *they* have in mind . . . it makes me laugh just to think of it . . . some ridiculous admixture of the Italian-American Civil Rights League and the Jewish Defense League. All by yourself. Noisy. That needn't be any trouble for you. Righteous. Liberal Jewish for those who like that sort of thing . . . hardline law and order for the Italian Americans. Nothing anyone can really focus on. Never a hint of what it's really all about . . . Catafesta. But loud. If you are loud enough, the mayor might even appoint you to something. How would you like that? Catafesta'll never be appointed to anything.

But you, you might get into a documentary on educational television. I can see it all now, so clearly." Tully laughed.

"You mean it, don't you, John?" said Grosbeck.

"I most certainly do, Harvey," said Tully. "You will be recognized as the man who stood up to *them.* Only they don't know who *them* is and you won't say. Oh, there are people in your building who do know . . . Catafesta and some others . . . and many, many more in the neighborhood. The former will cheer you and the latter will smile and nobody will hurt anybody. After a month or two, all that will be left of your indiscretion will be a sign in the lobby notifying outsiders that the tenants are watching their every move. Also, Catafesta will have found a very effective way of controlling his animals, in addition to the dubious kind of control he gets from the police right now. His problem is that he never knows when the cops are shaking the animals down at the same time they're on his payroll.

"Also, think of the warm civic glow you will have imparted to the squares. Almost as good as voting once every four years. You will have reached out and touched them. Isn't that what we all want and need these days? You will have shown them that the democratic process does work, that it *is* possible to work within the system, that the American way, for all its defects, is, in the end, the best of all possible systems. The right of the governed to petition their governors will have been exercised. We will all be safe in our homes. And we will have come to know one another, to end the dreadful isolation imposed on us in a *product-oriented* society in which *interpersonal relationships* have been so sorely riven. The words they use, the words. Oh, Harvey, when I think of the good you are going to do."

"It's very neat, isn't it, John?" said Grosbeck. "And sickening. It doesn't tell me anything I didn't already know, but it nearly, very nearly, tempts me to join the Catafestas."

"They wouldn't have you, Harvey," said Tully. "You think you're a cynic, but, I'm afraid, you are only a stupid idealist, much like the people you make fun of. No, stupid isn't the word; ignorant is, or innocent. You are an amusing man a good part of the time, Harvey, but not very perceptive. Perception comes to you only at the end of a stuffed club. I have watched you for years. I am even protective of you. But, except for your windy denunciations of the class of which you are as much a part as a heel is of a shoe, you are one of them. You think you are not, but, at bottom, you are. The nihilism you profess is *your* kind of thumb-sucking. Your capacity for self-deception is as great as theirs. You've sulked your way into the past and believed you could ignore the present. Well, now, you know better."

Tully sighed. "I hadn't meant to say all this, Harvey," he said. "Middle class is not the worst thing in the world to be," he said. "It's only that our people . . . I will use another piece of contemporary argot you won't like . . . our people don't know where it's at. It's fashionable to say that New York isn't the United States, but it is for the middle class. A murrain on the demographers. The sameness of the middle class everywhere in this country is what keeps our rulers in the seat of power.

"Are you going to do what I told you?"

"Yes," said Grosbeck.

"You had better, Harvey."

Grosbeck now found himself in the unique position of being hurt, frightened, reassured and ashamed, all at once. "I didn't think you lumped me in with the others, John," he said. "I thought you thought a little more of me than that."

Tully was both amused and annoyed. "Have you not yet

cast out the sin of pride, Harvey?" he asked. "Have I bruised you? You'll heal quick. And you'll be alive. Don't make me go on lecturing. If you do, I'll be no better than you. That's not bad, but it's not good enough for either of us. Go forth, Harvey. Get out of here and do what it is you have to do."

Grosbeck apologized. Tully said he didn't want any apologies. "I am going to Mass tomorrow morning, Harvey," he said gravely. "And I will light a candle for you. I mean it."

Grosbeck rallied. "Better a *yahrtzeit*, Dandy," he said. "And I will see a clergyman of my persuasion."

Both men laughed. In the cafeteria, in the clatter of trays and the tinkle of glass, and the sounds of other lives all about them, the laugh was the metaphor Grosbeck thought he had dispensed with. That morning, in the cafeteria, though he did not realize it. That would take time; the Tarot had seen that. Epiphany is many things and is not arrived at overnight.

❖

If epiphany is not to be experienced overnight, neither is the alteration of old habit; the pluck and iterance of reflex make their customary demands in charnel houses. The corn on the foot is not excised, except that it be pared away with a razor blade. Grosbeck was chary of handling razor blades: He might cut his big toe. Redemption lay beneath the corn, beneath layer upon layer of scorn and skepticism. Grosbeck's instinct or reflex had always been to buy a bigger pair of shoes and let the corn have its way.

The result was the Grosbeck, Grosbeck knew: Corns and shoes that swam on his feet; tics cultivated to avoid large seizures. He was the joke of the man who has been sold a suit that does not fit. In his attempt to salve his sucker's pride, to justify wearing a garment that is too short in one leg and too long in the other, the jacket of which is too tight, the collar too loose and the color wrong, he extends one leg and draws back the other, pulls in his stomach so that the buttons of the jacket lie flat and looks at himself in a mirror under bad light so that the color is in shadow. He is a cripple in a burlap bag. "Perfect, perfect," says the salesman, pinching the collar. The salesman is lying and Grosbeck deceiving himself and yet both play out the ridiculous business and Grosbeck makes do with the suit. Grosbeck is both salesman and self.

So that, though danger was at hand and Tully twice had held up salvation before him (holding his wrist the first time, and, the second, pointing the way), Grosbeck was not yet a new man and nothing showed that better than what he did on his lunch hour that day. He decided not to call Madeline at work; the thing was too complicated to talk about over the telephone; it could wait. He would take a walk on his lunch hour and buy a book. This was no simple matter: The day was a hot one; the office was cool; he would have to walk some distance. Also, he would have to contend with crowds and the ignorance or noncomprehension of booksellers who neither read books nor sold them but were placed in stores simply to make money and rebuff inquiry.

But he went. He wanted a book and death would have to wait. Also, in the back of his mind, he did not really believe that death would come uptown for him. It did for many people, but for Grosbeck life *and* death were experienced only south of Fourteenth Street. An insane conceit.

So, he went: walked through the scabby lazars on the streets around the newspaper; the lepers lolling on the sidewalks in front of the pesthouses which advertised books, movies, pictures and other enticements; the highwaymen with knives and pistols in their pockets and chains wound around their waists; the bullying police.

Over to Fifth Avenue and up. The Fifth Avenue he had known as a young man was gone. It was now banks and airline offices, cheap-jack stores and, who could have told, frankfurter stands. Enough to have made Childe Hassam or Maurice Prendergast break their brushes and slash their canvases with knives. How much the juxtaposition of these things told! Still, on this August day, it was Fifth Avenue. There was nothing else like it and he would make the best of no bargain at all.

The avenue had acquired a new character: As its architecture, never more than a fulsome bastardization of its European origins, had declined, the quality of sexuality on its sidewalks had intensified wildly. Not the cheesy brazenness in front of the lazarettos near the newspaper; something different. The women, in costume, posture, stride, made a play of boldness, each different from the other, all very much the same. They rioted before the men, seeking confirmation from one another of what they were doing and drove all before them, all the while pushing at their hair, pulling at their skirts, chewing on bits of food bought on side streets. Rotten Row. The Reeperbahn. They made the men sullen and anticipatory. The men shuffled at building lines, picked their teeth with their little fingers, eyed the women speculatively, bubbled inside themselves or made remarks. Their attaché cases were closed, their minds open.

Grosbeck was no less excited than the others. What about this one? That one? Hmmm. Walk right up to that one over there and take the afternoon off? The two nearby? They might not want to, might not have the time, any more than he had. Also, there *was* Catafesta to think about and the book. He arrived at the bookstore. Its aisles were so crowded that it was no more than an extension of the street, a *galleria*, a covered arcade. Incredible that so many people should be after books when, he knew, they did not read them.

He stopped three people who, he thought, might work for the store. No, customers. They resented his mistake. Who did work for the store and how could he be identified? Buttons. That was it. Buttons. He pushed his way through the mob looking for a body with a button. And found himself up against a cashier's desk. The cashier was not wearing a button, but she was, plainly, a cashier, and there was a long line in front of her, waiting to give her money. The people had been there for days, hungry and irritable, but passive. In their hands, they had books, the names of which Grosbeck did not care to know, and money. The cashier accepted it disdainfully and when she felt like it, which was irregularly, addressed herself to the machine before her, adjusted her glasses, which were suspended from a chain around her neck, looked over the heads of the customers and down at a pad, tickled the keys on the machine with a finger, did many other things, but seemed never to complete a transaction. Behind the glasses, one eye was sclerotic, the other clear. The clear one was made of glass and it saw more clearly than the other. The store closed every night with the line before the cashier, and the customers slept standing up. The men had not shaved for days; the women were in need of fresh linen and makeup. No one would ever serve them.

Grosbeck realized he would have to look himself for the book he wanted, and, possibly, steal it. He looked, but could not find it. Rage took him and he returned to the cashier, pushed his way to the head of the line of the moribund book buyers, and said:

"I would like," as precisely as though he were practicing Swahili before a Greek proctor giving a quiz in Hindi, "to buy a copy of *How the Other Half Lives,* by Jacob Riis. With photographs. It has just been released. I cannot find it. I have looked under sociology, photography, history, biography, social work, crewel work, under any conceivable category this store could think up. I cannot find it."

The cashier, to whom Grosbeck meant no more than the permanent line of customers, said, "Have you looked under current fiction."

"Miss," said Grosbeck, "the book is neither current nor fiction, although it *has* just been published again."

"Try 'Books in Print,'" she said.

"Where is 'Books in Print?'"

"Over there," she said.

"Where?"

"There."

Grosbeck found "Books in Print" and then fought his way back to the cashier.

"It's not there," he said.

"What's not where?"

"How the Other Half Lives. By Jacob Riis. Reissued. In 'Books in Print.'"

"I'm sure I don't know what to tell you. I'm terribly busy."

"You probably don't even remember me," shouted Grosbeck.

"Oh, I remember you well enough. Believe me, I do. Please don't raise your voice."

"What do I do now?"

"I really don't know."

The line of customers sagged a little and mold dropped from a number of them.

"Would it be possible to *order* the book?"

"I suppose so, but you'll have to see someone else."

"Who?"

"I can't say. Most everybody's out to lunch."

"Just when people are trying to buy books on their own lunch hour?"

"Sir, I don't set the hours here."

"Who does?"

"I don't know. Yes, I do, but Mr. Mangin is out to lunch. He has to eat lunch, too. You'll have to take it up with him when he comes back."

"When's that?"

"I really couldn't say. Besides, we're beginning to take inventory today and he'll be busy."

"Inventory? Inventory of what? Inventory of this mess?"

"I beg your pardon!"

"What would you say if I told you I was ready to murder or pull everything down on the floor?"

"Sir, you'll have to step aside. There are people here waiting to make purchases and you've kept them long enough."

"Have I?"

"I'm afraid so."

"This *is* a bookstore, isn't it? And you *do* offer books for sale, and you have been in business for over a hundred years? And you are interested in bringing the finest that has been thought and said to those who would like to have some of it rub off on them?"

"That is our intention, sir."

Grosbeck's voice grew deeper and deeper, graver and

graver. His face was red, but there were lines of white on either side of his nose. Edwin Booth play-acting on the stage of his marble theatre on Twenty-third Street to an empty house.

The lady at the cash register pursed her lips with an air of finality and then opened her mouth again, for the last time. "I will refer you to the manager," she said. "I don't have time to stand here arguing with you."

"I'm not arguing," Grosbeck said. "All I have done is state my case. I do have a case," he continued. "I do." The whine of the beggar. "Here is a book published within the last week. I want it; you sell books." The beggar cast off his rags to reveal the prince. "I'll damned well have it if it's the last thing I do."

The woman pressed a buzzer and played songs on the cash register. Presently a man came up, a small brown man in a tight brown suit, large eyes swimming brownly in bruised sockets; white, even teeth gleaming, one hand caressing the other. The woman had lied to him; this was not the manager, but an Indian. An Indian Indian. In pursuit of a doctorate on a resident's visa and gainfully employed while doing so.

"Sahr?" asked the Indian. Grosbeck explained himself again, faintly. The ordeal had weakened him and he forgot to be precise in Swahili. He said he wanted to order the book. And, for some reason, he added, "My name is Grosbeck. Grosbeck. Grosbeck."

The Indian smiled at him conspiratorially. "Come with me, sahr?" he said, crooking a finger at Grosbeck. "We have it."

Grosbeck followed him through the mob in the maze into a distant corner of the bookstore. The Indian turned to a bookshelf and took something from it. Beaming, he faced Grosbeck and held it out to Grosbeck.

It was a book called *Group Sex*.

Group Sex. Grosbeck. Harvey Groupsex.

Motion was suspended. God smirked. The Indian winked.

Judgment had been passed on Grosbeck. He was a dirty old man. Not a condemned man, a connoisseur of the city, a taster of wines, an eater of foods or an appreciater of anything.

Someone had provided the eager Indian with a guidebook to the city. He had studied it faithfully, all its categories, and when he saw Grosbeck he knew instantly where to place him: Dirty Old Man.

❖

Grosbeck went home after the day's work, the victim of what his newspaper was wont to kiss off in situations where it could not figure out what people were thinking, as "mixed emotions." He told Madeline about Tully and the event in the bookstore. He said, "I am a dirty old man. How perceptive of the Indian. But I want to live. The grave's a fine and private place/ But none I think do there embrace. Dirty old men included. I doubt he saw that aspect of my dirty old manhood."

"Why should he?" asked Madeline. "Mr. Mukerjee, if he is to get his doctorate, has to hew to the line. Everything else has to be simplified for him. The guidebook has provided him with fifty easy ways to get through daily life in

New York City. Where to get hamburgers or a handful of brown rice."

"How to recognize a dirty old man."

"What *is* a dirty old man?" asked Madeline.

"Later, later, Madeline," said Grosbeck. "This is maundering."

"You started it, Harvey."

"All *right*. I started it. Now, I *stop* it."

"Don't, Harvey. Don't talk to me that way."

"I beg your humble fucking pardon. There's no time for that," he said. "Let's start to plan. That meeting has to be held quickly. But where?"

"In the lobby?" asked Madeline. "No," she said. "I know where. In the laundry room. That's where people meet naturally in most apartment buildings."

"And where the muggers go to meet them. I never thought I'd be doing anything like this."

"Why should you be different from anyone else?"

Heavenly discourse.

"Did it ever occur to you," Grosbeck asked his wife, "that people can't even quarrel gracefully? Quarrels have become an exchange of inventories of abuse, commonplaces flung at people's feet."

"My poor Harvey, my Ulysses. They took away your *agora*."

"That's the best you can say, Madeline?"

"Then don't lecture, Harvey. Don't slang the people on the way to Tyburn. The hangman isn't interested and the crowd is just out to watch you dangle. Do, Harvey, do. Common sense."

"All right. The laundry room. Now, how do we go about getting them down there? The notice. Typewritten. One copy in the lobby, near the front door, another in the elevator. And the meeting. When?"

"Not on the weekend, Harvey. A lot of people are away over the weekend in the summer. On a Wednesday. Next Wednesday. That gives us a week."

"Do you really think this will work, Madeline? All this crap Tully's laid out for me?"

"Do you have any better idea, Harvey?"

"You're so Jewish, Madeline. Always answer a question with a question."

"Write the notice, Harvey. Do a manifesto. Do it in your best civic style."

"I don't have a civic style, Madeline."

"Then assume one, Harvey. The ordinary people in the building will like it. Catafesta will know what you're doing and approve. And the rest, the peculiars, won't care one way or another. They'll be curious and come. Perhaps they'll light up and get stoned at the meeting."

"Sit with me while I do it," said Grosbeck. "I don't write manifestoes very often." Madeline followed him into the bedroom where there was a typewriter and he put a sheet of paper in it. Grosbeck was an editor, very swift and apt at putting other people's thoughts in order, very quick . . . much too quick . . . in conversation, but he didn't do much writing of his own. Composition was embarrassing and tended to reveal things. But it had to be done, and, little by little, this is what Grosbeck produced:

NOTICE

Last Sunday morning, at about ten-thirty o'clock,
my wife was returning from shopping, when she was
assaulted in this building, on the very floor on which
we live.

Fortunately, she was not injured. Her assailant, who
threatened her with a knife, escaped.

Increasingly, all of us have to live with assault
and robbery in this city and sometimes murder.

Madeline stood over the typewriter as her husband
worked.

"All right, so far?" he asked.

"Fine," she said. "But you'll have to try harder on the
civic responsibility."

"I'm not forgetting," said Grosbeck. "There'll be plenty
of that." He went on typing:

We have called the police repeatedly and made
representations to them. We have called other city
departments and talked with representatives of
the mayor's office."

"Have you?" asked Madeline.

"You know I haven't," Grosbeck said. "It's just a way of
getting into the civic responsibility nonsense. Watch."

He continued to type:

The responses have been, to say the least,
unsatisfactory. But, we are all in this together. In
the end, it is we who must make the streets and our
homes safe. That is our civic responsibility.

If the police cannot or will not control crime; if
the city cannot or will not, then we must.

"Easy on the vigilante stuff, Harvey."

"Don't worry, Madeline. I'm leading up to that, too."

I am not proposing that we carry guns or clubs or
that we use violence to protect ourselves. That

is the very thing we are trying to avoid: Violence
against us or against anyone else.

But, we do owe it to ourselves to take every precaution
we can. And, I believe that in doing so all of us will
come to know one another better; to trust one
another, to be better neighbors.

"How's that for bullshit, sweetheart?" asked Grosbeck.
"You don't seem to have missed anything, Harvey."
"I'm not through," he said. "Wait for the Garrison finish."
He looked down at the paper in the typewriter and then
up at Madeline. "Do me a favor, would you?" he asked.
"Get me something to drink. Club soda. Because if I don't
belch, I'll throw up. My unexpected talent at putting down
all these clichés is beginning to get to me. So, to wind up":

Therefore, I propose that we hold a meeting of the
tenants in the laundry room a week from the date
of this notice. I know that most of you work all
day at your jobs and that those who don't, your
wives, work equally hard at making homes for you.
It is those homes all of us want to protect.

My wife and I would be most grateful to you if
you would come to the meeting. Representatives of the
police department will be asked to be at the meeting,
too, to advise us, and the meeting will be thrown
open to anyone who comes. We need advice and
suggestions from all of us.

Thank you. I hope you will come.

Harvey Grosbeck, Apt. 3-B.

"That really is appalling, Harvey," said Madeline. "There's
just enough truth in it, too . . . If I didn't know what you're

219

really after. I didn't dream you had that kind of hypocrisy in you."

"Madeline," said Grosbeck. "I wasn't born into the middle class for nothing. I may not be with it, but I am of it. Forget Catafesta, the cops and what we're doing, for a second. You know what's interesting about proclamations of this kind? They are what pass for an *act* today. Whether it's government or business or an institution of some kind or whatever. Someone says thus and so is going to be done, or this and that will take place. And it's enough merely to say so. It doesn't have to happen and it doesn't. Tract, not act.

"Government knows this and business does and institutions and a good many people. Not my precious middle class. Not ever, but a good many people all the same. The substitution of word for deed may very well be the most important discovery we have made in the last hundred years. It is the one which will elude my class to the very end. It will go down in the ocean, giving off bubbles and clutching a petition to its heart. Real deeds are performed in darkness, in secret, nothing written down, talk in a room, a gesture, a nod or shake of the head; all of a sudden, the face of the city is changed and a man is murdered; prices go up and a war is fought. It is not even declared any longer; just fought.

"Balls," he said. "I have another trait of my class which I don't like. Talk, talk, talk. I'll put this up. Two copies, one in the elevator, one over the mailboxes. That should do it." He typed a second copy of the notice, found a roll of Scotch tape in the kitchen and went out to put up the notices of the meeting.

The next morning, Grosbeck found both copies of the notice on the floor, in the elevator and in front of the mailboxes. Neither had been crumpled or torn, just pulled away,
and thrown on the floor. There were heel marks on both.
They lay on the floor like handbills advertising specials in
a supermarket or a new beauty parlor. More likely than
not, the heel marks had been made not by whoever had pulled
them down, but by people simply walking over them in and
out of the elevator or in front of the mailboxes and who
had not bothered to find out what was on them.

Somewhere in the building was someone whose cynicism
matched his own; but someone who, at the same time, had
no idea why it was Grosbeck had put up the notices. The
difference between the cynical someone and Grosbeck was
that the skeptic could afford a certain philosophical detach-
ment. In the past, Grosbeck might very well have done the
same thing himself or, at the very least, ignored the notices.
He took them upstairs and showed them to Madeline. "I
think what's called for," he said, "is a little more. A notice
on the bottom of the notice. Something reproachful, something to the effect of 'It's your life, your property,' and on
the bottom a space where people can sign up, saying they'll
attend the meeting. What do you think? Why would anyone take these down." He already knew, but he wanted to
hear it from Madeline.

"You told me why yourself, Harvey, before you put them
up. Tract, not act. Maybe there are a few in your despised

middle class who think more like you than you're ready to concede. Give them the credit; they should. Everything that happens to you happens to them."

"You know what I'm going to do?" he said. "Just add the second notice to the first, put up the originals, heel marks and all, and the second right underneath. That should tug at their heartstrings. That should prove we mean it. Let's see what that does." He had forgotten, for the moment, what his real reason was for calling this meeting.

In two days, he saw.

Of the sixty tenants, more than forty had signed up to come to the meeting.

Over their signatures, someone had written, "Meetings suck."

Over the sentence about the failure of the police to do anything: "Why do you hate the police. Suport them, don't tear them down." Grosbeck did not fail to note the spelling.

Over the paragraph on guns: "What's wrong with guns."

Across Grosbeck's signature: "Jew bastard."

Under Grosbeck's signature: "Right on."

And elsewhere: "So what's new." "It's about time we at least tried." "That's the night I see my psychotherapist." "Is this a put-on?" "New York, love it or leve it, blow it up, sink it to the bottom of the ocean, I'm getting out anyway." Again, a misspelling.

In pencil and felt pen (red, green, blue, purple); handwriting crabbed, bold or like the marks made by a man pissing his name into the snow.

But there were more than forty names. And no one had torn down the notices.

Grosbeck had made his debut in the world. People stared at him in the elevator and in the lobby. Some spoke to him and introduced themselves. One woman asked, "It'll just be informal, won't it? We won't have to dress?" What? Jesus Christ. And Catafesta and his wife continued to pass him by going and coming, neither staring nor speaking. He had never heard either of them speak. Why not? It was to placate Catafesta, after all, that Grosbeck was doing this. By right, there should have been some acknowledgment, however oblique. Once, the Catafesta poodle jumped up on him and barked and whined. Was that the signal? Mrs. Catafesta coldly pulled the poodle away and slapped it on the rump. What would the Tarot have to say about that? Grosbeck had no intention of asking. Of the sergeant and the patrolman, and, of course, of the mugger, no sign at all.

At two o'clock in the morning, four days before the meeting, Perazzo's wife died of cancer, deliquesced until she was no more than a stain on the bed and an assortment of bent bones. Grosbeck found out when no newspapers were delivered. Perazzo, with an odd sense of dignity and fitness, or religious superstition or remorse, had forsworn the widow that night and sat at his wife's stinking bedside until she was gone, all the lights in the room on, all the medicines on the table, no one else there.

Perazzo had called the doctor and the doctor had said to him, "Let her go, Jimmy. There is no more to be done." And had come over, made his perfunctory examination, reached his foregone conclusion, put a death certificate in Perazzo's hand signed a week before (he dated it that night, in the Perazzo apartment), asked for brandy, settled for whiskey and left.

There was more to be done. Perazzo summoned the priest; not the monsignor, one of the curates. Priests, too, still made house calls in this part of the city. The priest came fully attired, as though it were the middle of the day, in the brown-wool cassock of his order, the rope around his waist as though it were the surcingle over a horse's back and belly;

With all of the proper paraphernalia, the oil, the Bible, the dollops of compassion and the dollops of ritual, some in Latin, some in Italian, some in English, the black shoes busy around the bed;

Anna dead; touched her with the oil, touched her lips open to form a blackish pit of mouth (the green-white false teeth, upper and lower, at the bottom of a glass of water on the table with the medicines);

Regarded Heaven first with his black liquid eyes and then Perazzo; took Perazzo by both hands and closed his nostrils against the smell. Then, with as much care as he had given Extreme Unction to Anna, he gave Perazzo his repertory of consolations. Silent glance of compassion; murmur in Italian; a smile with the hint of sorrow in it; an effort to deepen the lines in face and forehead (this was difficult; he was a young man and his face was round and smooth); blessed Perazzo; coaxed Perazzo into joining him in a drink; and, like the doctor, left; to take up sleep again behind the Roman walls of the parish house a block away.

Perazzo called the undertaker after the priest had left and said, "She's ready, Angelo." "My men will be right over," said the undertaker's assistant who had night duty. "She's better off."

And still more to be done. Perazzo telephoned the widow. "She's better off," said the widow. "Come over." She began to take curlers out of her hair as she talked on the telephone. "I will," said Perazzo. "But first the undertaker got to come. And I got to go down to the store and put up a sign we'll be closed today. Somebody else will have to handle the play today and it's a good thing today's not pickup day, too, for the cops. Later, I'll make a couple of phone calls."

"Don't rush," said the widow. "But come. You hungry?" "I could eat something," said Perazzo. "I bet you could do something else, too," said the widow. "I don't know if there's time," said Perazzo. "There's time," said the widow. "I never knew when there wasn't time." "What will God say?" asked Perazzo. "I don't know," said the widow. "I do know. You confess to the priest and I confess to the priest and God has no more to say." "I don't know if it's right," said Perazzo. "But I am hungry." "Suit yourself," said the widow. "You didn't waste any time when my husband died." "That was different," said Perazzo. "How different?" the widow wanted to know. "Different, different," said Perazzo irritably. "How am I supposed to know how that was different." "Suit yourself," the widow said again. "I'll be over," said Perazzo. "I'll be over."

The night undertaker came with another man who yawned and hid it politely behind a hand. There was nothing to the body and they carried it downstairs and away to the funeral home, refusing whiskey. "I ordered the coffin," said Perazzo. "I know," said the night undertaker. "Arculeo has it in the basement. We bring it up after we get done with Mrs. Perazzo. We got the dress, everything. You'll see. She'll look pretty good. The showing's at five o'clock tonight. Leave it to us."

Grosbeck came out of the building to find Perazzo locking up the store. "I figured, Jimmy," he said to Perazzo. "But, she's better off." Perazzo looked at him. "That's right, Mr. Grosbeck," he said. He, Perazzo, was not going to say, "She's better off" again, no matter how many times other people did. Whatever else they were going to say to him that day, they were going to say, "She's better off." Of course, she was, but he would go mad if he had to say it, too. *Meglio cosi. Meglio cosi. Meglio cosi. A fongool.*

"Where will she be laid out, Jimmy?" asked Grosbeck.

"Over on West Broadway, Mr. Grosbeck. You seen the place."

"I would like to pay my respects, Jimmy," said Grosbeck. "Anna was a nice woman. She was a lady."

"Thank you."

Grosbeck had not the remotest idea whether Anna had been nice or a lady. She had never done much more than nod at him when he went into the store for cigarettes or soda. She had seemed always to be sweeping piles of numbers slips into a pocket of her smock, and, to tell the truth, Grosbeck was not even sure she had spoken English. But some sort of bond had been established between himself and Perazzo and he was determined that Perazzo's dignity should be upheld. (Grosbeck had an obtuse way of dealing with the people in the neighborhood. He did not condescend to them so much as, hard as he tried not to, keep a distance. *They* enforced *that* by keeping their own distance. The result was that he finished by having to guess at their ways and meanings and they by knowing all about him.)

If Perazzo had no dignity, Grosbeck would confer it upon him. Besides, Perazzo knew all about Grosbeck's dilemma. Grosbeck asked when Mrs. Perazzo would be laid out.

"Five o'clock tonight," said Perazzo. "But don't come tonight; the first night is for the family."

"Anything else I should know, Jimmy?" asked Grosbeck.

"What else is there to know, Mr. Grosbeck? You been to funerals before."

"All I meant was, is there anything special I should do?"

"Nothing," said Perazzo.

"All right, Jimmy," said Grosbeck. "I'll be there tomorrow night. Mrs. Grosbeck, too. Not Jason? I suppose not. He's a little young for that."

"Young?" asked Perazzo. "Not so young. It ain't a party, but that's life, too. How old were you you went to your first funeral?"

"About that age. About fourteen," said Grosbeck.

"There you are," said Perazzo. "Never too young. You'll see lots of even babies if you come."

"Well," said Grosbeck, "we'll see about Jason. Again, Jimmy, I'm sorry. If there's anything Mrs. Grosbeck or I can do . . ."

"Nothing," Perazzo repeated. It was almost as annoying as *Meglio cosi.*

At seven o'clock the next night, Grosbeck presented himself and Madeline at the funeral parlor. They had dressed carefully for the occasion: he in a dark lightweight suit; she in a dark dress, no jewelry, very little makeup. They had often passed the funeral parlor and observed the swarthy chauffeurs lounging on the fenders of the Cadillac limousines at the front door, at the mourners going in or coming out, none of whom seemed to be mourning anything, but rather attending the première of a play everyone knew was going to be mediocre. This was to be the first time either Grosbeck or Madeline had entered the place.

Grosbeck was a little disappointed to find in the main lobby the same sort of black bulletin boards to be found in any non-Italian funeral parlor; boards with white, removable letters on them, telling people where the defunct Mister This or the defunct Mrs. That lay. And the lobby was lighted by hard white fluorescents, as though it were an automobile showroom. It was not so different from the Jewish funeral homes he had been in, although both Jewish and Italian, he could see, were totally dissimilar from the interior of Frank Campbell's up on Madison Avenue, where the middle-class liberals, the intellectuals, the show-biz atheists and the indefinable *goyim* were carted off to, there not to have a funeral service said over them, so much as to be eulogized by their indefinable kind and then cremated.

He had hoped for more: some kind of Renaissance chapel; some tomb built for Greeks and adapted to Roman Catholic uses centuries later by Sicilians. The suspicion crept into his mind that even funeral parlors now were all owned by one corporation, whatever the professed religion of the dead; that all of the embalming was done in one central embalmery; the funeral clothing picked from the racks in another building; the special needs of one group or another attended to from a warehouse in a third place;

A central control room full of consoles with flashing lights on them, a hum in the room, a man at a microphone dispatching a hearse to one place, coffins to another (everything from conspicuously plain, unpainted pine boxes for orthodox Jews to the conspicuously best bronze for those who, although they could not afford them, insisted on having them, to the conspicuously gray-steel military kinds for the pieces of soldiers brought back from Indochina); flowers, Mass cards, platforms, podiums, Bibles and pamphlets containing only the necessary service for the dead in whatever religion was required; wigs for the bald dead, *yarmulkes* for the living Jewish mourners, lipstick, base tone, eyeshadow, rouge, extra vats of embalming fluid to be sent around in tank trucks should the possibility arise that the embalmery might run out.

You name it; we got it. Necroglom, Int., Inc., Ltd., & Co. delivers the goods, delivers the dead, delivers whatever the living decide has to be delivered to the dead. Delivers everything. Except deliverance. That comes from higher headquarters.

The Grosbecks found the room in which Mrs. Perazzo was laid out and stopped for a minute before going in. A man dressed in a black, double-breasted suit (black cloth buttons on the jacket) and brown shoes, with a nose even larger than Perazzo's, but of the identical shape, was standing to the right of the door. Obviously a brother of Perazzo. Next to him, on a small table, was a black wooden box with a slot in it rimmed in brass, and next to that an open register and a fountain pen.

People going in handed Perazzo's brother envelopes bordered in black. The brother would open them and remove money, count it, replace it in the envelope, drop it through the slot and then enter the name and the amount in the register. That way, the family would know who gave how much, and when they went to someone's else's funeral, they, too, would know how much to give to whom. The system was crude but efficient. Grosbeck felt that it was far more discriminating than the orthodox Jewish system under which a beggar wandered around, in everybody's way, with a *pushke,* a can, in his hand, asking for alms, beneficiary unspecified. (He all but had a sign on his chest over his pinned-up, torn clothing reading "Beggar.") Necroglom was in the process of phasing out the *pushke;* at any rate, Grosbeck had seen fewer of them in recent years.

He and Madeline looked at each other and then at Perazzo's brother. The brother held up a hand and shook his head; they were outsiders and there was no need for them to contribute anything; it wasn't likely that the neighborhood would go to Grosbeck's funeral. Grosbeck was glad, however, that he had had the forethought (or, rather, Madeline had) to send flowers, a large spray in a basket with a small card, ordered at and delivered by an Italian florist who knew just what should be included and who, for an appropriate tip, had had the spray delivered at the right time in the right room of the funeral parlor.

They went in. The room was not large, but, mercifully, it was in shadow; no fluorescent lighting here; wall sconces of opaque glass, within which were electric bulbs, amber colored and molded to look like candles. The walls were paneled in walnut three quarters of the way to the ceiling and a dado of molded plaster ran around the top of the paneling. That's more like it, thought Grosbeck. The coffin stood out from a wall: Bronze. Yes. Anna had been given four thousand dollars' worth of bronze. Half the two-part lid was up, lined with satin and a crucifix pinned to it.

From where he and Madeline stood, just inside the entrance, Grosbeck could not yet see her face. But he could see, in the shadows, mourners, men and women, sitting in rows of chairs before the coffin. A few sat straight, looking ahead and mumbling to themselves (Grosbeck assumed prayers); most talked and gestured, occasionally laughing in low voices, or shook hands or acknowledged the presence of new arrivals; took out handkerchiefs to wipe beads of sweat from lips, mustaches and foreheads; for, despite the fact that the room was professionally cooled, it was not cool; death heats up things. It is hot, not cold.

The Grosbecks advanced into the room. Near the coffin, sat Perazzo, alone. That was the custom. He was there to greet mourners; if they were very close members of the family, or very special mourners or apt to lose their way, to get up from his seat and lead them to the coffin. The way to the coffin lay through a tangle of canopied jungle trees and thick underbrush and it was only meet that Perazzo should be there to lead effete tenderfeet to the coffin. Perazzo inclined his head, rose, and without touching either Grosbeck or Madeline, pushed them toward the coffin.

When he was no more than a yard from it, Grosbeck kicked something; it was a low prayer bench, placed before the coffin for those who intended to say something for the dead. Grosbeck had not seen it in the shadows. He looked sheepishly at Perazzo, moved the bench back to where it had been, and, with Madeline, approached the coffin. Perazzo left them and went back to his post, left them to appreciate the undertaker's handiwork, perhaps, and Grosbeck possibly to keep in mind that he might want the same man for himself when his time came.

Anna had been done up beautifully, as nearly girlishly as it is possible to confect a cancerous woman of more than fifty who had suffered until her body had fallen in on itself. Jimmy had had her dressed in pink. Grosbeck wondered whether the dress was a full-length one. Since the lid of the coffin was open only to Anna's waist, the undertaker could have provided just enough to cover her. Grosbeck had heard about funeral clothing. Did Anna have shoes on? Stockings? It was something to think about. Her hair had been marceled, probably for the first time in the last twenty years, and her face had been made up with more care than she had ever given it. The undertaker had made a mistake, outdone himself. He had left this poor semblance of a face with a slightly coquettish look on it. It was out of place, Grosbeck complained to himself, but he guessed Perazzo had decided on the works. Anna had a rosary in her hands, crossed on her chest; some of the beads almost covered her wedding ring. (She must have had a chest, even if the undertaker had had to provide it.)

The Grosbecks stood before the coffin for a length of time which seemed inordinate to Grosbeck, but could have been no more than a minute. They did not pray, because neither of them had anything to pray about. Grosbeck did think about his maternal grandmother, an entirely different kind of woman, with whom he had played *pishe pashe,* a card game, on the very day she died, a little gray woman who laughed often, and then stopped, finally, sitting erect, the cards clutched in one hand, the other hanging at her side.

After looking at Perazzo for a clue, the Grosbecks began to leave, having deposited their quarter pound of mourning. As they did so, Catafesta and Mrs. Catafesta entered the room. My God, thought Grosbeck, they didn't bring the poodle with them for a change. Mrs. Catafesta looked no different from the way she always did, groomed the way Italian women of her class always are groomed. In a coffin, she would probably look like the Medusa. Catafesta gave off his olive ectoplasm and seemed to fill the room. Madeline exerted pressure on Grosbeck's arm with the fingers of her right hand, but he did not heed her.

Instead, he moved off to the side of the room, not too far from the coffin and the banks of flowers about it, and waited. Perazzo rose for the Catafestas as he had for the Grosbecks, but not for the same reason, and led them to Anna. The Catafestas viewed silently and then Catafesta motioned to his wife to find herself a chair among the rows of mourners. She did. When she was seated, Catafesta turned back to the coffin and knelt. He knelt on the floor, not on the prayer bench, which he moved aside. He wished to indicate the depth of his obligation toward the late Mrs. James (Giuseppe?) Perazzo.

He made an Act of Contrition. In Italian. Grosbeck had never heard his voice before. All of his fears, magnified in the veritable presence of death, assailed him again. The voice was . . . it was simply a voice . . . but it had expressed displeasure with him to other people whom he had never seen and so he must listen to it. Shortly before finishing the Act of Contrition, Catafesta glanced up and looked at Grosbeck. That, too, had never happened before. I am exaggerating, Grosbeck swore to himself, but he is driving a spike through me and pinning me to the wall. Even Madeline had moved back. The reaction was much the same the two of them had once had on a deserted subway platform, deserted, that is, except for themselves, and a pockmarked man with a face the color of white wine who was deciding to attack them. A train had entered the station, a transit policeman had looked out the door and the pockmarks had disappeared behind a pillar.

Catafesta looked at Grosbeck for possibly twenty seconds. Then, deliberately, deliberately, he said the Act of Contrition in English:

"Oh, my God, I am heartily sorry for having offended Thee."

He had no accent; his was the enunciation of a simultaneous translator for the United Nations.

"And I detest all my sins because I dread the loss of Heaven and the pains of Hell."

Why is he doing this? Grosbeck asked himself. I shall faint.

"But, most of all, because they offend Thee, my God, who art all good and deserving of all love."

Am I not, too, asked Grosbeck.

"I firmly resolve with the help of Thy grace to confess my sins, to do penance and to amend my life. Amen."

Catafesta arose, signaled to his wife, and the two were out the door before either Grosbeck or Madeline could move.

I have been told, thought Grosbeck. I am heartily sorry for having offended thee. Amen.

❖

The last light of the summer evening was gone when Madeline and Grosbeck came out of the funeral parlor. He took her arm. Neither of them said anything. They walked for two or three blocks.

Catafesta had been unambiguous. Perazzo and the rows of mourners had borne witness. The Paschal lamb was being prepared. It was only a question of setting the date for the holiday.

"What did you think of that?" Madeline said after a while.

"I'll tell you something interesting," said Grosbeck. "First, I was paralyzed. So were you. Then, I was fascinated. Never to have heard that man's voice before. Always having wondered what he would sound like. It was disembodied. The voice wasn't his; it didn't belong to him. It was the voice . . . the voice of . . . wait a minute, it'll come to me."

"Señor Wences," said Madeline. "The ventriloquist."

Grosbeck was astonished. "That you should know that!"

"Why should I not?" asked Madeline. "What is there about you and your life that I don't know, that you haven't told me? Nothing. Señor Wences is the least of it."

The little wooden head in the black, polished wooden box with the door on the box and the red velvet lining. The *two* voices, so clever was Wences. One voice for the head when the door to the box was closed; another when it was opened. The voices of the head were, by turns, impatient, petulant, sepulchral. Wences implored it, reasoned with it, bawled it out. The head was impervious to any of this for most of the act, performed on a stage with black drapes behind the ventriloquist in white tie and tails, no light on him, save a powerful white Klieg which made a circle about the upper part of his body and caused the dead glass eyes of the head in the box to shine savagely.

Wences fought with the head and pleaded with it and devoted logic to it until it gave in grudgingly, until it said, "S'all right, s'all right; difficult for you, easy for me," and then had the door of the box slammed shut on it, the box carried offstage, the protesting voice inside shouting, almost not to be heard in the heavy applause that came from the audience.

Grosbeck said, "Catafesta does not speak for himself."

"You won't ever know for whom he does speak," said Madeline.

"That's what frightens me so much," said Grosbeck. "Who does speak for whom? It's so much more than just Catafesta. Or the cops. Or the hoods, who, for all I know, will get me tonight. But we've been over that."

"Not tonight, they won't, Harvey," said Madeline. "Remember, Tully told you all you had to do was have the meeting. Catafesta won't have you touched before then and not after. He plays with you, he warns you, but he will not do anything, provided only that you hold the meeting and bring it off right."

Grosbeck prepared for the tenants' meeting, for his part in a play reading to which an important agent and a group of investors had been invited in the hope that the piece would be sold. He telephoned Madeline at her office and asked her to give him something light for dinner; scrambled eggs and bacon, toast and tea. He went over what it would be best to wear and decided on a pair of chinos, canvas-soled shoes, a loose shirt over his pants, no socks. Shower? Yes. Shave? No, that wouldn't be necessary. The morning shave was good enough. Pad? Yes. Pencils. Clipboard. A written speech? No, he didn't intend to talk that long, and, besides, it would make a better impression if he improvised so that the agent and the investors would think his sales talk represented a conviction so deep that it didn't have to be read from a piece of paper. Chairs? They'd just have to bring their own. Or they could sit on the washing machines, the dryers and the covered laundry tub. Or on the floor.

At home that evening, he found himself clearing his throat continuously. He left most of his food and went to get himself a drink.

"I wouldn't, if I were you, Harvey," said Madeline.

"Hell," said Grosbeck. "Why not? There's nothing like a bowl of sauce to . . ." he waved at her ". . . to make you feel right. I don't feel that way and I have to."

"You're a bad drinker, Harvey. Not an alcoholic or anything like that. Just a bad drinker. You get excessive or foolish; you say more than you mean to and, as far as I'm concerned, the wrong things. Either you don't make sense at all, which is embarrassing, or you offend people. Tonight's not the night to offend anyone."

"Look," he said, "it's either a drink or I blow the whole thing. I'm counting on it. You watch and see. All that a little whiskey will do for me tonight is keep me straight. Nobody knows any better than I do what I've got to do."

He poured himself a drink and swallowed most of it in the first swallow. Madeline shook her head.

"Make me one, too, Harvey," said Madeline. She bit the nail of a little finger. "Only not as big as yours."

"A little *el belto* for the sake of your stomach?" asked Grosbeck.

"You're feeling it that fast, aren't you, Harvey?"

"Oh, come on," he said, handing her her drink. "I'm only trying to be offhand about this and the drink really is helping me do it. It won't hurt you, either."

"I'm not going with you, Harvey," said Madeline.

"But, you've got to, Madeline," he said. "Why not? Now what have I done?" He started on the second drink.

"Look at yourself, Harvey. In five minutes. No, you go. I'll stay here with Jason."

"But, he won't be home for another three hours."

The Victorian lady with whom he had regular assignations, with whom he got drunk when they were alone, whom he found so compliant, so adventurous in private and willing, or eager, or both, was elsewhere tonight.

He begged. "Please," he said, but he did not put down the second drink. He pointed at her with the glass and drank some more; Madeline drank a little.

"All right, Harvey," she said. "We both know I'll go with you. We both know I can't stop you."

Grosbeck said, getting up, "This was just what I needed. Enough. It's finished. See?" He finished the second drink. "There. Done. I'm ready. Let's go. It's time."

"In a minute, Harvey," said Madeline. "I've got to go to the bathroom."

"Certainly," he said gallantly, as she left him. He had both fists on the table and the table top seemed to move back and forth beneath them. Another little one before Madeline got out of the bathroom. He drank from the bottle, screwed the top back on and put the bottle away; washed both glasses in the sink and was sitting at the table, drunk, by the time she returned from the bathroom.

❖

In the elevator, the Grosbecks met a whey-faced girl and her husband who were going to the meeting. She had hypoglycemia, she had once told the Grosbecks, and she wore it ostentatiously with the long strings of wooden beads she wound around her fingers. She was proud of her hypoglycemia as she was of her breasts, which were enormous on a body so stringy. Between them and the hypoglycemia, she had something, this Jewish princess in diminuendo. Because of what she fancied to be her delicate condition, she had her groceries delivered, did little housework, brooding day long over two plants in the window and reading the recipes in women's magazines. She was a bad cook, the husband had said; he tried to keep her out of health-food stores, but she was not to be denied. Most of the stuff rotted. The husband was tall and thin and pale all over; his eyes were a light blue and he wore steel-rimmed glasses.

If one could not tell what he was thinking, he told one. He put up with his wife, possibly because of her breasts, probably because of something else at which no one could ever guess. For all of his talkativeness, he really said very little; and for all of her diffidence, the wife had a great deal to say. "Going to the meeting, eh?" said the husband, to the

238

people who had asked that it be held. The wife said to the husband, "No, they're going to Tangiers for a week." The husband pressed doggedly at a large natal lump on his forehead; the wife, under the pretext of adjusting her beads, three times made certain her breasts were still in place. Both the lump and the breasts stayed where they were as the elevator descended.

In the laundry room half a dozen people already had assembled: The black homosexual, a powerfully muscled, slender, agreeable man; his elderly white paramour, who had felt it unnecessary to wear his false teeth for the occasion; a tiny little man of about eighty, with an enormous head, a Greek whose English was startling and whose understanding of what was being said about him equally so (once, upon being asked whether he thought it was hot enough for him, he had delivered a scathing indictment of the current Greek Government); two girls who lived together in a studio apartment and had no trouble accommodating, at the same time, the anxious men (usually not known to each other) who visited them; and a man whose sole distinction was that in all seasons he entered or left the building in spiked baseball shoes and a softball uniform. Where he played softball in the wintertime was a matter of much conjecture, but, so far as Grosbeck knew, no one had ever asked him directly.

The woman who had had an appointment with her psychotherapist that night came. She confided to the Grosbecks that her "man" had told her it might be good for her to get out a little more with all kinds of people. "He's not charging me for missing an appointment, either," she said. "He's wonderful. He wants me to reach out. You probably wouldn't have noticed, but I've stopped twitching on the left side of my face." She was about to say more when

Madeline interrupted her. "You must drop in at our apartment some night," she said. "Your doctor is absolutely right. I often think our compassion quotient is far too low." Compassion quotient, thought Grosbeck. Madeline guided Grosbeck past the woman to a centrally located washing machine on top of which he put his clipboard and pencils. "Shit," he said. "Where do you pick up that jargon? That woman is a barracuda. She'll bite you to death." "Save your eloquence, Harvey," said Madeline. "Don't waste it on mice."

"Speaking of mice," Grosbeck said to Madeline. "Look." It was the engineer from upstairs with his black Jewish wife and their two brawling children. The engineer was wearing his karate robe and belt, and he strode, rather than walked, like something out of a bad martial-arts movie made in Hong Kong. His wife had decked herself out in a purple turban made of some kind of anomalous synthetic. She jingled and jangled with ropes and ropes of tarnished metal beads and she had on a caftan. The children had on not much more than a layer of dirt on their hands, faces and legs. Tags of spittle had dried on their faces and they tore at their mother's caftan while she roared and slapped at them. They moved about her with the agility of mongooses. The engineer approached Grosbeck, opened one big fist and showed a pedometer in his palm. "I hope this won't last too long," he said. "I'm all for solidarity, but there's a couple of miles to be done tonight before we turn in. Hah!" Mrs. Engineer said to Madeline, "I find it simply disgusting that the sisterhood is so inadequately represented among us. Where is our voice, what our position?" Madeline murmured at her. Then, slap, slap. The children fell to the floor, but got up undeterred. The engineer regarded his wife without passion. She had a bruise under one cheekbone, placed there by the engineer during a philosophical difference one night. "Sisterhood!" he said. "Get over in that corner with the kids." Mrs. Engineer opened her mouth, closed it, swept herself into a corner with the children and was followed there by the Lord High Engineer, who did isometric exercises throughout the evening. Neither of them said another word that night, either to each other or anyone else.

By ones and twos, the tenants entered the laundry room and filled it. It was not a large room. The walls were painted gray, like the bulkheads of a Hog Island coal burner of six thousand tons. The room contained four washing machines, four dryers, two laundry tubs, a long, splintered bench and two wooden chairs on which no one ever sat because everyone knew they would collapse. Strings of pipe crossed and recrossed the ceiling, making gray sounds. The laundry room was about to get underway, to slip past the stone mole at Tananarive, at Cobh, at Mobile, past the blinker buoys and the bell buoys and the lights of coasting steamers, six knots, hull down, bound east for Cardiff, booms lashed, a cargo of copra, rats nesting in the dunnage and the straw; coffee aft in the urn that was never empty; the watch above and at the bow; the night foggy and the swells beyond the mole long and languorous, covered with oil and the discharge of the galleys of a thousand ships which had preceded the laundry room out of the harbor. Enough.

The Italians came with folding chairs of aluminum, shining green plastic seats: clubby, suspicious, off to one side, waiting, dressed formally. The others were . . . the others: A drunken man who wore glasses on a black silk ribbon and said he was a doctor; a manufacturer of baby furniture with a sweeping black mustache lately adopted with his advanced views on family life. These included a wife who wore batik blouses of a kind not seen in Greenwich Village since Edna St. Vincent Millay had lived on Bedford Street; a beautiful son who knew only too well what to make of his parents and his father's advanced views; a camper truck the family used on weekends and knapsacks to be carried when the three of them strode through the countryside looking for antiques at bargain prices. Grosbeck, with the omniscience of the uninformed, thought he knew his man: The manufacturer's liberal outlook had led him also to seek out an accountant who kept two sets of books for him and a young lady to whom he read long passages from *The Sorrows of Young Werther*, both before and after she entertained him nights in a Hudson River tenement when he was supposed to be going over a new lathe in his small factory near the big airport in Queens. For her part, the manufacturer's wife collected spices and cooked and cooked and cooked, standing naked before a stove for no other reason than that it was a form of defiance of her husband. They were both prigs, and Grosbeck felt sorry for the son.

Grosbeck was uncharitable in the extreme. They don't live, he told himself, they have a goddamned life style. He would have liked to compose vignettes of everybody who entered the laundry room, but there was no time for wool-gathering. And a policeman had arrived, dressed in a sleeveless white shirt and yellow chemical pants; he was getting paid overtime for community-relations work, but that didn't mean he had to wear a uniform. He identified himself to Grosbeck, who made himself shake hands with the man, and then leaned against the wall, arms crossed, waiting for things to begin.

The tenants disposed themselves anyhow, talking. Only the Italians were a large block of silence. How badly life imitated art, Grosbeck thought, how poorly these people fulfill anyone's grand design; how contemptible, in the end, all of them. They are nothing. And I am one of them. He had not yet fully absorbed the galling fact that he was not only one of them, but that his end was theirs, theirs, his. If anyone were to be contemptuous of anyone, they were to be contemptuous of him. Or contemptuous of no one. How now, compassion quotient; how now, brown fucking cow.

The whiskey had hold of Grosbeck. He was sweating; his brain was sweating, the drops running down the pane of coherence. They laughed when I sat down to play. . . . Unaccustomed as I am to public speaking. . . . He had never before addressed an audience this large, nor, indeed, been under the necessity of putting on an act to save his life. He reached back of him for the clipboard on the washing machine. It fell to the floor and he bent down, flushed with the difficulty of the movement, to pick it up. Nausea flooded him. Madeline had been right. He should not have had anything to drink. Too late. Catafesta was not there; there was no reason why he should be. Plenty of people would tell him. He wished Catafesta were there. I would have done to him what he did to me: Spoken to him in Italian as he spoke to me in English. He *was* speaking to me. But you can't speak Italian; you can't even speak Yiddish, you deracinated Jew.

The clipboard seemed so heavy to Grosbeck that it canted his body to one side. He looked around for a place to put it down again. He found the washing machine from which he had taken it and dropped it loudly on top. The clatter stopped the talk. People wriggled to attention. He could hear the drip of water in one of the laundry tubs. So many eyes upon him. He could not see Madeline. The policeman pushed himself away from the wall, whispered to Grosbeck, and then went back to his post.

Grosbeck moved out three steps. "We don't know one another very well," he began. No one disputed him.

"Here we are living in the same building, the same neighborhood, for years, and what do we really know about one another? Nothing. There's nothing new about that. New York's always been that way. O. Henry wrote hundreds of stories based on that theme. Stephen Crane . . ." The affectedness of what he was saying somehow penetrated to Grosbeck. The policeman closed his eyes. The audience, the lump of people in the laundry room, signified neither yes nor no.

"Well," he said, "isn't that so?"

"Isn't that rather self-evident?" asked a man with a pipe. Stick your pipe up your ass.

"Shhh," said someone else.

"Forgive me," Grosbeck said. Forgive me was the story of his life. "I don't feel too well tonight. I guess it's the heat. I'll do my best not to impose on you."

One of the Italians looked at his wife and tapped his head. There was some kind of disturbance in the miles of electrical conduits and cables in the streets outside and the lights in the laundry room became too bright and then too dim. They might go out. Or, Grosbeck in his drunkenness and distress might have imagined that part about the lights.

He held up both hands, palms out.

"We've got things to do," said a small woman with dyed red hair and a face like a peeled potato. "We can't be here all night."

"I promise you, you won't," said Grosbeck. If I had a corer, I'd deal with that face. I feel my fingers slipping.

"I think the best way to get on with this . . . I do agree

244

we haven't got all night . . . is to introduce Patrolman Whelan. But, before I do, there are one or two little things I'd like to say . . . or, rather, just one little question I'd like to ask. It seems to me . . . I'm afraid I seem to be falling apart . . . I'm sure you've all had that experience at some time in your lives. Be patient. I'll be out of the way sooner than you expect."

Grosbeck, if asked, would not have been in a position to identify the speaker.

"In any case, we all have something in common." He looked around the room. "Just now, ha, ha, it eludes me. Oh, yes. Mugging. Protection. My wife, as you all know . . ." He tried to find Madeline in the room. There she was, seated on the floor, next to one of the laundry tubs.

"My wife has had an awful experience. Right on our floor. There's no point in going back over it. She was fortunate. I heard her and ran out the door. Mind you, I'm no hero, it's just that the man saw someone there and bolted down the stairs. I could have been anyone in the hall. No credit to me. I'm not even sure what I would have done had he come at me."

Whatever was going on inside Grosbeck was deeply complicated by alcohol. The people in the laundry room seemed to know that he was drunk and he had the impression that they were whispering, whispering behind their hands, nudging each other, or covering their mouths to hide grins. The open fly. No, not that. Alternatively, they were sitting stiffly upright, not moving at all, not saying anything, thinking nothing, not judging, not reserving opinion, not even there. Perhaps he was alone in the laundry room. The swells would subside once it was out past Robbins Reef and Ambrose Light. There was coffee aft in the urn and he would have a cup before continuing.

No aft, no urn, no cup, no coffee. The laundry room.

"To go on . . . no, no need for me to go on. It's been long, long enough. I don't know if any of you will ever know, or if you do, whether you'll care. But that's another story. Here is Patrolman Whelan of the Fourth Precinct. He takes care of community relations. We all know what community relations are. They're relations who don't live with you, but drop in to eat three or four times a week at eleven o'clock at night. It isn't much of a joke, but Patrolman Whelan is, and here it is . . . here *he* is. Patrolman Whelan."

❖

The policeman came forward with slight, acknowledging nods of the head. As he passed Grosbeck, he whispered, "You sure are an example to these people, to all of us, Mr. Grosbeck. I've heard about you. Why don't you just get the fuck out of here. I need you like I need a hole in the head."

"You mean it about the hole in the head, don't you?" Grosbeck whispered back and put a hand on his eyes. "I don't need your sarcasm either, Mr. Whelan." Before Grosbeck could say anything more, the policeman was out in the center of the room. Grosbeck followed him.

"It'll only take a second more," he said to Whelan. "Give me just a second."

"It's your meeting," said the policeman. "But, if I were you, I'd try keeping my mouth shut for a while." This was a little more than the tenants had expected and they enjoyed it.

"I assure . . ." Grosbeck said to Whelan and turned to the

audience. "Whatever I said didn't refer to Patrolman Whelan," he explained. "It was an involved, intricate sort of joke, that's all. . . . Let me try to explain. I wasn't referring to Officer Whelan at all. What I was trying to do was make a mild joke about community relations. Relations. Community. Get it? Nothing more."

"They get it, Harvey," said Madeline from where she sat. "Go and sit down."

"Right away, Madeline, I swear," said Grosbeck. "But I've *got* to explain . . . I've got to establish that there was no malice . . . simply an accidental connection, that's all . . . community relations and Officer Whelan. Like *napwins* instead of napkins, like your sister used to say when she was a child . . ." Nobody else said anything and Grosbeck walked over to Madeline, talking as he went: "Can't I do anything right? Ever? They've got to be made to understand. . . . You've got to understand . . . I didn't have anything in mind . . . I was trying to get the meeting going."

"Sit down, Harvey. Quickly." Grosbeck nearly fell to the concrete floor and bruised his behind. "It was an unintentional ellipsis," he cried.

"Ellipse this," said someone.

"This is getting silly," Grosbeck said to Madeline. His tone was pleading, not declaratory.

Patrolman Whelan, who had been chosen for community-relations work because he had the kind of face known as frank and open, and who, as far as anyone knew, wasn't pushing drugs, began his speech.

"I know you're all upset," he said. He looked in Grosbeck's direction. "Particularly Mr. Grosbeck. I would be, too. My wife's been molested where we live."

"I thank you, Mr. Whelan," Grosbeck said from the floor. "Profoundly."

"Nothing, Mr. Grosbeck," said Whelan. "But you've got to stop interrupting. It was you who called this meeting and these good people were concerned enough to come and maybe if you'll just stay quiet. . . . Mrs. Grosbeck, I appeal to you. . . ."

"Not necessary, Whelan," said Grosbeck. "There won't be another word out of me."

"That's nice, Mr. Grosbeck." Whelan smiled at the tenants. "It's all in a day's work. You live with it."

Grosbeck struggled up from the elbow he had been leaning on. Madeline pulled him down. Whelan talked.

"First," he said, "there's something I'd like to tell you. We get plenty of calls at the precinct asking for more protection, for men on foot, for a quicker response to perpetrators and assailants. Possibly you don't know this, but you live in a precinct which has the second-lowest crime rate in the city."

"You could fool me," one of the tenants said.

"I expected that kind of reaction," said Whelan. "Get it all the time. But, that's a fact, and I have the figures to prove it." He didn't produce them. "We do know that Mr. Grosbeck's wife was attacked and that others in the neighborhood have been from time to time, and, of course, that calls for action. That's what we're here for. But, we do need your cooperation. And we're getting it. All over the city, people like yourselves are forming block associations and patrolling their own buildings and staying on the alert and there's no reason why you shouldn't be as successful here as the others are. We're for it down at the precinct. High time."

An Italian woman, black hair, pasta complexion, got up, brushing off her husband's restraining hand. "Why, I want to know, block associations, tenant patrols, if there's so little crime down here. Why, if we pay you more and more every year, the rent goes up, the landlord gets rich, the police aren't here when we want them. You know what? *Tu puzza.* You stink."

The husband got up, yelled, "*Stai zito*," at the offending wife and dragged her down on her folding chair. "I apologize," he said to Whelan. "To you, to the people here. She gets excited. Down here, we don't talk that way. We have our problems, you have yours, officer. Please."

"We *are* here, missus," said Whelan. "You might not think so, but we are. I can show you from figures how often the patrol cars pass the entrance to this building."

"On the street, walk on the street," said the Italian woman. "Don't tell me patrol cars."

"We have found," Whelan said, "it doesn't help as much that way. Things have changed, missus. Everything moves much faster now, including the perpetrators we have to apprehend. Foot patrol only slows us up, lets them get away."

"Then, how come crime goes up all the time?" the Italian woman asked.

"It doesn't, missus, not in this area," said Whelan. "I showed you."

"You show me nothing," said the woman. "I'm going."

"You're not," said the husband. "She will stay," he announced to the room. "We will all stay. The policeman has something to tell us."

"Thank you," said Whelan. "I can practically tell you what you're going to ask. 'Why don't we keep a gun? Why don't we get a knife? Mace spray?' I'll tell you why. Violence. That's what we're trying to prevent."

"What's wrong with violence, with a gun or a knife?" asked the man in the softball uniform. "That's what they use on us. Or a baseball bat. Forget the mace. You can't get it out of your pocket in time. I tell you, I feel safer when I go out of this house with a bat and wearing spiked shoes. I'd kill one of those sons of bitches he tried to lay a finger on me." He gesticulated. "I'd beat his head to a pulp with the bat and I'd stomp his guts into the sidewalk with the spikes. He'd think twice after that, the animal, the junkie son of a bitch."

"Watch your language, mister," said one of the Italians. "There's ladies present."

"I'm sorry," said the man in the softball uniform. "But, you know what I mean. How much longer can we take it lying down?"

A young girl in a smock, cradling a bundle of laundry in her arms, murmured, *"Hare krishna."*

"I'll tell you why you don't want a gun or a knife or a baseball bat," Whelan said. "Because *they* can use it better than you. That's their business. *They've* had lots of practice."

"Want to get to Carnegie Hall?" Grosbeck said loudly. "Practice."

Whelan continued. *"They* been using them for years, they know how to use them, you wouldn't stand a chance. And violence just isn't the answer."

"What do you mean by *they?*" asked a young Negro in a dashiki.

"Why, nothing," said Whelan. "Just *they,* these people who are perpetrating crimes of the person and property on you. And you're you. *You're* what they're after. That's who *they* is."

The Italians looked dubious.

"You don't mean nigger?"

Whelan rubbed his nose with thumb and forefinger. "No, mister," he said. "And I don't mean mick, kike, wop, polack or bohunk, either. You know how many Negroes we got in the department these days?"

"Blacks," said the Negro.

"Blacks," said Whelan.

"How many captains, how many inspectors?" asked the Negro.

"My buddy is black, the guy who rides with me," said Whelan.

"He going to be commissioner next year?"

"Why not?" asked Whelan. "He's got as good a chance as I have. You all know this city's not like the rest of the country. Here, a man gets to get ahead regardless of race, creed or color. Take you, yourself. You look to me like a man hasn't been held black . . . I mean back. . . . Can I ask you, what do you do? It has to be pretty good to live in a building like this. The rents can't be cheap in an elevator building like this."

"It's none of your business, officer," said the black, or Negro. "But I'm a first teller in a bank."

"There, then," said Whelan. "That proves it."

"Proves nothing," said the Negro. "What about the rest of the brothers and sisters? You think I'm ever going to get to be a vice-president of that bank?"

"Mister," said Whelan, his head rolling slightly on his shoulders, "I can't take on the problems of the world. I'm just a cop, that's all, a cop. And what I'm here for tonight is to try and help you people protect yourself. You want to come out later and have coffee with me, I'll be glad to talk to you all night about it. But not now. I can't take that one on now. Who could?"

"You're not being responsive," said a voice from the audience, a clear, resonant, liberal, self-satisfied voice. "You're not addressing yourself to the issue." Grosbeck, in

his fuddlement, was both amused and infuriated. "Responsive." "Addressing yourself to the issue." Bullshit language.
These people would be smothered in the garbage of the
way they talked to each other.

"I do what I can," said Whelan. "You people want to go
on?"

There were cries of "Yes, yes."

"That's about it for guns and knives," said Whelan. "You
know they're not going to work. So what do you do?" He
talked about the tenants patrolling the building themselves,
about special locks on the doors, how to get in touch with
the police quickly, about getting together with other groups
in other buildings, about carrying whistles: the whole
manual of decay and desperation. Whelan neither knew
nor cared whether anyone believed him. That was what he
was supposed to say and he said it . . . at time and a half
for overtime when he had to do it nights. He declared the
floor open (declared the floor open!) for suggestions and
questions.

Another of the Italian wives raised a hand. "It's up to the
landlord," she said. "He's got to do for us. We're entitled to
a doorman. Twenty-four hours. We pay enough rent."

"Forget it," said someone else. "Also, how's that going to
help you out on the street?"

"The street, the street," said the Italian woman. "That
takes care of itself. It's around the building we need help.
You saw what happened to that lady." She pointed to

Madeline. "Only by the grace of God and the Blessed Virgin is she sitting here among us tonight."

"That's right," said Grosbeck. "They watch over the least sparrow, even a Jewish sparrow."

Whelan realized he was through and retreated from the center of the room. Let them get off steam. He would have liked to put the boot to the Negro in the dashiki. The black bastard. Not all of them. This one. What was it his old man used to call them? Biggety niggers. No, that wasn't the old man. His grandfather. His grandfather had picked that up from an Alabama redneck in the infantry in the First World War and passed it on. The grandfather had got tired of plain "nigger" or "coon" or "shine" or "spade" or "smoke." Besides, whenever he said "biggety nigger" people looked up to him as some kind of intellectual . . . that was one they'd never heard before. Ah, America! How would the grandfather have felt if there'd been a darky around in Europe during that grand war to call him "peckerwood," a northern peckerwood. Would he have thought of Rastus Biggety as an intellectual? The hell he would.

The tenants' meeting began to get clotted with nonsense as one suggestion after another was put forward. Some of them were beauties. Someone wanted to lock the outside door at midnight so that nobody could get in at all after then, even if he had a key. "Decent people don't come any later than that," said the proponent of the idea. "An hour later over the weekend. Anyone who does come in after that, let them sleep somewhere else. We know what they're up to." That was a man.

A woman answered him: "Welcome to the twelfth century."

"You think . . . never mind what you think," said the

man. "How else are we going to keep them out? Drastic things have to be done, Draconian things. . . ."

"Draconian!" said the woman. "My, aren't *we* well educated."

"Fudge," said the man.

"Why don't you say it straight out, buster?" said the woman.

"I said 'fudge,'" said the man. "And 'fudge' is what I meant, you nasty dyke."

The quality of the meeting deteriorated steadily. There was talk about putting a red light on the canopy outside to alert the police, but no one was able to say where the button for the light should be inside the building; whether the victim would be able to get to it, or whether a police car would be passing when the light was turned on. A buzzer system was proposed. It would be heard throughout the building; there would be buttons all over the place, from basement to roof; everywhere anyone turned, there would be a button. Once the button was pushed and the buzzer went off, everyone would burst from his apartment and get involved. The victim could, however, be in any one of a hundred places in the building, bleeding all over the button until someone found him. The button idea was dropped; so was the light-on-the-canopy idea. There were more ideas along the same lines until Grosbeck understood that his neighbors had no more grasp on the essentials of survival than he did.

The Italians said, "Hmmmph" and "Pssss," and rolled their eyes and offered no suggestions.

A divorcée, a woman in her early forties, who lived alone and was so consumed by her condition that it made her face seem no larger than a persimmon, and not unlike one, contributed an idea. Doorbell drill, she said, rotating her hips as she spoke in a blond voice. Her lips were overred and suggested another part of her body, which she had covered with the tightest black pants she could find.

Doorbell drill. That is: One of the tenants, every night, would act as a monitor, go downstairs and ring doorbells. There was an intercommunications system and the person at home was supposed to ask, "Who is it?" and ring the downstairs bell only when satisfied that it was someone he knew. If the careless householder rang the bell without asking, he was to be censured. How was he to be censured? Why, all the tenants on his floor would be summoned by the monitor, and, in a body, they would go to his door and bang on it with their fists. If he opened to them, they would point accusing fingers at him and tell him never to do it again; if he did not open the door, they would keep banging on it until one of them had written a note and slipped it under the door.

The laundry room began to smell bad from all the people crowded in it and from their brainlessness: perfume and sweat, cigarettes, cigars and pipes and effluvia of crotches; the odor of garlic and scallions and Limburger; the miasma of behinds imperfectly tended and that of soap gone bad; and alcohol, particularly the alcohol that Grosbeck had drunk. He was getting sicker and more annoyed and more afraid and more impatient. He no longer lay on his elbow. He had risen to face the babble.

Out of it rose another voice, that of a girl who, up to then, had said nothing and had been so inconspicuous that she seemed to be one of the pipes running from the floor to the ceiling. "Dope addicts are sick people," she said.

The Italians rolled their eyes again.

"Rats," said the girl. "They sneak in from the streets. The rats, creeping out of their holes, creeping up from the cellars, out of the hallways, into the empty lots and down into the subways. All the dark and evil places they come from. Has anyone ever counted them? There's a devil on earth and the devil is in all these rats. Pieces of the devil, making one whole devil. I've seen them by the hundreds, in packs, running down the tracks in the subways. Then, I don't know, they jump up on the platforms before the trains come and that makes me run away and take a taxi."

"Cut it out," shouted Grosbeck.

"We've got to kill the rats, have no mercy on them," the girl went on. "Or we'll be overwhelmed by them. You should see the size of them. The color. I can't stand the color. Packed close together and running. Not fast, either, because they're not afraid of us. We're afraid of them. And, because they don't run very fast, we can get away. Up into the street and into a cab. I don't always have cab fare and I have to run for blocks and blocks until I'm out of breath and my eyes are closed all the time. I might run into something. What shall I do? Tell me."

"I'll tell you, God damn it," Grosbeck shouted again. "Cut it out. Stop it. Get the hell out of here." He made brushing motions with his hands, brushing the girl out of the room. She became docile and sat down on the floor, her lips puffed out, her hands working at her hair.

"I've got something to tell you people," Grosbeck said at the top of his voice. "I've had something on my mind and you better know about it. All this crap has nothing to do with anything. You're just not very bright, that's all." He tried bracing himself against himself and spread his feet wide; there was no support, so he swayed in order not to fall. A physicist could have told him what he was doing, but he didn't want to hear from any physicist about the dynamics of standing on his feet. Nor did he want any further cautions from Madeline, who, pale and wretched, came up to him and was pushed away.

"What I've got to tell you," said Grosbeck, "is . . ."

"No, Harvey," said Madeline.

"Yes, Madeline," Grosbeck mimicked, looking away from the tenants for an instant. "Yes, indeed." He tried to straighten his tie and it took him a while to absorb the fact that he was wearing neither tie nor suit. He spat on the floor. Drunk or sober, he had never done anything like that before. You've never, never done anything like that before, he sang aloud, the tenants responding, silently, you've never done anything like that before. Outside of the noise he was making, there wasn't a sound in the room.

"So, if I did," said Grosbeck, "I'll clean it up. But there's a . . . I've got to clean all of you up before I do that. You need it. Here it is." He breathed heavily. "You want to know why my wife got mugged and how she got mugged?

"Well, here's why. There's a drug dealer in this house, a pretty big drug dealer, that's why, and that son of a bitch with the knife who got my wife in the elevator was on his way to make a pickup from him and she happened to be in his way or he just felt like playing with her or I don't know what.

"But . . . a dealer. *In this house.* Mafia. Mafia. Mafia. You all know who he is." He addressed himself to the Italians. "You know I'm not talking about Italians. I'm talking about Mafia. Jews are Mafia. Anybody. Evil Mafia." Then why not say Catafesta's name right out? Well, why not? The drunken mind gives no accounting of itself; the little rivulets of alcohol wind their way through the tiny capillaries, through the blood and brain; and the pool of thought is darkened; left becomes right, right, left; the feet are fixed in concrete while the head rises to the ceiling, coming down with a lump under the thinning hair. The larger the lump, the less the logic. Drunken cunning; drunken stupidity, is what it really is. Grosbeck had decided, through the blearing of the alcohol, not to say Catafesta's name aloud. There was, actually, no need to.

There was a rumble among the Italians, a rumble distinct from sounds made by the other tenants . . . those were chitterings and twizzlings. All motion ceased in the room. All motion, but the swaying of Grosbeck and the waving of his arms, and the rolling of his head.

"You don't think so?" he demanded of the people. "You don't think the cops are in with him, that's how things get done in this city. But when it's my wife, my home . . . I'm not accustomed to this. Why me?"

Whelan, impassive, left the room quickly, unnoticed.

"Harvey, Harvey, Harvey." Grosbeck knew the voice.

The Italians rose as one and left; the rest of the tenants bobbed and moved, but did not leave at once, the sensation-seekers. They formed an inquisitive circle about Grosbeck, which none of them entered. Then they got out of the laundry room.

Madeline put an arm around Grosbeck's waist. Grosbeck raised a forefinger to punctuate something more he was going to say. He dropped his arm and the forefinger at the end of it. He did not fall; he did not vomit; he no longer swayed.

"I'm going to take a walk to clear my head," he said to Madeline.

"Why not," she answered in despair. "What possible difference can it make."

Suicide. The late Harvey Grosbeck.

"Let's take a walk," said Grosbeck. "Let's have a party." He pulled his shirt out of his pants and scratched his belly. "Let's run around the block."

The dying runner would never get to the corner.

"A party. That's what we both need. Take your mind off it. Take your clothes off it. No, just take your clothes off."

He had read somewhere that when a man is hanged, he is cut down with an erection.

"Come on, Madeline. I don't feel so bad."

"I guess you don't, Harvey."

"What's the matter?" asked Grosbeck. "You think you got a monopoly on fucking? Hasn't been a monopoly on fucking in this town since Lucky Luciano."

No answer.

"I wish Catafesta had been here."

The water in the laundry tubs dripped loudly and the bulbs in the ceiling of the laundry room shone yellowly.

"Jason."

He repeated the word drip for drip until he had worn a rut in it and was tired of it.

"Tell you what. Forget fucking. I'll call Tully again."

Madeline shook her head.

"All right, then I won't call Tully. Haven't you got anything to say? So I had a few drinks. Didn't all that need saying tonight? I was only trying to defend you. I was only . . ."

"No, you weren't, Harvey."

"What can I do?"

"I don't know."

"Wait."

Time passed.

"I hope it won't hurt. I hope it comes quickly."

Time passed.

"You haven't said anything, Madeline."

"You've never heard anything I said."

How trite the dialogue. And then it was over; there was nothing more to be said. Grosbeck lay down on the floor of the laundry room and slept. Madeline sat next to him, cross-legged. At eleven o'clock, the superintendent came in to lock up.

"Your husband has no brains, Mrs. Grosbeck," he said.

"You have brains, don't you, Mr. Cavanaugh?" Madeline said. "You know and I know and he knows."

"Good luck, Mrs. Grosbeck," said the superintendent.

"Good night, Mr. Cavanaugh. You've been a big help."

"You got me wrong, Mrs. Grosbeck. Any other situation, I'd make an effort. But this one I stay out of. I got a skin to keep in one piece, too."

"You knew. They all knew. Perazzo. Everybody. Somebody could have said something to him."

"I can't afford to, Mrs. Grosbeck."

"Good night, Mr. Cavanaugh."

Cavanaugh went away to his basement apartment.

Madeline got Grosbeck to his feet and out into the lobby. Standing in the lobby were the Negro homosexual and the old, bald white man with whom he lived. Madeline pushed the button for the elevator.

"Don't go upstairs right away, Mrs. Grosbeck," said the white man. He had put his false teeth back in.

"Why not, Mr. Allison?" asked Madeline. "I'm afraid Mr. Grosbeck needs bedding down right now."

"Please," said the Negro. "Come out with us. We like you."

"We do," said the white man.

Grosbeck's chin came up from his chest and his eyes opened: "You love us?" he said.

"Yes," said the white man. "You and Mrs. Grosbeck have never been other than kind to us."

"Should we be any other way?" asked Grosbeck.

"I don't care, personally," said the Negro, "but *he* does and if he does, I go along with it. And you have been kind."

"How kind? Kind? How?" Grosbeck was getting interested.

"Let him tell you," said the Negro.

"But we never meet outside of the lobby or in front of the house," said Grosbeck. "The most we ever say is hello or lousy day or I'm tired."

"That's not it," said the white man. "It's the attitude. The feeling. We know what's there."

"Don't get maudlin," said Grosbeck. "I can't stand that. You're setting me up. Drunk as I am, I won't be set up. There's a man in my office named Tully tried to do the same thing. So, don't you do it." He waved a finger at the two men. "See that finger?" he demanded. "There's more cunning in that finger than you think." He showed the finger to Madeline. "Pardon," he said, and belched.

"I've seen too much," Grosbeck said. "What I haven't seen, I've heard about and what I haven't heard about can't amount to a damn. I'll not be set up. We've all of us been fooled too many times."

"Come," said the white man. "Nobody would dream of trying to set up a personage like you." "Personage," said

Grosbeck. "Regardless," said the white man. "Let's the four of us have a drink."

"Please not," said Madeline. "As you can see, Harvey's in no condition. . . ."

"Something soft, then," said the white man. "We have an idea of what's going on. And he ought to know that he's not so much alone as he thinks. There's nothing practical, really, we can do, but we would like your company for an hour or so, and I think the two of you might like ours."

"You better believe it, Jack," said the Negro to Grosbeck. "Yeah, not just good morning and good evening. Company, baby."

"Can you make it, Harvey?" asked Madeline. To the two men, she said, "It is so very kind of you."

"I shall kiss you, Mrs. Grosbeck," said the old man, sucking in his papery cheeks. "I don't think people kiss enough. Unless, of course, you have an objection. In which case . . ." He kissed Madeline. "And you, too, Mr. Grosbeck. May we call you Harvey?" He kissed Harvey. "Now, you, Arthur," he said to the Negro. "You, too."

"Nothing nicer, baby," said the Negro. "First, Harvey, because he do need it most, then Madeline." The four stood in the lobby, in the heat, embracing.

"I don't live by symbols, I want to warn you," Grosbeck said, extricating himself from the clump.

"This time, shut up, Harvey," said Madeline.

"But, I don't, Madeline," said Grosbeck. "We both just happen to like Allison and Arthur."

"I don't know what you're talking about, Harvey," said Allison. "Symbols, I mean."

"Don't make any difference, either, baby," said the Negro. "Liking someone. It's no big world deal. Have a good morning; have a good evening. Go to Mass Sundays."

"The two of you go to Mass Sundays?" asked Grosbeck.

"That's what we do," said the Negro. "You better believe there's no two better Catholics around."

"That's *your* symbol, Arthur," said Grosbeck.

"Don't know about that, Harvey," said the Negro. "I just want God so bad I can taste it."

"Even when he's loaded and been a bad boy," said Allison.

"Well," said Grosbeck, "I don't want God. I can't have God. And, whether you know it or not, something bad is going to happen to me. God can't do much about that, nor love. I'm drunk and sick and they can't do much about *that.*"

"I'm not recommending God," said Allison. "I'm not even recommending love. But there they are, the both of them; both one."

"Keep it clean, Allison," said Grosbeck. "You really think so?" he asked, looking from one to the other and then at Madeline. "You think so, too?" She nodded. "You, too. Just wanted to confirm it. All right. Let's go. Where? By the way," Grosbeck added, "you two have one hell of a high compassion quotient."

The four of them walked toward the North River in the dark, paired off, Grosbeck with Allison, Arthur with Madeline. "You know the wholesale meat market?" Allison asked Grosbeck. "I've been around there," said Grosbeck. "Picturesque. But I'm not looking for a side of beef this time of night."

"There are several pleasant bars in the district," said Allison.

"I'm not stupid," said Grosbeck. "I know what kind of bars. Cuddle up and don't be blue with the sex of your persuasion."

Allison pinched his arm, not in anger. "We're not fags,

Harvey," he said. "We're husband and wife." He clacked his false teeth. "Arthur and I have lived together a good many years. Isn't that right?" he called ahead to Arthur. "Can't hear you, baby," said Arthur. "But if you say so, that's right." "I was saying," Allison said loudly, "we've been husband and wife for many years." "Love every minute of it," said Arthur. "Except when you get the dysentery. Then, I got to put you to bed and put you on and take you off and, oh, what a drag that gets to be."

"You used the word 'fag,' Allison, I didn't," said Grosbeck. "I don't care what you do. I'm a closet heterosexual myself. Some day, I'll be right out there with the rest of us. Provided, of course . . . I have my prejudices, but that isn't one of them. Besides, who cares? You and Arthur waited for us in what I shall call . . . ahem . . . our hour of need." Grosbeck pinched Allison's arm.

"Arthur does what he does; I do what I do and people don't seem to understand. He's a rash young man. We fight all the time. He gets drunk when he shouldn't and we wind up quarreling. He can be bad."

"I wouldn't have believed it," said Grosbeck. "Looking at the two of you. The perfect couple."

"You're making fun of me, Harvey," said Allison.

"I *am* kidding," Grosbeck said. "Nothing malicious. A joke between old friends."

By now, the four were in the meat market, walking under the overhang of corrugated-iron sheds, passing open stalls in which could be seen men in long, white, bloodstained coats pushing carcasses hung on steel hooks, the hooks in rails on the ceiling. Twelfth Street, Little West Twelfth, Gansevoort, Hudson, Greenwich, the sagging Pennsylvania Railroad and Erie piers, the profanation of the West Side Highway.

Grosbeck stopped under a street light, the better to see Allison. "You do go back a long way, don't you?" he observed.

"I'm sixty-five," said Allison. "Still go out to work every morning. I'm sort of a semiexecutive. Arthur wants me to retire, but I want to die in the saddle."

Die in the saddle. Grosbeck marveled. Allison, too, was a landmark and should be preserved; he was not ready to be torn down.

"I don't like the word 'homosexual,'" said Allison.

"Neither do I," said Grosbeck.

"That's why I said 'fag,'" said Allison. "And, besides, we're not. I wanted you to understand."

"I do, I do," said Grosbeck and put his arm around the older man's shoulders. Let the dialogue go where it would. Together with drunkenness, it pushed Catafesta away. Who would have dreamed that here, in this place, in the company of these two, Grosbeck would have found what he had found in Tully.

"I'm worried about that dysentery of yours," he said to Allison.

"Don't be," said Allison. "I do prefer constipation, though. When you've had dysentery the way I get it, you want, you *need* constipation. Dear God, there's nothing better when you take a dump than constipation. You strain and push; it's hard and it hurts. Glory. And when it's over, you go and lie down on the bed for a few minutes. Worn out but satisfied."

"You're making me self-conscious," said Grosbeck. "I mean, I prefer the middle way. Nothing sensational; just regular, steady, no shocks. Clean. No strain. I'll take that every time."

"You two all right back there?" Arthur called. "We're at the Cave."

"I think so, Arthur," said Allison. "This should do as well as any."

They passed a sign. It read:

Shells	Jobsoloma
Ribs	Lomo
Hips	Palomilla
Butts	Bola
Eyes	Boliche
Tops	Bola Filete
Bottoms	Tira de Piennes
Fillets	Filete

"This the Cave?" asked Grosbeck. "That what they call fags now? All these different kinds? And in two languages."

Arthur doubled up in laughter. Allison hugged Grosbeck and said, "Next door, Harvey, that's a packing house."

Next door was more like it. The door was open, but the windows were painted black. To the right of the door was a huge plywood figure of a cowboy. Maybe a cowboy. It was wearing a ten-gallon hat and a leather vest and boots; a leather belt to which was attached a pair of handcuffs; in its left hand was a tire chain; its right was pointing a huge penis at the observer. A legend beneath the figure read: "Power to the Penis."

"It looks a little rich for my blood," said Grosbeck. "I've got tired blood."

From the doorway issued the music of a jukebox; laughter, cackles, screams, talk, the clink of glasses and a series of clunks. "Clunks," said Grosbeck. "What's clunking in there?"

"Go in, go in," said Arthur.

"I'm not sure," said Madeline. "A woman . . ."

"Sweetie, the way you dressed tonight, them jeans, that

shirt, the dark glasses, you might as well be a boy, baby," said Arthur. "They look twice at you, it be for other reasons than usual for you."

"We don't usually come here," said Allison. "But, you know, we thought you might like a diversion tonight."

"Let me look inside first," said Grosbeck. He leaned in the doorway.

Two men, naked, were dancing with each other to the music of the jukebox.

Grosbeck looked over his shoulder. "The cops allow *that?*" he asked Allison.

"Two ways," said Allison. "Some are gay, some come for pay."

"I should have known," said Grosbeck. "What's the percentage either way?"

"I really couldn't say, Harvey," Allison answered. Grosbeck looked inside the door again. The lighting in the place was minimal green, red and yellow. A sign on one wall said, "Do It At The Cave." Another said, "Let us come together once again . . . as in the beginning. Better to have loved and lost than to have married and always lose." The clunking noise came from a half-size pool table on which two blond young men in tight leather pants and vests which exposed hairless, or, at least, depilitated chests, were playing bottle pool and exclaiming over every shot. The ceiling was hung with fish nets from which lanterns had been suspended. Pieces of driftwood hung in the nets.

"If you would prefer something less flamboyant . . ." Allison said to Grosbeck.

"No," said Grosbeck. "I guess this'll do. It doesn't hurt to get off the beaten track every now and then. Isn't that what you always say, Madeline?"

Madeline said nothing and the four of them entered the

Cave. They stayed for about an hour and Grosbeck went back on his intention to drink something soft.

The dancing partners put on their pants after a while and went to a corner table where they kissed each other over and over, all the while keeping their hands on the table. Ultimately, one of them ordered a ham sandwich and the other a frankfurter and two glasses of chartreuse. When they were through eating and drinking and kissing, they spent a half hour with their hands under the table squirming and turning their eyes upward until only the whites could be seen. Apparently, they both reached a climax at roughly the same time; Grosbeck couldn't tell, because he had looked away and when he looked back, the two seemed to have sagged in place.

The Grosbecks and their companions were treated with the utmost courtesy. The bartender shooed away a patron who tried to approach Madeline, with the explanation that she was Grosbeck's son.

Grosbeck got drunk again. He told his story again, about Catafesta and the police and what he expected to happen to him. Allison clucked and Arthur tit-titted.

"Don't cheer, lads," Grosbeck admonished the two of them, "the poor devils are dying."

"Take heart, Harvey," said Allison.

"Perhaps the good Lord will be good to us fatality-wise," said Grosbeck and put his head on the table.

Arthur reached out for the head and tried to pick it up. He couldn't. Grosbeck's hair was cut too short.

"Baby, I think he's had enough," Arthur said to Madeline.

"He had enough years before you knew him," said Madeline.

"Hey, sweetie," said Arthur. "You pretty funny, too. But I think it time we took him home."

Madeline nodded. "How?" she asked.

"I get the bartender to phone for a cab," Arthur said. "Be around in ten minutes. I think this did Harvey the good we said. He sleep it off and do his worrying another day."

The three of them pulled at Grosbeck and got him away from the table; the cab came; two of the customers took Grosbeck by the legs, two others, by the arms, and, followed by Madeline, Arthur and Allison, they got him into the cab. At the apartment, it took the cab driver and the other three to get him to bed, but not before he had dirtied them all with his retching and tried to pray on the floor of the elevator.

"I have high hopes for him," Allison said as he left the Grosbeck apartment.

"Cat wants to pray got to be going *somewhere*," said Arthur.

Madeline did not answer either of them.

The Festival of San Gennaro began on a cool September Saturday. From the north end of Mulberry Street, at the porous, fieldstone walls of Old St. Patrick's Cathedral, south to Mulberry Bend, stopping at Bayard Street in Chinatown, green-and-red-and-white pennons, the national colors of Italy, hung across the street, from window to window of the tenements. All traffic was kept out. There were carts lined up on either side of the roadway selling *calzone, zeppole,* hot sausage, sweet sausage, red and green peppers, strings of nuts, chicken, crab, oysters, clams, *tortoni, spumoni, cannoli,* the sweet *ricotta* oozing. Smokes and smells rose from the steel bars of the grills, under them charcoal.

Italian popular songs were played over public-address systems at the volume of Doomsday; if the songs were not heard five miles away in the parish of Our Lady of Mount Carmel in East Harlem, the Festival of San Gennaro was not a fact. The songs were meltingly of love and betrayal and redemption and gain and loss, sentimental and sardonic, and in the windows of the music stores were bad, heavily retouched photographs of the Roman singers who had recorded them. The music sounded hopelessly out of date, off pitch, unbearable, yet one could not help liking it and wanting to hear more. The tenors and the baritones were so bad the Roman police kept their Rolls Royces off the Via Veneto and prescribed the hours when their admirers could offer their supplications.

The Italians were in Mulberry Street; the uptown people were there; the Chinese slipped in and out unobtrusively, their numbers now augmented by the slim young toughs from Hong Kong who entered the country like maggots. People's feet squushed in the offal of the Festival. Tenants looked out the windows of their tenements, bored with the yearly intrusion on their lives. It was all very well for San Gennaro and for the church and for the fathers and for the conniving, murderous commercials, who, in the back rooms of the dingy social clubs along Mulberry Street, made arrangements, split up this and shared that and made life hell for the householders the week of the Festival. It was all for God and these others, not for the people who lived in the buildings, but, after all, it was only a week. It was noisy until two o'clock in the morning, but it was safe noise. Clam shells were thrown out of the clam bars but there was no gunfire for the week of the Festival.

Grosbeck, as he always did, went to the Festival on the opening day with Madeline and Jason. He carried his apprehension with him this year, a tumor in his belly; he counted the days to retribution and they stretched out, one upon another; he could not tell how many they would be and he became almost hungry for resolution; but inevitability, like canker, would take its own good time. Meantime, the first day of San Gennaro.

The day was bright, carts and booths at the curbs, the people packed together, movement near to a halt, hoarse cries from venders, the click and clack of gambling wheels, dolls with pink faces and purple feathers on the shelves for prizes. A regular *geshrei*. The street would have to be cleared for the religious procession, for the passage of the Virgin. Grosbeck wiped away crumbs of *calzone* as a private policeman pushed him and others out of the roadway. The procession had begun in the distance. Trumpets announced themselves up the block above the joinery of noises.

Grosbeck found himself between two of the carts, one foot on the curb, the other in the road, people before him and in back of him and on both sides of him. Madeline and Jason had become separated from him, but that did not bother Grosbeck. That always happened at the Festival. Later, they would find one another, pushing through the crowds.

Not today.

He received a sharp blow in the ribs and went "H-h-h-h-h . . ." and bent over in pain, disbelief, belief and wished to fly straight upward, holding his side. Not in years had he been hit so hard by anything. He straightened up. The blow was not accidental, not someone's elbow. It came from a fist. He looked to the left. A young white man looked at Grosbeck, a laboratory technician gauging the effect of a procedure, then past Grosbeck, causing Grosbeck to turn his head. There was a young Negro at Grosbeck's right. He was grinning.

Now? Now. Beyond doubt. It was time. The place was wrong, but it was time.

"Please," said Grosbeck. He tried to put a hand in his pocket, but the white man restrained him.

"I was just trying to get out my money for you," Grosbeck said. "If it's not enough, I can get more. You're not from Mr. Catafesta, are you? It is money you want, isn't it?"

He looked intently into the white man's eyes; the intensity of his gaze would evoke from him an answer, the truth. The Negro kicked him in the shin, the white man punched him in the ribs again. The pain, the pain. And no answer.

Each of them seized one of Grosbeck's arms and began to pull him backward toward the doorway of one of the tenements. Grosbeck shat his pants. The distance across the sidewalk was no more than eight feet from curb to doorway. There were people all about Grosbeck and the two men. Yet he did not ask for help, did not raise his voice in a cry, as they grappled him toward the doorway, an awkward, smelly bundle. He felt intensely private between the two. They would be sure to kill him instantly if he said anything outside the privacy of their affair, notwithstanding all the people about. They were having trouble getting him through the crowd on the sidewalk, so they stopped to catch breath. They had to, pressed in as they were, with the procession about to pass them.

So that was how it was to be. At three o'clock of an early fall afternoon, in the narrow doorway of a tenement on Mulberry Street. One black, one white; perfect symmetry; ineluctable proof of the doctrine so agonizingly held by all right-thinking people: that you could, regardless of race, creed or color work together in companionable harmony . . . yes, to maim and murder.

So it would not be cancer of the bowel. That morning, in the toilet, his refuge from so many things, he had observed blood in the bowl, then blood on the toilet paper. Not for the first time, but increasingly of late and that had disturbed him almost as much as the creaking shoes of death at his back that he heard so often since the night of the tenants' meeting.

In the doorway of a tenement on Mulberry Street. Not even in an automobile junkyard in Brooklyn or Queens or on the green shoulder of an expressway. Bullet? Knife? Did they have time to punch and kick him to death in that doorway? Certainly; in decent solitude, in dim light, two feet away from the crowd.

The brass band: a compost of old men in white shirts, black trousers, peaked caps manufactured on Pearl Street half a century ago, dust on the brims; black ties; an array of bobbing noses and uncertainly blown brass. The drums beat slowly, the rhythm as bad as that of the shuffling feet. Vertigo. Bright colors.

The Virgin: Plaster? Papier-mâché? Not marble or metal. They wouldn't have been able to carry her, the old men bent beneath the platform on which she sat complacently.

So bright the day, so garish the colors, so thick and palpable the smells and smokes of food and what was in Grosbeck's belly; so varied the people, so closely pressed; so close, indeed, that that was another reason why he could never escape these two. There is nothing like propinquity to promote indifference.

The five-dollar bills, the ten-dollar bills, the dollar bills hung limply from the jeweled caftan of Our Lady; pinned there by the faithful and the skeptical and the superstitious

and the gamblers. Fresh from the ticking wheels run by con-
cessionnaires, they tacked on their occasional winnings for
Our Lady. She could be soiled, but not they, once they had
made the offering. Her eyes stared out at nothing; her lips
were testy, where they should have been full of benison.
The craftsman's hand had slipped years ago in some monument works on the East Side and he had been too tired to
slap another trowel of plaster on the face of Our Lady.
And so her lips had hardened into short temper.

She was not a cynical Virgin, but her annoyance with
the world was plain. She held the Infant in her arms with
patient disdain. He would not come to a good end, any
more than all these people beneath her. Like Him, all she
wanted was peace, but He would be a touchy man and
make trouble.

The cornets whined; the clarinets pestered them, like
moronic children poking at dogs; the drums tried, desultorily, to enforce a discipline among these quarreling in-
struments, but failed, and so beat on unheeded.

And loud. Everything was so loud that nobody could hear
what was being said to Grosbeck ("Move, you son of a
bitch; move, or you get it right here"); and no one could
see what was happening to him. A private policeman stood
two feet away from Grosbeck. Whatever his concerns, they
had nothing to do with him, although Grosbeck, conclusively
aware, threw up a hand and waved at the policeman, tried
to shout, tried to create an agitation that would, like ripples
in a pool, spread outward from the doorway to which he
now had been wrestled, and sprinkle the mustache of the
private policeman, upsetting his composure and attracting
his attention and bringing him to the terrified man, cornered
in the doorway by the two men who had come to kill him.

The men were so powerful. They had him inside the doorway, back to the wall, the Negro holding both of his arms tightly, effortlessly. So enigmatic: The white man went through his pockets and took everything he had, including his identity cards. Catafesta must have paid them adequately for the job. Why then, would they bother with his money and what ends were served by taking away his identification? That was unimportant: In seconds, he reasoned, he would be unidentifiable not just to the world, but to himself. He would be dead.

"Don't," he whimpered. "Don't." As much whisper "Don't" to a plane dropping bombs; Baleen discharging him; Milton Michaels breaking his arm; "Don't" to computers; "Don't" to all of the things, abstract and concrete, which oppressed him and the rest of the human race (in that order). It had been his fault not to embrace sooner all mankind as he had Arthur and Allison. So there was, after all, a Higher Power waggling a finger at him and saying, "Naughty. Naughty. Live no more. Feel no more. Thou shalt not even have hell."

They beat and kicked Grosbeck terribly, broke his nose and smashed at his ribs and belly; punched his face until the eyes were shut and the planes of the cheekbones altered. They had put on gloves to do it so that their hands would not be injured. But Grosbeck did not know that. He lay unconscious in the doorway, blood from his eyes and nose running down him until he was blood all over and his head lay at a peculiar angle to his shoulders.

There, in the doorway, not much later, Madeline and Jason and a regular policeman found him.

The late Harvey Grosbeck.

In accordance with the desires of the newspaper, and in plain contravention of the known wishes of the deceased (he had left no will, dying intestate, with a joint checking account overdrawn to the end), a memorial service was held for Grosbeck at the Frank E. Campbell Funeral Chapel on upper Madison Avenue, in a rich and antiseptic neighborhood. The service was decreed by the paper because he had fallen, not in the line of duty exactly, but he had fallen, bleeding, at the hands of contraveners of the law by which all men must live or we shall perish in anarchy.

Grosbeck had been a newspaperman, and, *de mortuis nil nisi bonum,* a seeker of truth, a carrier of that torch the light of which illumines the world, pushes back the borders of darkness; he had been a defender of the public's right to know. The most imposing defender of that right on the newspaper was Baleen and he intended to eulogize Grosbeck, who was in no position to contradict him this time. The opportunity to make a speech was irresistible to Baleen and Grosbeck's death, however beside the point, was not to be passed over. Baleen decided that Grosbeck had died for all newspapermen, an upholder of probity, a lance against the forces of evil which plague our great city and the nation and which we all, however much at times their errors bear heavily on us, love. A better day will come. Grosbeck will not see it, but his widow will and his offspring. Baleen wiped the corners of his eyes at what he planned to say and picked out a sober tie. Shalit drove in from the suburbs to attend the service. He sighed at the wheel: You take your symbols where you find them, he thought.

There had been some thought of holding the service at Temple Emanu-El, but that had been dropped on the ground that Grosbeck had not been a high executive of the newspaper: Temple Emanu-El services were reserved for Reform Jews above the rank of assistant city editor. Also, Grosbeck had been the kind of Jew much deplored by the Ashkenazim and Sephardim who owned the paper; he had often said the temple was so reformed that it was closed on Jewish holidays. Besides being an old joke, that was untrue; the temple *was* open on Jewish holidays.

Grosbeck had been a *shonda*, a scandal, for the neighbors, for what he said about Baleen and others around him, for his cheap cynicism. Any cynicism which was not theirs was cheap. There was an element of revenge in Baleen's insistence on a memorial service. Grosbeck's behavior at editorial meetings, his immature intransigence, his way of getting out of line . . . In death, he would be brought back in line, although not at Temple Emanu-El. All that callow talk about driving money changers out of the temple . . . and handing real-estate speculators their coats at the same time!

Only the boundless tolerance of Baleen had kept Grosbeck on the job all those years. Baleen knew himself to be an enlightened man, above all a forgiving man. But, not to be uncharitable about it, it was a relief to be rid of Grosbeck and he might as well make the most of it. Baleen had had the chapel banked with flowers. He did not know one flower from another; he had simply ordered flowers, suitable and discreet. Remember, he had told the funeral director, this isn't the Tournament of Roses.

After consultation with Mrs. Grosbeck, Baleen arranged

for a selection of songs about New York City to be played and a rendering of street cries common to the early half of the nineteenth century, by a very *recherché* group of folk singers, these to be interspersed with the calls of birds to whom New York was home: the common English sparrow, the grackle and the pigeon. On the wall of the chapel, behind the podium, Baleen had had hung an enlargement, three feet wide and six feet deep, of the last piece of copy edited by Grosbeck: Of the twelve paragraphs in the piece, all but one had been eliminated by Grosbeck.

Members of the staff had been dragooned into coming and the hour of the service was set early enough so that the operations of the newspaper would not be disrupted. There were no prayers. As a man who, inexplicably, had seemed to like Grosbeck and was, therefore, suspect himself, John Tully was called on to say a few words. He declined and Baleen had everything to himself. The body, in a substantial but not showy coffin, was placed before the podium. At a signal from Baleen, the songs, bird calls and street cries were faded gradually. The lights were dimmed and Baleen stepped to the podium rattling a sheaf of notes.

"I will not dwell upon the accomplishments of Harvey Grosbeck," said Baleen. "You all knew them well . . . the passion for accuracy, the determination that each fact should be placed after every other in a progression allowing of no deviation; which hewed to the line of enlightenment, of clarity and of precision for which so many of us strive and so few arrive at. He was not known widely outside of our editorial offices but among us his was a blade which hacked away at the dross of inaccuracy." Baleen's gift for mixing metaphors was amazing and quotations from his articles were treasured, sometimes framed.

"Hey, Baleen," a voice called out of the dark. "You're the

dross which hacks away at the blade." There was a rustling among the colleagues and three guffaws.

Baleen gripped the podium with both hands. "I have only this to say . . ." he began, when the music unexpectedly started up again. The cooing of a pigeon was heard and then a tenor voice: "Buy me some peanuts and crackerjack;/ I don't care if I never get back;/ So, it's root, root, root for the home team;/ If they don't win it's a shame;/ For it's one, two, three strikes you're out at the old ball game." In his coffin, Grosbeck turned over and lay on his side, a smile on his lips; he regretted being out of it.

Baleen took a different tack. "I have no objection to high spirits," he said. "But there is a eulogy to be delivered and deliver it I shall." He rapped for order with the carriage of Grosbeck's typewriter, which was to be buried with him.

"Harvey Grosbeck," he went on, "was, perhaps, indiscreet at times in the pursuit of truth, unable or unwilling in his burning zeal to keep his feet on the invisible line which divides interpretation from advocacy. But it was precisely that form of indiscretion which endeared him to so many of his colleagues, myself included. If he had to be reined in, it was in the interest of a higher good. He could, to be candid, be a trifle wearing at times. . . . I will hide nothing. . . . But all things in a man go together and he would not have wanted me to paint him in bland strokes; he would have wanted to be limned warts and all."

Tick. Tick. Tick.

"Extrapolated, the act he performed [what act, what performance?] on that tragic day further insures, in however small a way, the right of the public to know. For the newspaper has done more than record his death." Grosbeck had been given a three-paragraph obituary under a small headline, bottom left, of the obituary page, and no picture.

"Even now, as I speak," Baleen continued, "all of our resources are being devoted to aiding the police in tracking down the murderers of Harvey Grosbeck and when they are found they will be punished to the full extent of the law, which, as you all know, now forbids capital punishment and with which I agree, whatever the temptation to exact an eye for an eye. The search for the men who took his life is but a part of a greater quest, the rooting out of crime in our daily lives, the extirpation of the cancer which afflicts us. I notice that among you sits our commissioner of police. His presence here today is no accident. . . ."

Baleen had to end the folderol sometime and he finally did. "Taken all in all," he said, "we shall not see Harvey Grosbeck's like again. We are the poorer for the loss of him.

"And now," he said, "the ushers will pass among you and distribute reproductions of prints from the pages of I. N. Phelps Stokes's *The Iconography of Manhattan Island*, a multivolume work which Harvey Grosbeck knew well and which sustained him daily in the hurly-burly of news gathering. These will be modest mementos of Harvey Grosbeck."

Baleen looked to the left and to the right, but the ushers were already on their way up the aisles. They were women dressed in white: white dresses, shoes, stockings and caps on the back of their heads. They carried piles of the prints in the crook of an arm and wore stethoscopes around their necks.

Then, the service was over and the procession to the place of burial followed. Long black cars and the hearse. Grosbeck had died, the city was dying. He had asked Madeline, years before, either to have him cremated, or, if he had to be buried intact, to take a prescribed route to the cemetery. He wanted to be laid to rest in Green-Wood, the last home of William Marcy Tweed, after the Ludlow Street Jail.

What could be nicer, Grosbeck had said, than to await eternity next to so famous a thief, a thief who, unlike the present rulers of the city, was as direct as a steam locomotive.

The shrieks of the dispossessed and the derelict echoed around the limousines as they passed slowly through the streets. . . . Guns went off and clubs fell on flesh. The blind, dead towers which froze and killed anyone within blocks of them, stood in serried lines, contemptuous of everything about them. Curiously, the dome of the Merchants' Exchange glinted in the sun on Wall Street. It had not yet been burned down in the fire of 1835. The City Hall sat in its Frenchified prettiness before the columned, porticoed hulk of the Post Office. The Post Office was a pockmarked, slashed phiz with a plug hat on, summoning the City Hall like a pretty whore in one of the river wards.

Grosbeck had made the detours to Green-Wood circuitous and the limousine chauffeurs didn't like them. Shit, they'd be all day getting this stiff in the ground. They passed the Greek Revival of Washington Square; the vernacular of S. Klein's department store on Union Square and the statue of George Washington, shifted from time to time to suit the convenience of traffic; Madison Square, where the Jerome mansion had been torn down, but where the vultures had not yet been able to touch the marble courthouse of the Appellate Division, cowering in the lee of the Metropolitan Life Insurance Company; Gramercy Park (Samuel Ruggles, solid, humane bourgeois); Grosbeck had never owned a key to the park. He had envied those who did and fought for their right to exclude the dirty, grubby public.

The cortege was diverted downtown to Leonard Street for a look at the last remaining building standing to be built by James Bogardus. It avoided, at Grosbeck's request, the land upon which the Washington Market once stood (that, he had said, would have been more than his bones could endure); it went up one narrow street and down another, from Canal to Houston, from Sixth Avenue to Broadway, so that the body of Grosbeck this one last time could pass the cast-iron buildings, the warehouse of Charles (Broadway) Reuss; everything, everything. The truck drivers cursed the funeral procession. No one had ever seen one around there and it had no business being there. The hearse and the limousines got in the way of everything. It took them two and a half hours to go a dozen and a half blocks.

It was late in the afternoon when the funeral procession finally got over to Brooklyn and the broad sweep of the expressway to the place where the dead lay under the rolling hills . . . the bones beneath the monuments; the monuments grown over with brown-and-white autumn grass; the crucifixes worn and the Stars of David; the cherubs chipped and noseless; neat legends, extravagant ones, outright lies on many of the headstones . . . all eroded in the fierce weathers of the city.

Grosbeck was to be laid away by small, lumpy men with unshaven faces and dirt-stained hands. For a change, the gravediggers were not on strike. His widow stood at the edge of the grave as the box was moved toward it on slings. She wept. Grosbeck pushed up the lid of the coffin and took her hand tenderly. Then, he subsided, waited for the lid to be screwed on, the box to be lowered and covered with the acid earth of New York City; the small burial party to turn away in grief and to leave him one with the city forever.

But tears coursed down the furrowed cheeks of the corpse, wetting the crusted lips and the round chin; dampening the hands neatly folded above the neat paunch. The corpse was afflicted by light and opened its eyes. It moved its head and saw one of the lady ushers from the funeral parlor, in her white dress and cap, with the stethoscope around her neck.

The lady usher smiled at the corpse and said, "There we are, Mr. Grosbeck. You certainly gave us a few anxious moments. How do you feel?!"

The corpse croaked.

"Good, good," said the lady usher. "Do you know where you are?"

Croak.

"Mrs. Grosbeck is waiting to see you. I'll bet you've missed her. I know she's dying to see you."

Croak. It was the best Grosbeck could do under the circumstances. There were tubes in him, around him, under him; in his nose, up his ass, between his nose and left ear; he lay in a tangle of nickel and rubber contraptions on a white catafalque thirty feet above the floor, waited on by a forty-foot nurse.

Madeline entered the room. It was her tears which had fallen on Grosbeck's face as he lay in the coffin. She bent and kissed him. His face was badly swollen, black, blue, green, yellow and purple. His lips were drawn back to reveal a number of gaps in his teeth, upper and lower. He felt pain but could not localize it. Several of his ribs had been broken and he was tightly bound.

"They didn't kill me," he croaked.

"No, Harvey, you're alive," said Madeline. "You never died. You said you were dead, but you weren't. Don't try to talk too much. That's what put you in here."

Grosbeck mumbled and closed his eyes.

Early in November, Grosbeck sat with John Tully in the restaurant across the street from the newspaper and ate with good appetite. "No change in the sauerbraten," he said. "The new teeth work just fine."

"You had to get drunk, didn't you, Harvey," said Tully. "So self-indulgent, the innocent of the world."

"No lectures, John. I'll lecture. Dandy," Grosbeck said, "I have, through an act of supreme rashness, become a man. It has to be beaten into some people. I am one of them and that is my metaphor. Let us suppose, for a minute, that it wasn't Catafesta had me beat up, that it had nothing to do with Catafesta, that it was one of the consequences of being a New Yorker. Suppose that."

"I'll suppose it for your sake, Harvey," said Tully. "But all the evidence is against it."

"We'll never know, Dandy, will we?" Grosbeck said. "But, don't you see how irrelevant it is. Whether I got it purposefully or not, I have survived it and I have found my metaphor."

Tully shrugged.

"When a man has risen from the dead," Grosbeck continued. "When the stone is rolled away, he has got to live with a little more assurance, something I never had, and . . . and . . . I don't know what else. But I feel it inside of me. Don't get me wrong. Don't expect me to love Baleen or Shalit. Don't expect me to embrace the world. Fuck that. But so long as I have Madeline and my children and there are meals to be eaten and books to be read, so long as there is a bracket or a corbel or a pilaster or a spandrel on some building before which I can stop and be pleased, so long as I am alive . . ."

"What an incredibly sentimental and romantic man you are, Grosbeck," said Tully. "All this uplift and moral conversion. Go on back to work." The two men rose from the table.

It was the day of the presidential election. Shortly after midnight, an election story on the man who had lost was laid on Grosbeck's desk. It began:

> "The defeated candidate's long day's journey ended at 10:37 Tuesday night in cheers and tears for a desperate odyssey that produced the penultimate but not the ultimate miracle."

Not Beowulf, not Chaucer, not Fielding, Swift, Smollett, Defoe; not Joyce, Proust, nor Faulkner could have produced a sentence like that . . . so perfect in its ignorant absurdity, so well-packed with the *Dreck* of language . . . tired allusions, misdefined words and phrases . . . an encyclopedia of shit. "Long day's journey . . ." "Cheers and tears . . ." "Desperate odyssey . . ." "The penultimate but not the ultimate miracle." Hoo-hah.

Grosbeck filled his lungs with the stale air of the city room and bit with relish into a bagel with Nova Scotia salmon and cream cheese at his side. Life was very, very good. Then, he crossed out the sentence and rewrote it in English.